A FAMILY OATH

A FAMILY OATH

CHRONICLES OF AN URBAN DRUID™ BOOK 3

AUBURN TEMPEST

MICHAEL ANDERLE

DISRUPTIVE IMAGINATION

Copyright © 2020 LMBPN Publishing
Cover by Fantasy Book Design
Cover copyright © LMBPN Publishing
A Michael Anderle Production

LMBPN Publishing
PMB 196, 2540 South Maryland Pkwy
Las Vegas, NV 89109

First US edition, November 2020
eBook ISBN: 978-1-64971-328-5
Print ISBN: 978-1-64971-329-2

THE A FAMILY OATH TEAM

Thanks to our JIT Team:

Jeff Goode
Dave Hicks
Dorothy Lloyd
Deb Mader
John Ashmore
Diane L. Smith
Kelly O'Donnell
Rachel Beckford
Paul Westman
Micky Cocker
Peter Manis
Larry Omans

Editor
SkyHunter Editing Team

CHAPTER ONE

"Do you think my spear clashes with my outfit?" I pivot in front of the entrance mirror in my new kickass leather boots, silk blouse, and my ass looking fabulous in a pair of black culottes. Birga's jagged Connemara marble spear tip is an olive green with veins of gray, brown, and black. My blouse is a vibrant emerald green to set off the russet red of my hair.

I'm not sure it's working.

"I think you're the only druid on the planet who would worry about it," Calum shifts in behind me at the mirror, "but no, you're totally rocking it. Isn't she, Kev?"

Calum's partner winks from the couch in the family room and finishes chewing his bagel. The guy is the blond, all-American type, and Calum was smart to snatch him up when they were young because he's the real deal. "Nailed it. That is, if you're going for badass sexy warrior chick."

"As a matter of fact, that is *exactly* what I'm aiming for. Glad you picked up on that." I flex my fingers and invite my enchanted spear into its resting place as a tattoo on my right forearm.

"I don't like it one bit," Da says, for the eleventh time. "Fiona, yer meetin' the heads of all the most powerful magical sects in the city. Ye need to take me or one of yer brothers with ye."

"Da, no. We've been over this. *I* was invited to have lunch with the Lakeshore Guild as the representative of Clan Cumhaill. There was no plus one on the invitation. Besides, I'm already sneaking Bruin in as my Killer Clawbearer party crasher."

Da raises his finger with his scowl locked firmly in place. "Och, don't fool yerself, missy. That is the only reason I'm lettin' ye out the front door."

I loop my purse's strap over my head and free my hair from the collar of my fall jacket. "The fact that you don't think I'm safe without a mythical grizzly bear to slaughter my way clear of enemies is insulting. And you can't *let* me do anything. I'm a grown woman."

"Yer twenty-three and think ye have the mysteries of the world figured out. Yer sorely mistaken, and I'll not have ye losin' yer life to learn that lesson."

I fight the urge to roll my eyes, knowing it'll only set him off more. "Love you huge, Da. I'll tell you all about it when you wake up tonight. Get some sleep. You're super cranky."

Dillan opens the hall cabinet and retrieves his sidearm from the gun safe. He's dressed in his blues and ready to start on afternoons. "Spending all night in a tactical van with three sweaty men can do that to you. It's even worse when you get absolutely nothing to show for it."

Da grunts. "Ye don't catch the big fish on yer first cast, my boy. Patience is a virtue, after all. Ye must play the game to win it."

I grab my keys and zip them into my purse. "Which is why I'll be perfectly safe taking this lunch meeting. Garnet has guaranteed my safety and will be my escort for the whole thing. I'll play their game, and we'll be more prepared with the added intel on what Toronto's got going on."

"Garnet Grant is a notorious criminal and old enough to be yer father. Remember that, Fiona."

I crinkle my nose at the latter half of that sentence and won't even open that for discussion. "I'm well aware."

Emmet sticks his head out of the family room and points toward the front of the house. "Either your ride is here, or Janine and Mark ordered a limo to go to prom gangsta style."

All righty. I check myself over once more in the mirror and head for the door.

"Ready and steady, Freddie." Emmet holds his fist out for a bump. "You've got this, Fi. Represent."

"Have ye got yer phone?"

"Yes, Da." I lean forward, kiss his scruffy cheek, and give him a reassuring look. "Clan mac Cumhaill for the win. As Emmet said, I've got this."

"I bet Daniel said the same thing while headin' straight into the lion's den. The man is literally a lion, Fi. Don't let his smarmy smile fool ye."

I wave over my shoulder as Da's warnings follow me off the porch in the crisp, autumn air.

"Locked and loaded, sista," Dillan calls after me.

"Always."

As I approach the curb, Garnet Grant slides out of the black Hummer limousine's back seat and straightens. The man is equal parts elegance and arrogance in a black-on-black suit and possesses enough sculpture in his frame to make a girl's inner butterflies flutter.

He also has a gift of coercion—less sexy—but thankfully, that doesn't work on me.

I'd like to think I'm immune because I'm not *that* girl. You know, the type of girl to get swept away by the man's stunning amethyst eyes and panty-dampening deep voice.

Truth is, it's more likely my shield protecting me.

The Fianna crest that appeared on my back the day this whole

3

druid adventure started is a double-edged sword. It protects me from the dangers of the hidden realms of magic, but it's also a beacon that draws those dangers straight to me.

Ironic, right?

"Lady Druid." Garnet dips his chin. "It is my pleasure to be your escort for the next few hours."

"I want her back in one piece, Grant," Da snaps. *Oh, goody, he followed me out.* "Not a scratch on her, or I'll raze the fuckin' city and burn down yer house of cards."

"Da, stop," I hiss.

"It's fine." Garnet straightens beside me. "You have my word, Niall. May I call you Niall?"

"No."

Emmet chuckles as he slides into the mix.

Garnet doesn't seem to care one way or another. "I give you my oath, Mr. Cumhaill. For this luncheon, I will guard your daughter with all I am and return her to you exactly as she is now, breathtaking and whole."

Okay, I appreciate the solemn vow and all, but I could do without the bit about me being breathtaking.

Because, *ew*, Da's not wrong.

The man might look like he's in his early fifties, but aside from being the Grand Governor of the Lakeshore Guild of Empowered Ones, he's also Alpha of the Toronto Moon Called. As a lion shifter, he's bound to age well and could be sixty or seventy for all I know.

"If he tries anything," Dillan joins the testosterone party at the curb and pats his gun at his hip, "send him to the dragon queen to get munched."

I catch the slight twitch of Garnet's lips as they rise over his canines. Yep. Good one, Dillan. Rub salt in the wound. I did send one of Garnet's men to their death at the hand of the dragon queen—well, at the teeth of her, I assume.

I didn't mean to.

Well, I sorta did…and sorta didn't.

Hey, I told him to stop groping me and roughing me up. He deserved it. I think so, anyway.

By the look on Garnet's face, I doubt he'd agree.

"No one will be sent to the dragon's lair to get munched." I offer Garnet an apologetic smile. "The only munching today will be lunch. Now enough jabbering. Goodbye, family, go inside and let us leave."

As my grand protectors turn and grumble their way up the walkway, Da stands his ground and crosses his arms. "Not one scratch, Grant."

Garnet straightens, and a growl rolls from his chest that echoes and vibrates through mine. When his eyes flip from purple to gold, I feel the magic of his lion ascending. "I gave you my oath, Cumhaill. You would do well not to question my honor."

Awesomesauce. "Okay, buh-bye. Love you all."

I close the distance to the passenger door, but before I grab for the handle, Garnet reaches around me and opens the door. I offer him a smile and slide into the back seat.

He rounds the truck limo and climbs in on the driver's side. By the time he looks at me, his eyes are amethyst once again. "Never a dull moment with your family, is it, Lady Druid?"

I rub a hand over my face and sigh. "Nope. It's endless fun, twenty-four-seven."

Garnet leans forward and knocks on the opaque privacy glass that divides us from the driver. The truck engine rumbles to life with a beefy growl, and we pull into motion.

"I'm sorry they were rude. They get a little heavy-handed when it comes to my safety."

"They are your pride, and you are their only female. I don't suppose it's much different from how the males of the Moon Called protect our females."

My seat belt *clicks* as we pull away from my house. "I suppose not."

"Males posture when they get protective, Lady Druid. It's a fact no female has much control over."

I glance out the window and track our progress as we drive off my street and head along Wellesley toward Sherbourne. "It occurs to me that I don't know where we're going. Does the Lakeshore Guild have a head office? Are your gatherings catered? Are we meeting in a restaurant? What should I prepare for?"

Garnet sits back and runs and a strong hand over the knee of his fine, tailored slacks. While I've never noticed him wearing rings before, today he has a large, silver signet ring on the ring finger of his right hand.

"What does the symbol on your ring mean?"

Garnet flexes his fingers to show me and points. "This is the insignia of the Lakeshore Guild. The pentacle, of course, represents the unending connections of the elements—earth, wind, fire, water, and spirit. The Centurion's helmet in the center represents the honor of battling for our people. And this sigil dates back to Babylonian times as the symbol for truth and justice."

"Does the Guild live up to all that?"

Instead of giving me a quick, pat answer, Garnet thinks about it. "We strive to, although like any organization, there are things that can be improved and those who fail to share the long-term vision. We are a work in progress, but I'm proud of what we do, yes."

"Is this luncheon something you often do?"

Garnet sighs. "These are all the wrong questions."

The snap in his voice is harsh, but I try not to let it get to me. "Okay, then what are the right questions?"

"You need to worry less about the location, the lunch arrangements, and my ring and more about the intentions and alliances of the people you will encounter."

I'm not keen on his tone, Red, Bruin communicates on the mental frequency he and I share from our bond. *Are we walking into a hostile camp?*

I rub the spot on my chest where I feel his spirit wriggle inside me. *Not sure. I get the feeling that I might end up owing Da an apology. Damn, I don't want to eat crow on this.*

Forewarned is forearmed. We'll take whatever they throw at us and be ready.

I draw a calming breath and focus on the "right" questions. "Are you saying I'll find this luncheon unpleasant?"

"Physically, no. I gave you and your family my word that you'll come to no harm and I meant it."

"*Buuut?*"

He lifts his knee and turns toward me on the wide bench seat. After stretching his arm across the back of it, he taps the leather of my headrest. "I did as you asked and looked into the events leading up to the Vow of Vengeance leveled against you by the hobgoblins."

"And?"

"You were indeed targeted from the beginning. I apologize that Barghest took out personal grievances against you using their power and standing within the Lakeshore Guild. That's not what our organization is about."

As we move through the streets, I track where we are. If something happens later, I'd like to know where to take my complaints. "So, if you know they targeted us, and you know Barghest is a bunch of dark, necromancer dickwads with an ax to grind, why do you think I'll have an unpleasant meeting? Shouldn't people apologize and make nice?"

Garnet arches an ebony brow as if that suggestion offends him somehow. "You assume the other Guild Governors care about internal sect squabbles. To them, you're an unknown startup who possesses more power than you should and has become embroiled in our business."

"Embroiled? I'm more of a slow roast girl myself. I don't recall getting embroiled in anything of my choosing."

"Be that as it may, you and your family have killed close to thirty card-carrying members of the Guild over the past few months."

"In self-defense."

He lifts his broad shoulders and tilts his head from side to side. "That's your take on it. The leader of the Barghest has a different tale to tell."

"Who, Droghun? Yeah, I'm sure he does. That creeper tried to drug and paralyze me so he could drag me into the shadows of the forest and do goddess only knows what to me. He offends me on every level. Forgive me if I don't put much faith in anything spewing out of his mouth."

Garnet frowns but I have no idea what part of what I said offends him. "He claims you have illusions of grandeur and conspire to take his seat as Druid Guild Governor."

I laugh. "And join a bunch of creepy, power-driven misogynists out to squash anyone who doesn't play by their rules? Yeah no, I can't see me fitting in at that roundtable."

His lips purse and the truck fills with the low rumble of his lion's growl. "Is that how you see me?"

I sigh and take a moment to consider. "I think you are definitely power-driven and would have no problem squashing someone who crosses you, but no, I don't believe you're creepy enough to try to strip me down as a blood sacrifice or overpower me with drugs and paralytics because you don't have the balls to come at me head-on."

He shakes his head. "But that's all I get? I rank just above rapists and spineless psychopaths. Well, one thing's for certain, a male always knows where he stands with you."

I bite my bottom lip and groan. "Sorry. It's a family trait. I don't filter well. I've ended more than a few friendships by telling it as I see it. In truth, you rank quite a bit higher than that, and you're gaining points all the time."

He flips his fingers and waves that away. "No need to apologize. Your experience thus far with our organization is tainted, to say the least. I do, however, intend to prove to you that the Lakeshore Guild of Empowered Ones is more than what you think."

I doubt that but where there's life there's hope, amirite?

"Even if I think your boy's club of dictators and delinquents should come out from behind their iron curtain to get a fresh air perspective on what's going on in the city streets?"

He dips his chin. "Yes, even then."

I'm not sure what to expect as Garnet opens my door and offers his hand to help me out of the truck. A corporate center in the heart of the city maybe? A private dining room at a swank restaurant? What I *don't* expect is to step down from the chrome running board of the Hummer-sine and be standing at the Toronto Harbourfront looking at the *Jubilee Queen* Riverboat Cruise ship.

"Shall we?" Garnet gestures toward the long, red carpet that leads from the parking drop-off loop to the white and blue riverboat bobbing at the end of the dock.

"Sure, why not?"

"Take my hand, Lady Druid."

I chuckle and strike off under my own steam. "Pass. I've been walking on my own since I was eleven months old. I can make it a few hundred feet to a boat."

"That's not the point." His voice is tight. "By entering the meeting on my arm, a message is conveyed that you are here as my guest. There will be a great many powerful people in the room. Having them know I won't tolerate aggression toward you will go a long way toward me keeping you safe for the next few hours and upholding my oath to your father."

I sigh and look up at him. "Seriously?"

Garnet arches an ebony brow, his long, wavy hair framing his face and brushing his pecs. He's an easy foot and a half taller than me and a hundred and fifty pounds heavier. As far as the intimidation factor goes, between him and me, he wins hands-down.

"Fine, but I want it on the record that it rankles everything in me to play the part of the swooning female to your big and brawny."

"Noted."

I step closer, and when he bends his arm at the elbow and holds his hand up ahead of us, I rest my palm on his wrist. "And I may not have the heightened hearing of a lion shifter, but I heard the amusement in your voice when you said that."

He chuckles and runs his free hand over his mouth to sober. "Apologies. I find your lack of pomp quite entertaining. I admire your transparency. It's refreshing."

"Yeah, but we're still in the honeymoon stage. You'll likely change your mind once we spend more time together."

"Then I suppose time will tell." As much as this guy might seem like the consummate gentleman, I hear my father's warning playing on a loop in the back of my head. Da doesn't make accusations lightly, and he's come across Garnet Grant enough times in the past years in the police stations to take a serious disliking to him.

The wind coming off the lake holds the bite of winter, so I flip the collar of my jacket up to protect my neck. We stop our stroll along the red carpet to collect two champagne flutes from a server stationed as a greeter.

I feel bad for the guy. It's chilly out here.

There's another arrival ahead of us, so we amble to the side and wait for the congestion to clear.

Garnet offers me my glass of champagne, and I stare at it. He chuckles and leans down to speak directly into my ear. "It's a mimosa, not poison. Would you like me to take the first sip and be your royal taste-tester?"

I flash him a haughty look and accept the glass. "In honor of transparency and before we embroil ourselves in more guild business, may I ask you something?"

He sips from the edge of his glass and shrugs. "Ask away."

"What is it that gets you and your men arrested so often that my father has you pegged as one of Toronto's biggest crime lords?"

He chokes on his champagne, and I give his broad back a couple of whacks to clear the pipes. "Is that what he told you?" He guides me farther off the red runway and lowers his voice. "Your father thinks I run a crime syndicate?"

"Well, not in so many words, but I know my father. He's a father first, a cop second, and a druid third. For him to take such a disliking to you, it's because you offend something he values. Since it's not my brothers or me, the next most important thing to him is his sense of law and justice."

Garnet nods to a male in a double-breasted suit and waits until the man passes before talking. "I've researched him extensively over the past weeks. He's rather rigid in his moral code. I'm sure living up to that level of censure was tough."

I swallow my drink and laugh. "Nice try. I see what you did there, but no, we're not turning the conversation around on me. I am very clear about the lines my father draws between right and wrong and agree almost completely with how he views the world. My question is what *you* do that lands you in the station enough to be put on his naughty list."

By the change in Garnet's demeanor, I know I've struck a nerve. He studies me with a cold gaze and takes another long sip of his drink. "Honestly, Fiona, there are people in the world who simply dislike those who have more than them."

I stiffen and step back. "Not my father, which—if you

researched him as you said—you know. Niall Cumhaill wouldn't care less if you owned half the city as long as your moral codes aligned. Which they don't, or you wouldn't have tried to front."

Garnet narrows his gaze as his frame grows rigid. "Just because someone doesn't want to get into defending his personal life in a public setting doesn't mean he's fronting."

"Maybe. Or maybe your admiration of transparency doesn't extend past protecting your king-of-the-castle image. Too bad. I was genuinely starting to like you."

I swig back the rest of my mimosa and stride over to the ship's purser, who is greeting the guests. He's adorable in his sailor suit and white gloves, and I figure if all else is a bust on this riverboat to Hell, at least there is some nice scenery.

He reaches forward when I arrive at the boarding planks and takes my hand. "Welcome aboard the *Jubilee Queen*. Your party is gathering for appetizers on the upper deck. We hope you have a wonderful cruise."

I step across the boarding planks and smile. "I doubt that very much hotness, but thanks for trying."

CHAPTER TWO

The *Jubilee Queen* lets off a long blast of its foghorn to signal us disembarking from the dock. The jostle of the engines gearing up rocks the ship, and I sway. Garnet is there to steady me and places a possessive hand at the base of my spine.

"Say what you will against me in private, Lady Druid, but I take my oath seriously and won't leave an opening for you to be harmed. I would rather you be angry at me than have to kill a colleague I respect because my position on the matter is unclear."

"Um...thank you?" I'm not sure where I fell by the end of that oration but whatevs. "I get it. You're better at appreciating honesty than you are offering it. As an alpha, I expect admitting flaws and exposing weaknesses to others is unsettling. I'm sorry I hopped on a soapbox."

The relief on his face gives me hope. At least on some basic levels, I understand where Garnet Grant is coming from. After we take off our jackets and hand them to the girl behind the coat-check counter, we head off.

He lets me take the stairs first, and I feel the warmth of his gaze on my ass. I'm not sure whether to be pleased that my ass really does look awesome in these pants or weirded out because he's old enough to be my father.

"Huh," I mumble as I settle at the top of the stairs.

"Something wrong?" Garnet asks.

"It's just…this *is* the luncheon for the Empowered Ones of Toronto, isn't it?"

"Your point?"

I shrug. "Nothing. I guess I expected it to be more Hogwarts majestic dining hall and less next-door neighbor's bridal shower. You know her, remember? She belongs to your quilting guild."

He arches an ebony brow and chuckles. "Right, how could I forget? Janine. We're BFFs. Is she the one standing on her porch holding a yappy ball of fur?"

"Yes, that's Skippy. What that dog lacks in size and character, he more than makes up for in incessant barking at anything that moves."

"Charming."

"You have no idea."

"Grand Governor," a man says as he steps up to Garnet. His skin is mossy green, and he smells a little like he took a bath in swamp water before coming. "If I knew we were free to bring arm candy, I would have done so as well."

I stiffen as Garnet's hold on my hip grows tighter. "Malachi, now, now, we both know you've never had the grace or the charms to secure arm candy. If you'd like to say Lady Cumhaill is beautiful, perhaps make your comment as simple as that. Women appreciate transparency—or so I've been recently reminded."

"We do." I force a smile for Malachi and muster as much sweet and sincere as I can summon. "Thank you, by the way. I like to think my pleasing exterior distracts men from noticing I'm both intelligent and deadly. In a battle, it helps to be underestimated from the beginning."

Malachi cants his head to the side like a puzzled dog.

"If you'll excuse us," Garnet says in that amused tone of voice he seems to get around me.

He uses his hold on my hip to guide me away from that conversation and straight toward a lithe girl a little older than me with long silver hair and more fringe than John Wayne. Animal hide bellbottoms ride low on her hips, and beaded braids fall on both sides of her slender face.

When she turns to greet us, I notice she has the same tipped ears and panther grace as the French-kisser I met in the Doyle grove.

"Suede Silverbirch, this is Fiona Cumhaill."

Her face lights up with genuine warmth. "Fiona, a.k.a. the girl who's finally more annoying to the males of the Lakeshore Guild than me? Nice to meet you. Happy to have you around to shake things up."

I like her immediately. "My pleasure. If truth be told, so far, all my offenses have been reactive, not proactive. If it weren't for the members of the Lakeshore Guild coming after me and mine, you'd likely still have your place at the top of the annoyance list."

Her grin is wide and infectious. "I'm sure I would. Come, have you tried the appetizers? They're delish."

I look back at Garnet, but he holds up his hands and surrenders me to the force of nature that is Suede Silverbirch. When we're out of earshot of the men, she hugs my arm against her side and faces me toward the food selections. "Let's talk fondue. Are you a cheese or chocolate girl?"

I laugh. "Chocolate. One hundy percent."

"Oh, thank the goddess. I didn't want to be the only one. Come, let's dig in and make them all puff up in protest."

"Hey, one of my specialties."

The two of us set up in front of the chocolate fountains, and she hands me a small white plate. "Okay, here's the lowdown. Me, Garnet, and Zxata—you see that swarthy guy with blue hair standing in front of the picture of the queen? That's Zxata—yeah, we're trustworthy."

With a tilt of her head, she draws my attention to a tall, Korean man in a blue suede blazer. "Xavier is head of the vampires. He and his sect are only as loyal as greed allows. If you have an understanding with them and they get a better offer, you'll lose out. Count on that."

She picks up a few pineapple chunks and a couple of strawberries with the metal serving tongs. "The hobgoblins are all assholes, which you know because Kartak of the Narrows already took a run at you as a favor to Droghun. That's not over, so don't take your eyes off him in a crowded room."

Not over? *Awesomesauce.*

"I have no grievance with him. I wish he'd drop it."

"Sorry, sweetie. Never going to happen. You denied him his vengeance, you killed his men, and you brought their dishonorable behavior of attacking outside the scope of the charter to light. You're walking dead in their opinion. That fight is coming your way, so be prepared."

"Forewarned is forearmed, right?"

Suede grabs a wooden skewer, stabs it into a chunk of pineapple on her plate, and holds it under the flow of dark chocolate. I do the same but pick milk chocolate.

"Okay, what else?" She looks around the room while she chews on her fruit. "Make friends with the mages. They're cool. Witches be bitches... Oh, and do you see the blond in black leather looking bored in the corner?"

"The kid tatted up with ripped jeans and the guitar?"

"Yep. That's Nikon Tsambikos. Old money. Arcane powers. As much as he despises these mixers, he's hands-down the most powerful being in the room."

"Being? What do you mean by that?"

"I mean he's one of the immortals. Not sure how or when but the rumor is that sometime way back when in ancient

Rome—maybe medieval times—his family tapped into eternal magic."

"He looks like he's ready to audition for a heavy metal band but will need a fake ID."

"Looks mean nothing with the empowered. Take a guess how old he is?"

I cast a sweeping glance his way and assess his punk spikes and guyliner. Seeing her amusement, I tack on a couple of extra years for good measure. "Twenty-one?"

Her smile widens. "Try twenty-one hundred."

"Hubba-*wha?*" I dip another chunk of pineapple and swing around for another look. "Yeah no, I'd never have guessed that. I thought when you said ancient Rome you meant his ancestors, not his parents.

Suede catches one of the passing servers and snags us two more mimosas. "That's about it for the hierarchy. The rest of us are lesser fae and shouldn't give you any trouble. Oh, and remember that most of the people in this room can hear your heartbeat, smell your emotions, and tell if you're horny. Try not to be horny. It makes the men cocky and stupid."

"I'm not horny." I scan the forty or so people in the room and nod. "And I won't be getting horny while I'm here."

"Okay, good." She takes a long sip of her drink and smiles. "So, we're girlfriends now, yeah?"

I blink. "Um… Yeah, I guess so."

"Okay, then from one girlfriend to another, tell me. Why do you wear the kiss of a woodland elf?"

Now it's me choking on mimosa and Garnet patting my back as he comes up behind us looking amused. "Yes, Lady Druid. I'm curious to hear the answer to this one too. Woodland elves don't offer magical favors for no reason. What did you give him?"

As I glance around the room, I realize that at least half of the attendees are staring at me in a sideways glance. My cheeks flame hot, and I turn back to the chocolate fountain. "Nothing salacious. I saved and restored his grove. Barghest imprisoned fae and drained their essences. The elf was grateful we were able to stop it and right the balance. The kiss was unsolicited and rather unexpected."

Suede giggles. "I've heard they are very good kissers."

I offer her a small smile. "Yeah, you heard right."

The *twang-clang-twang* of metal startles me, and I jump nearly out of my skin. The captain is smacking a metal baton around the inside of a triangle to get everyone's attention. "If you'd be so kind as to move to the main deck, your luncheon will be served."

I pat my hand over my racing heart and frown. "If you'd be so kind as to provide fresh undies in the loo, I may have just peed my pants, thank you very much."

Garnet, Suede, and I happen to be standing at the back of the boat and take another couple of spears of fruit dipped in chocolate before we join the end of the pack.

I like being the last to move. It gives me a chance to study the players while no one's at my back—except Garnet, who has rarely taken his palm off the base of my spine since we boarded. "Am I really in such grave peril, or do you like to have a hand on me?"

"Will you judge me if I say a bit of both?"

"I value honesty, remember? And I *try* not to judge."

He lifts a muscled shoulder. "Then both."

The crush of bodies ahead of us thins into a single file at the top of the metal stairs, and we make our way down. The chatter of close to forty people swallows the hollow *clank, clank, clank* of my boot heels on the steps.

The main deck is set up for a sit-down meal. With two short and two long tables pushed together in a linen-draped rectangle down the center of the ship, the empowered guests and governors are seated so everyone faces inward.

It's a massive banquet table, and my skin tingles with magic the moment I'm fully in the room. I follow the energy and focus on the table's centerpiece.

It's a low rock wall fountain that runs the surface's length and provides a visual division of space complete with little cascading waterfalls of fae-enriched water.

It's the only thing remotely interesting or magical in the room, and I have a feeling it's directed at me. What I'm not sure about is whether the nod is in my favor or not.

That sparks another thought. "Have you had one of these lunch meetings on a boat like this before?"

Garnet flashes me a knowing smile. "No. It's a first."

Okay, so the entire location is directed at me. *Nice.*

I take another gander around the room and wonder what other messages might point my way. On the far end of the room, the cutie sailor sits behind the bar. On the near end, beside us, a table sits heaped with all manner of daggers, swords, and guns.

"I assume it's rude to be armed at the table?"

Garnet dips his chin. "These luncheons have been known to come to bloodshed. It's best if the weapons of greatest temptation not be too convenient. Have you anything you'd like to surrender, Lady Druid?"

I shake my head. "Nope. I'm good."

Birga and Bruin are part of me, so tough noogies. I'm not surrendering them.

"I'll catch up with you after, Fiona. Good luck." Suede pats my arm, but before she peels away, I catch her wrist.

"Don't abandon me now. I thought we'd sit together."

"I can't, sweetie. The tables are grouped by power rankings. Druids don't sit with elves. You can call and command magic. I possess nature magic. That's two different worlds in this crowd."

I'm not sure what she sees in my face, but she shakes her head. "Don't get gnarled up about it. It's the way of things. We'll reconnect upstairs for dessert."

Without waiting for an answer, Suede glides off and takes a seat on the opposite side of the room.

I scowl at Garnet. "Segregated seating based on race and power levels? Seriously?"

Garnet arches a brow and sends me a warning look. His breath is warm against the shell of my ear as he whispers close. "As a guest, remember that your footing in the community is tenuous at best. Inciting a civil uprising would be unwise for you and your family. I hope you'll win a few members over with your presence, not alienate more."

"Right. Sorry. No filter, remember?" He straightens and points at two empty seats near the front of the ship. "What? We aren't together either?"

"I'm the Grand Governor of the Lakeshore Guild. You're a druid only months into training. *No*, we don't sit together." He escorts me to my seat and pulls out my chair. When he tucks me under the table, he leans close once again. "Not yet, anyway, but at the rate you're progressing, who knows."

CHAPTER THREE

I'm seated fourth from the end on one of the long tables, between the human representative for the rugaru and a hairy man with a unibrow that I can only guess is a troll.

Both seem disinterested in striking up a convo, so I nibble on my breadstick and study the other guests as the servers lay plates in front of us.

I soon figure out the governors are the ones with the platinum pins of what looks like a lightning bolt. It's very *Harry Potter*-esque, and I look forward to telling Garnet I think so. Garnet's pin is on the lapel of his black suit jacket, some wear them on their ties, and one woman has hers on the tail of her silk neck scarf where she's tacked it to her bolero jacket.

Contrary to what I thought, the Guild Governors don't fill the tables in the power seats to my left. They sit either on or near the left, but others apparently outrank them—in power if not guild position.

At the center of the left table sits the emo goth god *sans* his guitar. Great bone structure. While burgundy lipstick and black guyliner isn't normally my thing, in a game of Marry, Fuck, or Kill, I know where he'd go.

Nope. I wouldn't kick him out of my bed.

He doesn't look like the marrying kind, and he's a god, so I'm not going to try to kill him.

He looks as bored as he did before, and I take pity on him. If I were immortal, I'd think coming to these meetings to measure the size of my dick would suck too.

Suede said he's the all-powerful one in the crowd, so the hierarchy of power must begin there.

Beside him to his right is Garnet. Makes sense. The man is the Grand Governor and Alpha of the Moon Called. I'm sure that's a big deal in these circles.

Beside emo god guy to his left is a rake of a woman with a weird aura. I'm pretty sure she's a witch. When I try to look at her, my shield tingles, and my back itches.

I recognize the sensation.

Having been through illusion bullshit with a bitch of a witch before, I decide to look under the hood. I slide my hand into the pocket of my pants and focus on seeing through her veil of illusion.

As I call on the ambient power in the air, her visual deception melts away and I yelp.

All conversation stops, and everyone turns to stare.

Okay, not my smoothest moment.

I raise my hand and wave. "Sorry. Thought I saw a spider. Big one. My mistake. S'all good."

I slink back in my chair and make a big deal about chewing my breadstick. *Mmm*, so yummy. Garnet gives me a suggestive look, and I realize I shouldn't be so engrossed with gnawing on my breadstick in a room full of men.

I stop that immediately and scratch the side of my face with my middle finger.

He covers his laughter with a cough.

I focus on eating my salad for a while, and when the room goes back to ignoring me, I give the top woman a cursory glance while pretending to study the seagulls flapping and squawking outside.

Man, someone seriously whacked her with the ugly stick—a lot—like, a real beating. What the hell happened to her face? It's not nice to stare, but I'm mesmerized.

It looks like she stood too close to the radiator, and half her face melted and hangs down past her collarbone.

How does that happen?

Although she looks like a survivor of a nuclear meltdown, I give her the benefit of the doubt and assume she's a very nice person.

Ehhh! Wrong answer.

I blink at the voice in my head. *Bruin? Was that you?*

Was what me?

Didn't you hear someone talking in my head?

No.

Okay, weird. I pick up my wine and give it a suspicious glance. Am I being drugged? Dammit, *again?*

The laughter in my head isn't mine, and it isn't Bruin's.

Hello? Who's there?

I'll give you three guesses, and the first two don't count. In a game of marry, fuck, kill, I'm the bored emo guy you invited into your bed.

My eyes flick to the center of the head table, and he's smiling. He lifts his wine glass, and for the first time in the past hour, he looks less bored.

Eavesdropping is rude, and I didn't invite you into my bed. I simply said if you were there, I wouldn't kick you out.

Then tell me where you live, and you can expect a visit. Oh, and will it be the two of us, or do you have a man warming your sheets already?

Laughter bursts up my throat, and I cover my mouth to stifle my nerves. Unbidden, images of Sloan come to mind.

Nice. I wouldn't kick him out of my bed either. I'm game.

I roll my eyes. *Okay, enough talk about horizontal hijinks and magical ménages. Not happening.*

Disappointing. Talk about a bait and switch.

I laugh. *This isn't a bait and switch. I can't be held accountable since you were infiltrating my cranium at the time of the supposed offer to do the dance of twenty toes.*

Or thirty. You forget the male model. His laughter echoes inside my mind, but nothing shows on his face.

Do you have a name, or should I call you Tom?

Tom?

You know...Peeping Tom.

Oh, I like that, but my given name is Nikon of the island of Rhodes.

You're from Rhode Island?

No, the island of Rhodes.

Isn't that the same thing?

No.

Nikon, like the camera?

It was my name first.

Can I call you Nikky?

No.

"Lady Druid?" Garnet's voice invades my focus and tears me from my mental chat session with Nikon. "Is everything all right?"

I bat my eyes and take in the disdainful looks I'm getting from all around the rectangle of rebuke. "I'm sorry, what?"

"Emperor Kartak of the Narrows expressed his discontent about you and your family holding magic hostage, and I asked if you would like to counter."

"Sure. Who's Emperor Kartak?" By the way the room stiffens, and Nikon smirks, I'm pretty sure that was another one of those "wrong question" moments.

I follow the startled gazes to the man at the corner of the short table of power. He's fourth to Nick's right and three positions away from where I sit on the opposite side of the room.

Man, it would help if I knew how the ranking of this seating system works.

Emperor Kartak looks like a character out of one of my brother's role-playing modules. He's decked out in a blue and gold tunic with a leather chest plate beneath, and even with his weapons checked at the door, he looks the part of the fearsome warrior.

His face is almost animalistic, his nose wide and flat, his ears extend off the side of his head to a four-inch point, and his long, straight hair is slicked back into a samurai topknot.

When I meet his cold gaze, I lock down my reaction and give him a little wave. "Hey, there. Sorry about that. We haven't met yet."

"Are you not smart enough to learn the faces of the men you scorn?" Droghun snaps.

"Men I scorn? Seriously? You were so pee-your-pants scared about another group of druids moving in on your turf, you sicced your creepy subway-dwelling minions on us, and we mopped the floor with them. You can't blame us. If anyone has the right to wave the scorn flag, it's us."

"Enough," the drippy-faced witch says. "The matter of the Vow of Vengeance is not up for discussion. You were asked to answer to the fact that your family possesses the ability to take the ambient power from everyone in the city. How do you speak to that point?"

I shrug. "We wouldn't do that."

"But you *did* do that," someone with a raspy voice shouts to my right. "You stole the ambient power."

I lean forward, but the speaker is on my side, and I can't see who it was. "That was an accident...and we only borrowed it. As you all may or may not know, our family has some of the longest and deepest roots in the druid world, but we're new to the game. When we realized we impacted the city's magic, we rectified— and improved—the situation within days."

"How did you do it?" Droghun snaps. "How do you explain a family of startups sashaying in and releasing enough magic into the air to fuel an entire city?"

"She's made a pact with demons," the raspy heckler from the far end shouts.

The room looks appalled, and I take it that demons are as undesirable in the magical world as they are in the human world.

"First off, I didn't know demons were a thing until you said that. Second, I love how Droghun used the word sashay. Most men wouldn't be comfortable using such a pansy-ass word. Kudos on your manhood. Third, druids are gifted to connect with and command the natural physical world. My family and I used maps we found on the internet to locate the natural ley lines beneath us and unclogged the drain so nature magic could flow freely."

"Bullshit." Droghun slams his fist onto the table, and his Cornish hen flies over onto a witch's plate beside him. "You're lying, and we're going to prove it."

"Well, have fun trying because it's the truth. While setting up our lives, we realized we drained the limited natural magic, so we rectified it. Now, fae magic runs freely and fills all our lungs with every breath. You're welcome."

"And you profess you can add to it?" Xavier, the king of the vampires asks. He didn't seem scary when Suede pointed him out earlier, but having him focused on me makes my skin crawl. "There's more power to be had?"

My shield tingles against my back, and I recognize the danger without the cosmic warning. "Fae magic is like other forms of energy. It can neither be created nor destroyed. It can, however, be utilized and, if we're not careful, abused. We replaced and stabilized the ambient magic at a greater level than before. We did that by connecting the ley lines into the water table. If you want more power, you're welcome to draw it from there. We're not the magic police. You are. Or at least you're supposed to be."

"What's that supposed to mean?" a witch across from me snaps.

"It means that since the moment Fionn mac Cumhaill marked me as his successor and the leader of the Fianna, powerful people from within your organization have targeted my family and me with no reason and on no grounds. Why? We had done nothing except exist. That doesn't fill me with confidence in your organization's commitment to govern. Where's the safety and justice for all?"

Droghun barks a laugh. "You think you're the chosen successor? You are so full of shit that your eyes are brown."

"No, they're Irish blue, and you're pissy because your days of calling your Barghest psychopaths druids are ending. Your connection to nature is tainted by blood sacrifice and enslaving innocent fae to siphon energy. It's disgusting. No wonder you couldn't increase the ambient magic. Nature doesn't respect you."

Droghun stands and leans heavily into his palms on the table. "Bite your tongue, bitch. No one here believes your lies or your slander."

I stand and match his pose. "Well, they should. If they can read my heart rate and smell lies, they know I've only spoken the truth. Since the moment Fionn called on me, I've grown stronger with his blessings. I stand as a follower of the Ancient Order of Druids, which means a connection to nature and respecting the cycle of life. Your practices are appalling."

Droghun's lips quiver behind his snarl. "You don't know what you're talking about."

I bark a laugh. "Seriously? I was kidnapped and tortured at the druid stones a few months ago. After being strapped to that altar stone, staked down by my palms, and read the ritual for holy exsanguination with a spear tip pointed over my chest, I have a pretty clear idea about what I'm talking about."

"Is this true?" the leader of the mages asks.

Droghun lifts his chin and glares. "What she describes is unbelievable."

"And your way of not denying it. What I describe is one hundy percent true. The altar stone is still there if any of you would like to test it for blood. Human police have found numerous bodies discarded at the bottom of the raised stones. I can get you the police reports. This isn't an isolated occurrence. Barghest's practices are abhorrent and threaten your anonymity living among humans. I, for one, find them holding the druid seat in an organization like this disgusting."

"You see?" Droghun shouts and points at me. "I told you. The bitch shows her true colors. She's after a seat at the table."

I roll my eyes. "Not bloody likely. I said that you and your Black Dog assholes don't deserve the right to hold a *druid* seat. You are filthy necromancers, plain and simple. Keep your damned seat, but don't associate it with druids or what we stand for."

I plop down in my chair, swig back the rest of my wine, and hold my empty glass in the air. "Can I get a refill?"

"Wow, dinner and a show," Suede says.

I look up from where I'm hiding behind the dessert table and stuffing my face. "And a good time was had by all."

Suede's gaze dances. "You did well to stand up to Droghun. There are murmurs of respect hovering throughout the whispers in the crowd that weren't there an hour ago."

I pop another brownie into my mouth and put another three on my plate.

"What are you doing?"

"I couldn't stomach lunch after Kartak and Droghun, but the wine went down smooth and easy. I figure I better carb-load or

I'm liable to do something I'll regret before we get back to the dock."

"Maybe there's hope for the afternoon yet." Nikon sidles up to join us. "Any chance the regrettable actions involve lewd acts of one-on-one or mortally wounding certain members of the guild governing body? Either would be acceptable."

I smile and plug another brownie into my mouth. "Those are exactly the two things I'm trying to avoid."

"Don't fight it, lass." He leans past me to grab a crème Brulee. "Go with your first instinct. It's the right one." He brushes close as he leans back, and I can't help but notice how delicious he smells.

Gawd. That can't be natural.

When Nikon leaves, I chuckle. "Is he always like that?"

Suede blinks and picks up a blue shortbread with a red berry glaze. "I couldn't tell you. I've never seen him interact beyond a yes or no answer with anyone—ever."

"Huh, weird. I'm not sure what that's about. He's pretty cool. We chatted cranium-to-cranium earlier. He's funny."

"If you say so."

"Miss Cumhaill, a moment." I die a little inwardly as Malachi saunters over with a plate full of sweets. "Is it true you bonded with a mythical grizzly bear?"

Suede makes a *tsking* noise and scowls. "That's a rather personal question, Malachi. Did she ask you about your tail? I don't think so."

The tightening around his eyes tells me he's not fond of talking about his tail, and that makes me all the more curious. What is he that he has one?

"So, is that a yes or a no about the bear?" He chooses to ignore Suede's disapproval.

There's no real reason not to answer. The Moon Called know about Bruin, and so do the hobgoblins. I don't suppose it's much of a secret. "Yes, my animal companion is a bear. You heard right."

"May I see him?"

"I'm sorry, what?"

"I'd like to see him and see what he can do."

I'm contemplating the political fallout of Nikon's advice about going with my first instinct. Instead, I shove another brownie in my mouth. "Sorry. He's not a party favor I bring out to amuse people. He's a lethal battle warrior."

"You won't show him to us?"

I lean closer and lower my voice. "If you threaten me with bodily harm, he'll come out for you. You'll be dead before you see much, but yeah, you might catch a glimpse of him before your innies become outies and someone is called to swab the decks."

The emo god snorts across the room and raises his glass to no one in particular.

Yeah, yeah, yuck it up Nikky.

Garnet takes that as his hint to rescue me. "Having a nice time, Lady Druid?"

"The best."

He slides that hand around my back again and whisks me away. "Come, we're about to dock. Let's get our jackets."

"Fiona." I turn to meet the warm smile of the swarthy, blue-haired male that Suede pointed out as an ally earlier. I recognize the species traits of vertically slit eyes and pale silver skin cracked with darker tones beneath. He's an ash tree nymph, like my boss. "I'm Zxata. It's nice to meet you finally. I've heard a lot about you."

My smile falters a little. "I'm sure everyone here has. Why be famous when you can be infamous, amirite?"

He waves that away. "From my sister Myra. She speaks fondly of you, and in all our years, she's never been wrong about a person yet. You must be truly special for her to sing your praises."

No wonder he reminds me of Myra. They're siblings. "I adore your sister. Best boss *evah*. I'm so happy to meet you."

Zxata bows his head and a sad look passes between him and Garnet. "I won't keep you two. I simply wanted to introduce myself and extend a warm hello. I'm sure I'll see you at the emporium at some point."

I squeeze his hand. "I look forward to it. Thanks for saying hi. Have a wonderful weekend."

The boat bumps against the dock, and he backs away. I have no idea what the shift in emotion between him and Garnet was about. I hope it wasn't something I said.

Honestly, with my history, there's no telling.

CHAPTER FOUR

B y the time I get home, change, and head down to the kitchen, I'm pretty sure I've put us squarely in the crosshairs of at least two or three more magical sects. Hobgoblins hate us. Barghest hates us. I have no idea who the raspy-voiced heckler was down the table. The drippy-faced lady didn't seem keen on me either, and they were only the ones I spoke to.

"Hey, chicky-poo." Calum comes down the stairs dressed for his shift. "How'd your first meeting with the Justice League go? Did you charm the pants off them?"

"That would be a no. Although I did get an offer of carnal pleasure from an immortal god and I made friends with a cool lady elf named Suede."

Calum chuckles and grabs his lunch off the counter. "Suede is a cool name for a cool lady. You'll have to tell me about the indecent proposal in the morning. I'm out. Laters."

"Laters. Safe home."

I finish peeling the carrots and potatoes and toss them in olive oil and Gran's special blend of herbs. After I dump them around the chicken, I cover the whole thing in foil and pop it in the oven.

I'm setting my timer when my cell rings in my hands. I smile at the name that pops up. "Myra, how's things? Do you need me to come in tonight?"

"No, sweetie. Tomorrow's soon enough. I've got some new occult texts coming in first thing, and the book I ordered for your man's father should arrive with that too. Any idea when he'll be back in town?"

I think about Sloan and sigh. "No plans to see him until the next crisis hits, but the way things go around here, you never know."

There's a long pause at the other end of the line, and I wonder if a customer is beckoning my boss.

"Do you need to go?"

"Uh... No, I was wondering how it went this afternoon. You know, with the guild?"

"I met your brother. He seems awesome."

"Zxata, yes, he *is* awesome. If you ever need someone at your back at one of those meetings, you go straight to him. He'll protect you with his life."

"Hopefully, I won't have to have anyone laying their lives on the line for me. Garnet was all alpha protector for me today. It was rather over the top but well-meaning and sweet."

"Sounds like Garnet."

I hear the subtext pulsing through the line loud and clear. It's not the first time she's reacted to the name. "So, you and Garnet were a thing, eh? When was that? What happened? And why didn't you tell me this before?"

"Garnet and I are ancient history. I don't need to go into all that. I simply wanted to ask you about the meeting."

I laugh. "Sure you did. Well, the meeting went about as well as things around me go these days, but Garnet was great. He was attentive and protective and a true gentleman escort. He impressed me."

"Good. I'm glad to hear there are still moments when he can get out of his way and be the man I...uh, knew."

"*Knew?* Are you sure that's what you were going to say? It sounds like you might say something more."

"No. That's what I meant to say. Okay, then, Fi. I'll see you in the morning. Sweet dreams."

"You too." I hang up and stare out the kitchen window at my beautiful grove. "Myra and Garnet. Huh." Somehow, the idea that the two of them have a history gives me the warm and fuzzies. I can see how they'd be good for one another.

I'm still staring out at the magical forest in my back yard when the buck and doe from my grove step out of the trees and trot over to look at the fish in the koi pond.

After the chaos and emotion of my afternoon, the pull of wanting to spend time out there is undeniable. I grab Beauty off the table, gather my chunky sweater off the hook by the back door, and cross what's left of my back lawn toward my sacred grove.

Sacred is a funny word when you think about it.

Before being a druid, it brought to mind images of the Sistine Chapel, the rites and rituals of the Native Canadians, and the few things of our mother's we keep on the top shelf of the glass curio in the family room by her blue chair.

I never really considered anything that I owned could qualify. I was wrong. Our sacred grove is truly cherished as hallowed ground by me and mine.

As I step under the shade-bearing canopy of the leaves above, it's like falling under a spell of calm. A family grove is a place of power for a druid. It's also a place of quiet contemplation, reverence, and gratitude.

I'm thankful for every leaf at the end of every twig, every blade of grass beneath my feet, and every creature—fae or otherwise—living within.

Over the past week, I've worked on getting to know each tree, every plant pushing up through the rich soil, and every creature and colony making this their home.

When I reach my woven basket swing, I set Beauty down, pull on my sweater, and move the thick wool blanket on the cushion to take my seat. The moment I'm settled, Flopsy, one of the Ostara rabbits, flies over and I make a little nest in the blankets beside me.

"Hello, pretty girl. How was your day?"

The magical bunny looks up at me, her nose and whiskers twitching with what I'm sure is a fascinating tale. Sadly, I don't speak woodland like Emmet.

Pip and Nilm climb down from one of the larger trees and into the woven swing opposite mine. It's the same as the one I'm sitting in, and I love it as much as mine. Every time I see it, I chuckle to myself.

Sloan bought it because he knew I'd never share mine.

Smart man. He gets me better than most.

Pip grips her elbows and shivers, her antennae bouncing over her round, cherubic face.

"Are you cold, sweetie?" I guess they would be. Canadian summers are hot but short. September and October bring cooler temperatures as the trees start to go into hibernation and by November and December, it'll be colder still. January through March is stupid-freakin'-freezing, and anyone who can do it avoids going out as much as possible.

Minus forty is redonkulous.

"Okay, cold. Good point. You're not used to weather like this. I'll find a way to fix that for you." I lean forward and touch their little arms. *"Internal Warmth."*

The rush of heat builds in my chest and extends down my arms and into my touch. When Pip and Nilm sink into the hold and sigh, I know it's taken hold in them as well. "There, that's better for now. I promise I'll think of something more permanent."

With images of Ostara rabbits wearing ear warmers in my mind, I wonder about expanding the *Internal Warmth* spell I've already mastered. I finger through the pages of my druid spell-book, Beauty, and am grateful to have her.

I've loved her from the first moment I saw her at Myra's bookstore, and she loved Sloan's worn, brown leather spellbook from the moment she encountered him and got it on in the cabinet drawer.

It was crazy to me, at first, to think of books as having conscious will and instincts. I like to think my outlook on life has broadened considerably over the past few months.

I look at the cursive flourishes in the penmanship of my book and smile. Sloan Mackenzie is a modern thinker with an arcane soul. I pull out my cell and call up his contact.

Sitting in my swing, flipping through Beauty, and thankful for you.

Are ye drunk?

No. Do you know how to take a compliment?

From most people, I do. Sorry. How'd today go?

I stare at the screen. I didn't tell Sloan about the parley with the Lakeshore Guild. I thought he'd think it was too dangerous to go on my own and would start an argument.

How does he know? Who ratted me out?

The phone rings in my hand, and I jump. Big surprise. It's Sloan. I roll my eyes and accept the call. "Hello."

"Stop tryin' to figure out who told me about the luncheon, and tell me about it."

I chuckle and lean deeper into my swing. "You sound very sure that's what I was doing."

"Because that's what yer doin'. Now, how'd it go?"

"Mostly fine. I may have put my foot in it and rubbed a few people the wrong way."

"So, nothing out of the ordinary."

"Har-har. It was fine."

"*Buuut?*"

"I don't know... I guess I'm having an off day. I miss the sun of summer. My fae are cold, and I realized the hobgoblins aren't going to let things go, and Dillan's sad because he and Kady called it quits."

"I'm sorry to hear about Dillan and Kady, but there's not much ye can do about that. I'll send ye a few ideas about how to enchant yer grove's thermostat. As fer the hobgoblins—be incredibly careful. They're not known for their sunny dispositions, and I worry."

"I know you do. I will."

There's a long stretch of quiet, then he sighs. "Da is callin' me, so I'll have to run. Listen, have Emmet pick up some of those mint brownies you like from O'Landry's bakeshop. He's on afternoons and should be heading home soon. That will brighten yer outlook."

Honestly, if I ate another brownie I'd barf. "Yeah, thanks. Maybe I will."

"Are ye sure that's all it is, Fi? Anything I can help with personally? Just say the word."

I know what he's getting at, and I can't.

Before he left earlier in the week, he made it clear that he intends for us to get together, and he's willing to wait until I sort out all my druid stuff. When I'm ready to give in to what he thinks is the inevitability of us being a druid super-couple, all I have to do is "say the word." But before I can be half of a druid super-couple, I have to learn to be a super druid.

"It's only a case of the blues. Go. You gotta run, and my timer's going to go off in the house any minute. Nobody likes burnt chicken."

"'Kay. Be safe."

"You too."

I set my cell in my lap, close the spellbook, and give myself a shake. "I'm not sure what's bringing me down in the dumps, but I'm over it. I'm Fi-freaking-Cumhaill, and I don't do mopey."

"Good to know."

I jump and squawk. Flopsy flies off, her butt raining rabbit droppings down as she goes.

Nikon's eyes pop wide. "I've never had that effect on a female before. I'm not sure how to take it."

I pat my chest to get my heart pumping again and extricate myself from under my mound of blankie. "Maybe it's showing up where you weren't invited. You literally scared the crap out of her."

"Hey, there was no way to predict that would happen."

I stand, fluff out the blanket, and tuck it around Pip and Nilm in the opposite swing. I don't know if Nikon can see them or not, but it doesn't matter. My fae are cold, and I'm finished with it for now. "Did you come over solely to scare my woodland friends, or was there some other reason for you being here?"

"I wanted to say I enjoyed meeting you today. You were the highlight of an otherwise boring and predictable gathering of mediocrity."

"Ha! If I was the highlight, your bar is incredibly low. I wasn't even memorable today. I was on my best behavior."

He chuckles. "Then I look forward to being around in the moments when you're not behaving."

I wave that away. "What's this about? I've got dinner in the oven and things to pretend to do. If you're still angling for me to go to bed with you, the answer remains no."

"Your loss, but not why I'm here. Something you said stuck with me and I thought we could have a bit of fun." He holds out his hand and waggles his brow. "Would you care to join me for a little mischief and mayhem?"

I laugh. "You do realize that I live with five cops, right? Mischief and mayhem aren't things I strive for."

"I promise you'll enjoy this."

Studying his gaze, I reach out with my senses and get nothing back but a guy seeking companionship in an otherwise tedious existence.

"I won't be arrested or embarrass my family?"

"You won't be arrested. I can't say what embarrasses your family. With you, I'd guess *that* bar is quite high."

I laugh again. "All right, I'll give you that. But I *do* have dinner in the oven. I can't be long."

"Fifteen minutes, and you'll be in your kitchen with a smile on your face and a little mischief managed."

I slap my hand in his knowing I might well regret this later. "Sure, why not? I solemnly swear that I am up to no good."

———

Nikon flashes us from the grove in my back yard to the ring of druid stones where the Black Dog thugs took me to sacrifice me on the altar. Set in a flat clearing warded to prevent human discovery, seventeen rugged stones, each reaching about eight feet from the ground, encircle a stone slab with a hole in the center. Beneath the opening sits a wide-rimmed earthenware urn buried in the earth below.

"Is that the blood bucket?"

I nod. "Charming isn't it? It's supposed to be an authentic replica of Drombeg Circle in West Cork, except the original altar didn't have a blood-letting component."

"You sound very sure."

"I am. When Fionn mac Cumhaill named me his successor, he took me back in time to have an *airneal*. We sat in the original stones and shared a meal while he told me fireside stories about my ancestry and his hopes for me."

Nikon suddenly looks much older than his twenty-something visage. "It's cool that you got a look at the past without having to live all the years in between."

As quickly as the clouds set in behind his eyes, he pushes them away. "So, lady's choice. Shall we destroy it, hex it, or have you got a better idea for it?"

I blink as my hamster trips in my mental wheel. "I'm sorry, what? What are we talking about?"

"The altar stone. You said it offends your druid sensibilities to have it here and know it exists in your city."

"True story."

"All right then, what are we going to do about it?"

I raise a brow and chuckle. "Are you inviting me to be a vigilante vandal?"

"Are you saying you don't want to?"

"Are you trying to enlarge the enormous bullseye already on my back?"

"Do you expect me to believe you're conflicted? Because I don't."

I chuckle again. "Okay, I'm not, but my father taught me to at least consider the consequences of my actions."

"Then ignore them?"

"That's usually my go-to, yeah."

His mischievous smile makes him look even younger. Man, it must suck to go through life looking like you're eighteen. I still haven't wrapped my head around him being over two millennia old.

Annnd he's waiting. "Okay, pros and cons. Destroying it gets rid of it, but they can come along and replace it with another easily enough. How could we hex it?"

Nikon shrugs. "What would set your scales of justice back to balanced?"

I think about that and smile. "Whatever ill intent is done on an innocent is transferred to the one inflicting it instead."

"The old Leviticus theory. 'Fracture for fracture, eye for eye, tooth for tooth; anyone who maims another shall suffer the same injury in return.' Is that it?"

"Almost, but not in return—instead. I want the innocent to remain unscathed, and the injury to transfer completely to the one wielding the ill intent."

"A fine point of distinction, but the devil is in the details." He places his hand on the smooth stone of the sacrificial altar and closes his eyes. A moment later, he smiles and blinks us home. "All done and back before dinner as promised."

I chuckle. "Seriously? Just like that?"

He nods, his blond hair blowing in the autumn breeze.

"Well, thanks. I'll sleep better knowing those Barghest dickwads won't be able to hurt people there anymore. The stones are quite comforting to me, but not the way they're using them."

Nikon bows and his words hang on the night air as he disappears. "Mischief managed."

CHAPTER FIVE

The brass bell over the door chimes as I enter Myra's Mystical Emporium. I've been working here part-time for a couple of months and I *lurrrve* it. The otherworld bookshop has become one of my happy places. "Myra, who's your favorite protégé? Yeah, that's right. I come bearing gifts of java and sugary succulence—"

My footing falters as my shield burns hot on my back.

Hubba-wha? I freeze inside the doorway and listen. There's a muffled sound in the back, but it's quiet and could be anything.

"Myra? You okay?" The hair on my arms stands on end, and there's no response. "Myra? I need you to answer me."

When nothing comes back at me but a whiff of rotten stink and negatively charged air, I err on the side of caution. I've been down this road before in the store, and it ended with me getting kidnapped and Sloan getting poisoned by vampire venom.

Bruin, I need you. Something's got my shield in a tizzy and my gut tells me all is not well.

On it. There's a flutter in my chest, then a building pressure in my lungs until the *pop* of him breaking free of my body in his spirit form.

While he's on recon, I stash my Tim Horton's booty, flex my hand, and call Birga to action. With my intention clear, the ancient spear belonging to my many-times-great-grandfather materializes in my grip.

She senses my anxiety, and I feel her hopeful anticipation for bloodshed. "Olly olly oxen free."

Moving deeper into the bookstore in measured steps, I avoid the main corridor and take a meandering path through side aisles and around the displays.

As quickly as I can while still being careful, I make my way to the customer counter at the back of the storefront. The front section of the emporium is a standard bookstore displaying the mainstream tomes and texts.

Then, there's an offshoot section at the back that's three stories high with floor-to-ceiling bookshelves, iron ladders that hang on rails, and galleries to walk around.

Myra's home tree grows in the center of the floor back there, beneath a vast, ornate glass dome that arches over the entire space.

My nerves push at the base of my throat, and I try to swallow past the blockage. Nope. Doesn't help. I reach the antique display cabinet Myra uses as a customer counter and am both happy and sad not to find Myra here.

During the last attack, Sloan and I found her here unconscious. I'm not sure if it's better that she's not here or not.

Bruin roars in the back, and I launch forward.

I bolt through the entranceway to the back in time to see Myra crumple to the floor as her assailant shoots a bolt of black energy. Bruin goes into spirit mode, evades the attack and reforms behind the guy, and swipes across his head.

The dark magic hits the home tree, and Myra screams and twists in agony on the floor. As that guy goes down in a bloody explosion of claws to flesh, I harpoon-throw Birga at a second man who's bending down to grab Myra.

"*True Trajectory.*"

Birga is as swift and true as always. She cuts through the air and only misses piercing the man center mass because he vanishes into thin air.

"Is he gone?" I twist around, searching around me, waiting for another attack. "Can you check?"

I'll check that we're clear. Bruin bursts into a swirling gust of wind as I race to kneel by Myra. She's unconscious, but her pulse is strong.

Bruin returns and brings my hair up to tickle my face.

"Anything?"

Whoever they were, they're gone now. The store is clear.

"Awesome. Thanks, buddy."

I pull a pillow off one of the couches below the home tree and slide it under Myra's head. Then I gather my spear, thank Birga for coming to my call, and send her back into the tattoo on my forearm.

"Okay, who's that?" There's another man dead at the base of the home tree. "Did you get to him before I got in here?"

I didn't end him. Red, I'm offended ye can't recognize my work.

The mysterious dead guy's skull is cracked wide, and his head has basically exploded like a ripe melon. Very messy. He's not wearing the same black assault clothing the other two had on. He's in a brown uniform I recognize.

"Oh crap, Bruin, check the delivery door. If I'm right, I bet this is Murphy. Myra said she had deliveries coming this morning. Is there a brown box truck out back?"

There is indeed. So, do ye think yer Murphy fellow is in on the attack or in the wrong place at the wrong time?

"Option two. Except, if he's the reason Myra is here and alive, I'd say he was in the right place at the right time—sadly not for him, though."

A loud *crack* above me has me jumping out of the way as a

thick branch falls and nearly takes me out. I step back to get a better view of Myra's ancient ash, and my mind splinters. "Oh, no. Nonononono, Mr. Tree, what's wrong?"

Myra's home tree looks terrible.

I saw him two days ago, and he was healthy and strong, thriving after an infusion of Gran's fall nutrients. Now he looks weak, his bark is chunking off, and his leaves are all withered and droopy.

Do ye think it's because of the dark magic blast that hit him? It seemed to hurt Myra.

I see it then, the huge burn mark left in the trunk of the tree. And below the damage, crumpled at the base of the giant ash, is the dead guy Bruin ripped to shreds.

Ash tree nymphs are connected to their home tree much like we're bound. If the tree's ailing, there's a chance it's not about the tree at all— it's about her. Or vice versa. Maybe she's ailing because of whatever was done to the tree.

I rush past the leather couches beneath the broad canopy and try to avoid disturbing the body. "How do we figure out which way the sickness is flowing so we can fix it?"

No idea.

I'm overwhelmed by the scene and don't know where to begin. I point at the faceless delivery man. "What kind of spell do you think did that? Maybe if we can trace the magic back to a specific sect, we can narrow down who attacked her. What kind of spell do you think it is?"

I'm guessing a head explosion spell.

"Big help. Thanks. Okay, I'm in over my depth here. We've got two dead bodies, an attacker at large, Myra's unconscious, and Mr. Tree isn't doing well. I vote we call in the cavalry."

Agreed.

I call up Garnet Grant's number on my phone and hit send. The connection goes through and it rings three, four, five times.

"Lady Druid," he answers, sounding breathless. There's grunting in the background and the unmistakable sound of fist to flesh. "Miss me already, do you?"

Someone groans while someone else laughs in the background.

"Garnet, I hate to break up your beat-down, but we have a serious problem."

"So, this is an official call then. My ego takes a blow. All right, tell me. What have you stepped in this time?"

"It's not me. When I arrived at the bookshop... Garnet, it's Myra. She's been attacked. When I got to the—"

The connection crackles, and I pull the phone away from my ear.

"Myra?" Garnet's voice booms in the storefront, then he jogs into the back. His hair is windblown, his fists gloved and bloody, his eyes gold. "Where is she? What happened?"

I point at where she's lies on the floor and make my next call. "Hey, Da. Don't panic 'cause I'm fine, but..."

I meet my father at the door and hug him. "Thanks for coming. I hated calling you here straight after your shift, but you know... dead bodies in a bookshop human cops will never find. It makes it difficult to call it in. I could've called one of the boys but figured you'd only rush over here when you heard anyway."

"New rule. When yer dealin' with dead bodies, I'm always yer first call, *mo chroi.*" Da casts me a tight frown. "I never thought I'd have to say that, but there ye have it. I'm never too tired to stand at yer side and wouldn't be anywhere else when danger's afoot. Run it down for me, and we'll go from there. From the beginning."

I rub my hands up and down my arms and notice the tea and

treats I brought in. After cracking the tab of my tea, I take a few sips and feel a little more settled.

Growing up with my father and five brothers on the job, I know procedures almost as well as they do. I run the scene down for him from the time I arrived. "The door was unlocked when I got here. I took a couple of steps inside and my shield lit up, and stopped me in my tracks."

"Did ye hear anythin'? See anythin'?"

"The brass bell rang, and then boom, my shield went wacko. I did smell the rotten stink of dark magic though, and heard a slightly muffled rustle in the distance."

He nods. "What next?"

I recap the event in a detailed play-by-play and take him back to the scene. His pained expression when he sees the beautiful old ash tells me it's as bad as I feared.

"So, Bruin's defending Myra there by the couches. Shredded dead guy throws a dark magic fireball at him and hits the tree. Myra screams and collapses. Bruin deals with him, and I go for the last man standing when he tries to grab Myra."

I point at Myra lying on one of the couches. She's being tended to by two healers Garnet called but hasn't woken up.

"And that man is?"

"Gone. He *poofed* out."

Da sees Garnet and scowls. "What in blue blazes is he doin' here?"

"I called and asked him to come." Technically, I didn't get that far, but I would've asked him to come.

Da's scowl is instant. "I want ye to spend less time around the man, not more."

"I get that, but he's the head of the magical policing agency of Toronto, and he and Myra have a past. He'll know about things we don't. Also, he knows how to get in touch with her brother Zxata. I met him yesterday. He's one of the Guild Governors."

Da yawns and shakes his head as if trying to wake himself up. "All right, fine. He's here now. Carry on."

I hate to see Da looking so wiped. Another long night in a surveillance van, and the time spent here with me is catching up. "I'll call Aiden or Dillan to finish up. You go home and get some rest."

He shoots that down with a look. "Who's the officer in charge of this scene? That would be me. I'll not leave ye alone when there's a murderer close at hand."

I'm not sure if he means Myra's attacker or Garnet, and I know better than to ask him to clarify. Never ask a question if you don't want to hear the answer.

Getting back to the crisis at hand, I point at the damage on the home tree's trunk. "The burn of the spell has seeped deep enough to penetrate the meat of his trunk. We're not sure if what they did to the tree is affecting Myra or what they did to Myra is affecting the tree. I'm not sure how their bond works, but Bruin thought it's possible the suffering is shared."

Da frowns at the scorched gash, then straightens to get a closer look at the current state of Mr. Tree. "Och, it's more than possible, Fi. I'd say it's probable."

He looks from the tree to where Garnet hovers over his two healers tending to Myra and back again. "Text Emmet and tell him to come over when he finishes his shift. Have him see if he can put his nature healing to work. See what he can do to ease the ash while they work on helping Myra."

While Da pulls on his gloves, opens a field kit, and starts his cop thing, I text my brother as told.

The responding text comes almost immediately. *Are you okay? Do you need me now?*

No. I'm fine. When you're off-shift.

K. Love you, be safe.

LYT

I slip my phone back into the pocket of my khakis and join my father next to the dead guy in the uniform. "I'm pretty sure this is Murphy, our delivery guy. It's hard to know for sure without him having a face, but the uniform fits, and the build is right. There's also a delivery truck outside."

"Does he usually drop off on the stoop or come in?"

"He comes in. He's had this route for years. Myra pulled strings to have him assigned to her because normal humans can't find the shop with the wards up."

"Okay, so we can assume he came to make his delivery. Maybe he walked in on somethin' he didn't like. Is he the type of man who'd get involved?"

"Yeah, I think so. He was a good guy and a friend." I take another drink of my tea. "If him getting involved saved Myra, I'm thankful, but I'll be sorry if it is Murphy. He was a good guy."

"Is Murphy his first name or last?"

"No idea."

"Well, he doesn't have a wallet on him so maybe it's in the truck. If he drives all day, it's hard on the back to have a wallet in his back pocket."

"What kind of *other* was he?"

"No idea." Da scans the scene again and frowns. "Where did the dark magic come from? Does Myra sell to dark practitioners?"

I shrug. "As long as they don't bring their practices in here to taint the store's juju, she'll sell to anyone without judgment."

Da examines the weeping gash in Myra's tree and frowns. "She might want to rethink her policy and avoid mixin' it up with empowered people who do things like this."

Da works the scene. Garnet's healers work on Myra. Several shifters take away the bodies. I sit, worried and with nothing to do that will help.

"Hey there, Lady Druid." Garnet squeezes my shoulder and sits on the arm of the couch I flopped in. "Are you okay?"

I look at Myra lying there so still and shrug. "Not really, but comparatively, yeah, I guess I've got nothing to complain about. Did you get in touch with Zxata?"

"I did. He was out of town but should be here soon."

"What do your healers think?"

His expression tightens, and he pulls a small vial out of his pocket. "It's a catatonia potion or poison of some sort. They're trying to break it down to figure out an antidote."

"They poisoned her? Why?"

"To subdue her maybe? To make her easier to transport?"

I try to wrap my head around that, but I spin out. "Well, if they drugged her and put her into a catatonic state, they must have an antidote, right? The fact that they didn't kill her suggests they need her alive for something. They'd have to be able to bring her out of it to get what they want."

"That's sound logic, but without knowing who or why we can't narrow down what's been done to her easily."

"It's simple then. We need to figure out who and why."

He shakes his head and rakes his fingers through his hair. "Nothing about this feels simple."

After a long silence, Garnet gets up and paces for a little before ending up at the trunk of Myra's home tree. He places a gentle hand on the wounded tree and looks up into the withering leaves. "What happened to your mistress, old friend? Who did this to the both of you?"

"Can you talk to Myra's home tree?"

"Not anymore. It's been decades since our connection was strong enough to communicate. Zxata should be able to though."

Rockin' Robin starts playing in the front, and I jump to my feet. "That's Myra's phone. I'll get it. It'll give me something to do."

I miss the call. By the time I dig Myra's purse out of the drawer in the cupboard, it's gone to message. Still, now that I have it in my hand, I wonder about what we might learn from it. Maybe she got a call or an email that would start to answer some of our questions.

I swipe the screen to check and hit a roadblock.

Stupid password protection.

Da comes in from the delivery door with a wallet in his hand and sympathy in his eyes. "I'm sorry, *mo chroi*. It looks like you're right and the man in uniform is yer delivery man. Lukas Murphy, the license says."

He flips the wallet open, and I nod. "Yep, that's him. That's too bad. He was a nice guy."

Da sighs. "All too often, it's the nice guys who step in and wind up dead."

The bitterness in his tone is more about my brother Brendan than anything else. Brenny was an amazing guy. He stepped in front of a gunman as a shield for a woman and her daughter. The pain of that still burns hot in all of us.

Garnet joins us in the store and frowns. Then, he drops his mouth open and breathes in a couple of long, slow breaths. A lion's growl rumbles through the vast space, and he turns back toward the store proper. "I smell blood."

"Yeah, there's a giant pool of it in there."

"No. Another source."

Da and I watch as he rounds the counter and moves in measured steps toward the book display shelves. He isn't so much sniffing the air but breathing it into his mouth. It's weird—cool, but weird.

With slow, deliberate movements, he stalks through the bookshelves until he stops about ten feet from the customer counter.

He bends at the waist and closes his eyes next to a small stain on the counter's edge. "This is Myra's."

Across from where Myra usually stands behind the display case, he leans close, breathes in again, and raises his finger. "This isn't hers."

"Don't touch it." Da holds up his hand. "Let me get a swab first so your DNA doesn't contaminate it. Then you can taste it and see what you learn."

Taste it? Gross.

Garnet frowns but doesn't argue. Da jogs to the back to grab his field kit, and I'm at a loss for what to say. It's obvious I was right about Garnet and Myra, and by his reaction, I don't think the end of their life together was due to a lack of affection on either side.

"You still love her."

He blinks at me and arches a brow. For a minute, I think he'll front, but then the corner of his mouth lifts in a smirk. "How long did it take before you adored her?"

"It was pretty much instant."

He nods. "It doesn't fade over time. I wish it did."

Da rushes back with his kit and takes his swab. When he's done, he seals the evidence in its plastic zip bag. "I'll hand the dead guy's blood and fingerprints off to one of the boys before I go home. Maybe we'll get lucky, and our answers will be in the system. I'm not sure what your system is like, but I made duplicates for you as well."

Grant takes the offered samples, and his look of befuddlement makes me love my father even more. Da lives by a code and is a big enough man to see past personal grievances to ensure criminals are found, and victims receive the justice they deserve.

"Thanks, Da. Then go home and get some sleep. You look knackered."

His smile is solemn. "I'm sorry, Grant, that we're here for the reason we are. I'm fond of Myra. I'll do everythin' I can to help unravel whatever happened here today."

Garnet nods. "I appreciate that. Thank you."

I walk Da out and meet one of the regular customers as he comes in. "Oh, Fiona. Back from Ireland, are you?"

I nod and force a smile. "A couple of weeks now. How have you been, Mr. Simchas?"

Mr. Simchas is a tightly-wound little man who is always well dressed and never has a hair out of place. "I am well, thank you. Excited to see what Myra has in store for me this morning. She said she had a shipment coming in and thought one of them would be of particular interest."

"You'll have to come back, old man," Garnet snaps. "This isn't a good time."

I throw Garnet a glare and step between the feral lion and our customer. "Mr. Grant, perhaps you'd like to step into the back and take a breath. Mr. Simchas, do you know which book she intended for you?"

The man gives Garnet a harsh look, then offers me a smile. "I'm afraid I don't. She tends to surprise me, but I'm never disappointed. I'm sure she's got it ready."

I follow him to the back counter. I wish I were as sure as he is. Switching gears, I put on my business face and try to figure out what Myra intended. With her disappearance and possible kidnapping smacking me in the face the moment I arrived, I haven't even looked around to get started for the day.

There's a shipping order on a box by the counter. I grab the unpacking knife and unbox them for pricing. Thankfully, Myra set out the book order list and has made some notes. "If you'll give me five minutes, Mr. Simchas, I'll see if I can't figure out what she had in mind for you."

The man's excitement dims. "She's not here?"

"Not at the moment, no."

"Has she stepped out for a moment? I'll wait."

The feral growl from the back room has us both casting a wary glance toward the doorway to the other section of the store. "Three minutes," I offer, trying to appease them both. "Please, have a wander while I look through these and I'll be right with you."

Thankfully, Mr. Simchas is an accommodating man. Unlike the grumbly lion working himself up to a frenzy in the back. I focus on my task. Okay, the book request list has eleven titles on it. I'll start there.

After taking a stack of Myra's custom bookmarks, I check the first title on the list, find the corresponding book, write the customer's name on the bookmark, and set it aside. After drawing a pencil line through the first name, I move onto the second. I continue like that, doing a rinse and repeat until there are six books left.

Okay, one of the books not listed is *Ancient Aztec Healing Rituals*. This one is for Wallace Mackenzie. I know that for sure because I was here when Sloan ordered it.

That leaves five books.

"All right, Mr. Simchas, I've narrowed it down to five. We've got *Recovering from Demonic Possession, Rare Herbology, Dragons Myth and Modern Misunderstandings, The Unknown Truths of the Illuminati, Ancient Weapons,* and *Murderabilia*."

He looks over all the books and frowns at the pile. "Are you certain that's all there is?"

I show him the empty box. "That's what we received in today's delivery, yes. Was there something specific you were looking for?"

"No, no." His expression turns pinched. "What is murderabilia?"

I read the inside jacket and paraphrase it. "It refers to collectibles related to murders, homicides, and the perpetrators of other violent crimes."

His eyes widen. "I've never heard of such a thing."

"It says here that buyers typically seek collectibles that are artifacts either used or owned by murderers or serial killers and believe such artifacts offer power and control."

"That is disturbing."

"It sure is." I discard that as the selection. Mr. Simchas is the sweetest old man—

"I'll take that one. It sounds so macabre I can't resist."

I blink but try not to let my shock show. "Perfect. Let me price it for you, and I'll cash you out."

CHAPTER SIX

The rest of my Saturday is taken up with trying to heal Mr. Tree, cleansing the reading area of negative energy from the dark magic, and fine-tooth combing the entire store. When Zxata arrives, he and Garnet speak privately for a long while before he sits with his sister.

Seeing the three of them together, I'm surer than ever that they were once close, and something tore them apart. Maybe my discipline of empathy is growing because I feel the love between them.

There is pain too, but the love is stronger.

Sitting in the leather club chair under Myra's home tree, I drop my head back and close my eyes. Today has been a day already, and the empowered world has once again succeeded at knocking me off my axis.

"Hey, Lady Druid." Garnet crouches next to my chair to see me. "I'm heading out in a few minutes and wanted to say thank you and check on you. How are you holding up? Do you want me to flash you home?"

I shake my head. "No. I'll stay. My brother is coming, and we're going to try to heal Mr. Tree some more."

"You look tired, Fi."

I shrug, my name sounding strange coming from him. "I've had better days, but I've had worse too."

He nods as if he shares the sentiment. "Zxata and I have discussed it. I'm taking Myra home to my compound. I have tight security and staff who can watch over her, and if I know where she is, it will ease my animal side so I don't go on a rampage and slaughter half of the city."

I chuckle. "Avoiding mass slaughter is probably a good idea."

"I thought so, too. I'll let you and Zxata know when I have to go out if you want to sit with her. I think it's important she's not alone."

"Let me know where and when. I'll be there."

His smile is tired, but the hostile edge in his amethyst gaze promises violence and pain. I don't doubt that once we figure out who is behind this, Garnet's justice will involve bloodshed and loss of life.

I don't blame him.

"Hey, before you go." I pick up Myra's phone and tap her screen to bring it to life. "Her phone is password protected. I thought I might find something on her email or phone log that could give us a starting point. Would either of you know what she uses as her password?"

Zxata looks at Garnet and offers him the same sad smile he gave him on the *Jubilee Queen* yesterday. "It'll be Grant7."

My heart melts a little more, but I decide now's not the time. Garnet said it had been decades since he'd been able to connect with Myra's home tree, and yet, her password is still his last name. So sweet.

I enter the code, and it lets me in.

Garnet stands and looks over my shoulder. "What are you thinking?"

I shrug. "I live with cops. All the usual questions are swirling around like a dervish in my mind. Was she having trouble with anyone? Has anyone threatened her? Has anything stuck out in the past weeks or months that might indicate someone has a beef with her or is following her or interested in her for some reason?"

I tap on her call log and take a screenshot with my phone, then I page down and continue. "I'll check all the numbers without contact names and see what I can find."

Next, I tap her Gmail account and scroll through the list of her emails.

Zxata straightens from where he sits on the edge of one of the sofas. The resemblance between him and his sister even more striking with them side-by-side. "Do you see anything?"

I slide my finger over the screen, swiping and tapping while I check things out. "Just order confirmations, delivery tracking for today's delivery, and a couple of back and forth convos with a girl named Dayna."

"That's our niece who lives in the UK. The two of them stay in touch to keep us in the loop about what's going on back home."

I tap on sent emails and the subject line of the most recent one catches my attention. *"Eochair Prana."* I tap on an email Myra sent this morning. "All it says in the body is, 'No.' That sounds ominous."

Grant frowns and leans in to read it.

Needless to say, it doesn't take long to read one word.

"Who or what is *Eochair Prana?*" I ask.

"It's a what." Grant frowns. "The *Eochair Prana* is a book. An exceedingly rare, priceless book."

"Okay, so that explains how Myra got sucked into this, but what does she mean, 'No,' and who is"—I check the sender's email address—"ArcaneInc?"

Grant frowns. "Probably a rich man hiding behind a shell corporation. I'll find out. May I take the phone?"

I turn it off to save the battery and hand it over. "You're going to track that email to an IP address, yeah?"

"That's the plan. If we're lucky, we'll get a location. In my experience, people like this have their email sent from a burner email address that leads nowhere. Tracking them to the server will likely be fruitless." Garnet takes the phone, and there's no missing the worry clouding his gaze. Something more than Myra's current state bothers him now.

"Why did learning about a rare book put that look on your face? What aren't you saying?"

He scowls at me and sighs. "The *Eochair Prana* has been sought after for centuries by individuals, factions, and private collectors."

"It must be a good book."

"The lore suggests that it is the ensorcelled tome written by Morgan le Fey in a period when her duality of nature had taken a sharp turn toward being morally nefarious."

My mind stalls out on that one. "King Arthur's evil sister wrote an enchanted book and Myra gets kidnapped? I don't see the connection."

"Arthur's evil half-sister is only one iteration of who the Morrigan might have been. Some believe she was a sea queen, or the goddess mother, a rare and powerful fae, a witch, or the faery queen herself. No matter what historical description you follow, her evolutionary transformation to an antagonist of heroes and kings is undeniable."

"Yeah, she's a bad nut. What's her book about?"

"*Eochair Prana* translates to English as Prana's Key. The book is said to be an enormous info dump of all the Morrigan's arcane knowledge, light and dark magic, powerful spells, and incantations that could make and destroy worlds."

"Thus—Prana's Key." I let that sink in. "It's the key to fae power."

"Right, no one disputes that part, but there is a small group of zealots who believe the book also holds the means to resurrect high-level powers. They believe they can summon the Morrigan to them. It is said that whoever frees her from whatever existence she now inhabits will be rewarded with invincibility and immortality."

"So, not only does the Morrigan's spellbook unlock the secret of all fae power, but it also gives them endless time with no mortal consequence to play with it?"

He nods. "If the lore holds."

"That sounds like a fairy tale if I ever heard one. You don't think it does, do you?"

Garnet sits on the arm of the sofa next to me. "Honestly, I have no idea. I knew a fire mage, Ember Dant, who professed to own it in the seventies. He died of cancer, so either he lied or the book he thought was the *Eochair Prana* was a knock-off."

"Awesome. How many copies are supposedly floating around?"

"Ember believed there was one true tome and two copies made. He thought his copy wasn't original. Otherwise, why couldn't he summon the Morrigan and cure himself?"

"How could a buyer tell if their copy was authentic?"

Zxata groans and looks at his sister. "They'd seek an appraisal by an empowered member of the fae who deals in rare, magical books."

I look at where Myra lies so eerily still on the other sofa. "If I didn't know better, I'd swear she is Sleeping Beauty, and her eyes are moments from blinking open."

Garnet frowns. "It makes sense. Someone wants her to either authenticate their copy or figure out how to call the Morrigan. They approach her, and she refuses. They won't take no for an answer, so they come for her. She resists...and they drug her to take with them."

I frown at the blast mark on the tree. "Okay, now that I'm thinking about it, Mr. Tree expressed his concern for Myra a few weeks ago. I can't communicate with him like you, but he gave me the impression that he was worried about her."

Zxata presses his hand on the rough bark of the home tree and nods. "He says something was bothering her about one of her customers and she seemed concerned."

"Okay, well, maybe that's when the book buyer first contacted her. If she didn't want to get involved, I doubt he got the book through her, which means he may or may not be one of her customers. Still, I'll go through the ledger and see what I can find."

Garnet stands. "It's a start. Well done, Lady Druid. Keep me posted on anything you find, and I'll do the same."

I stand up and stretch, then walk with him back to the sofa where Myra lies deathly still. "Hang in there, girlfriend. We'll find the antidote and bring you back to life. I promise."

When Garnet takes Myra and flashes out, I'm left with a despondent Zxata staring at an ailing home tree. We reexamine the dark magic blast mark on the trunk, and Zxata rubs his chest while wincing. I'm not sure if he feels the trauma physically, but as an ash nymph, I know he hurts emotionally.

As Myra's brother, his connection to her allows him to connect with her home tree. Leniya, as I learned is his name, suffers from both the dark magic blast and Myra's physical state of catatonia.

The nymph bond is less independent than my bond with Bruin. When my bear and I are apart, I miss him and feel hollow and a little achy, but it doesn't harm me. If I'm injured or he is, we're emotionally affected because we care about one another, but the injury doesn't transfer to the other.

"I'm so sorry this is happening." I bring Zxata a cup of the special tea Myra keeps in the back of the cupboard. She explained to me once that not offering it to me wasn't personal, it was simply a blend intended for ash nymphs, and I wouldn't like it anyway. "What more can I do for you?"

Zxata offers me a sad smile. "You wouldn't happen to have an herbology degree, would you? I've never seen anything like what's happening to Leniya before. It's tragic."

"No, sorry, but I'll look through the inventory. Oh, and I'll ask my gran. She's the most gifted druid in nature magic around. Let's call her now."

I pull my cell out of my pocket and send a video chat request. Gran answers right away, but it takes a few "Hold on now... Wait... Almost there..." comments before the video screen opens and I can see her pretty face. "Fiona, to what do I owe the pleasure, luv?"

I tell Gran an abbreviated version of what's going on, skipping the part about the dead bodies and focusing on Myra's ill health and the dark magic blast affecting the ancient ash. I step back far enough to take a wide shot of the tree, then focus in. "He was healthy and vibrant two days ago, and now he's so sick."

"Och, *mo chroi*. That gash is weeping. Ye need to poultice that straight away."

"What more do you think it is, Gran?"

"By the curl of his leaves, I'd say the dark magic poisoned him somehow. What does the wound smell like?"

Zxata places his hands on the trunk of the tree and leans close. "Like foul bitters with a reek of baby powder."

"Och, the poor dear. He must be suffering so."

"What kind of poison do you think it is, Gran?"

"Well, it's near impossible to guess without knowing the sect of magic the caster gets his power from. Until ye do, ye'll not be able to reverse the effects completely. I'm sorry, duck. I wish I were closer to help."

I sigh. "Me, too. Okay, maybe I can find an herbology expert or someone around here that knows about dark magic poison. Thanks anyway, Gran."

"Don't give up on me yet. I'll do some research and pull something together to ease him for the time being. I won't let the poor thing suffer as long as there's something to be done. Let me know if ye figure out who the caster is. I'll work on things from my end and get back to you as soon as I can."

"You rock my socks, Gran."

"All right then, luv. If you say so. Hugs to all."

"I'll tell them." I end the call and plunk down onto one of the couches. "Sorry. I wish that were better news."

"It is what it is," Zxata says. "If you don't mind, I'd like to spend some time meditating with Leniya."

"I don't mind a bit. Take whatever time you need."

I leave the two of them to meditate, and at the front of the store, I map out my next steps. Busy work is my best distraction. I finish pricing the new books, call the customers who were waiting for custom orders, and check Myra's ledger to update her regular customers' purchases.

The big, brown leather book takes up most of the drawer beneath the counter. I enter the date and book titles of those who paid upfront and leave the others for after they settle up. Mr. Simchas is my last entry.

When I finish penning in his title, I scan some of the other books he bought from us.

Crazy. He's a sweet, nerdy little old man with kind eyes and a warm smile but his reading tastes are hardcore dark. You truly can't judge a book by its cover.

To eliminate it as a missed lead, I scan the entire ledger looking for any mention of the *Eochair Prana* or Prana's Key. There's nothing.

When done, I check my watch and wonder what I should do next. The shop feels weird without Myra. She has an energy about her that brings everything to a heightened state of liveliness.

I close my eyes and send her positive vibes.

I think about the Tarot reading I got last week from Pan Dora, my ink spell artist, a.k.a. one of the most famous druids of all time. Super-secret, hush-hush.

The three biggest takeaway points from that session were, one, our quest with water isn't complete. Two, beware the stranger with ill intent. And three, there are trials on the horizon.

I think we got a handle on the water quest. Well, at least the part about freeing magic into the water and converting it to ambient power. I learned yesterday there may still be issues around that with the empowered community.

I think about the second point—beware the stranger with ill intent. Ominous, but I'm so new in this world of empowered ones that almost everyone is a stranger, and most of the people I meet have at least some level of ill intent toward me.

And the third point—there are trials on the horizon.

No shit.

I sigh, but that does give me an idea. I call up Pan Dora's contact number and press send.

It goes to voicemail.

"Hey, Dora, it's Fiona. Listen, I hate to tell you this over the phone, but there's been an incident at the Emporium. Two dead guys. One very poisoned home tree. And one beloved blue-haired friend spelled into catatonia. I thought maybe we could do a reading if you have time. Call me. Thanks."

Should I have mentioned *Prana's Key*?

Pan Dora lived through the days of Arthur and the Morrigan. Maybe she knows something about the ensorcelled book. It didn't seem like something I should mention in a message on her phone, so I'll apologize for springing it on her if we meet up later.

The chiming of the brass bell makes my heart jump, and I tense—which is cray-cray because I'm in a bookstore and we're open.

"Hey, Fi." Emmet emerges from the center aisle. "Has your day gotten any better? How's Mr. Tree doing?"

"Myra's brother is in with him now. We won't disturb them. Are you good to stay for a while?"

"I'm all yours until you're ready to go home." My brother looks good in his police uniform. He's only been on the job for a few months as the newest and last Cumhaill boy to join the Toronto Police Department, but it comes to him as naturally as it does the others.

That's how I knew it wasn't for me. I could do the work. I know the laws almost as thoroughly as they do, but the idea of toeing the line of procedure rubs me the wrong way more often than not. I'm not good with "have to."

So much so that if you tell me I have to do "XYZ," you can guarantee I'll do "ABC."

"Are you still planning on going to the pub for Liam's birthday toast tonight?"

I scrub my hands through my hair and groan. "Damn, I forgot. What time are we supposed to meet?"

"Dillan's off work at eight, so I told Auntie Shannon around nine. If you're bagged, you can skip it. I'm sure he'll understand. After the day you've had—"

"No, no. Of course, I'm going. I refuse to let druid drama pull me out of Liam's and Auntie Shannon's orbit entirely. I'm Irish, after all. I can pull myself together for a few drinks at the pub."

Emmet smiles, but it's strained. "Fi, someone attacked you in your workplace. Permit yourself to be shaken up about that."

"Oh, I am. As bad as it sounds, I'm getting used to shit like this. Still, I'm scared for Myra, and my mind is wandering in every direction."

He opens his palms. "What can I do to help?"

"There *is* something." I think about finding poor Murphy lying dead and faceless in the back and feel bad before I even suggest it. "Da told you that it was our delivery guy who got the dark magic blast to the face, yeah?"

"He mentioned you knew him. That sucks big."

"It does. Well, Garnet called the company, and they're sending someone over to pick up the truck after four. I wonder if he got killed before or after he unloaded our order. The shipping manifest I found on the desk says three boxes, but there was only one. I think he got killed before he brought in the other two."

Emmet flashes me a crooked smirk. "You want to make sure you get all the boxes the dead guy came to deliver?"

"Well, it sounds bad when you say it like that. I'm thinking about it more like busywork is good for a troubled mind. Menial tasks free up the subconscious. I'm carrying the baton in the face of disaster. Also, we think they might've attacked Myra because of a book, so I should be thorough."

Emmet shrugs. "Okay, I'll go see what I can find."

He trundles off toward the delivery bay at the back and my phone rings. I check the screen and answer. "Dora, I'm so glad you called me back."

"Cookie. What can I do? How's Myra?"

"No change. I wondered about having a reading. Maybe the cards will pick up something and give us a direction. We have an idea of what might've happened, and I want to talk to you about it. Fair warning, it would deal with your past life."

There's a long pause. Then she makes an impatient sound. "All right, then. I just got back from serving lunch next door at the soup kitchen. Give me ten minutes to change, and I'll grab my deck. Are you still at the emporium?"

"I am. Thank you."

"One thing you learn over a long life is that when troubled times hit, you gotta raise the bar. Anything you need to ask me to help Myra, I'll do my best to answer."

I let out a deep breath and feel a little better. "Thanks again. I'll see you soon."

Emmet returns with a two-wheel dolly stacked with two more boxes. "Ask, and ye shall receive. Where do you want me to put these?"

I point at the empty floor beside me behind the customer counter. "Thanks, Em."

"No problem. Can I get you to sign here, please?" He hands me an electronic pad and points at the stylus.

I chuckle and do as he asks before handing it back.

"Who were you on the phone with when I came in?"

"Pan Dora. She's coming over to do a Tarot reading with me to see if we can pick up a lead on Myra's attacker."

CHAPTER SEVEN

By the time Pan Dora arrives, Emmet is bringing the cafe table from the kitchenette into the store so we can do a reading and still watch the storefront. Thankfully, the emporium is relatively quiet for a Saturday. Most customers come to either speak to Myra personally or to pick up something specific. We don't get a lot of lookie-loo browsers.

"Fiona." Dora rushes in, her boot heels clacking on the old, hardwood floors. "Tell me everything from the start. What happened?"

I'm about to lay it all out there again but stop.

"I'd like to see what the cards say first." It's not that I don't believe in Dora's talents in interpreting the magical universe's messages. I want to see what an uninfluenced reading gives us.

"It's your dime, baby. Whatever cranks your handle."

The two of us sit, and I put Emmet on duty to watch the store so we won't be interrupted.

She pulls her well-worn deck from a black velvet bag with silk ties. "All right, do you remember how this goes? While I shuffle, I want you to focus on what you need to know. Then we'll pull the spread and see what the cards have to tell us. Yes?"

"Yeah, all good."

While Dora shuffles her deck, I focus on the backs of the cards and try to connect. I study the triple goddess moon symbol glowing against the galaxy pattern of constellations. My mind is solely on Myra and how to help her.

Who did this to her? Is it about the *Eochair Prana*?

Dora finishes shuffling, lays the cards face down, and fans them in front of me in a skillful and smooth arc. "Now, point out nine cards that hold energy for you, in any order, and I'll draw them from the deck."

"Oh, she doesn't get to pick them herself?" Emmet asks.

"No, cookie. Some Tarot masters allow others to touch their cards, but not me. I have an intimate trust and flow of communication built up with my deck, and I don't allow anyone else's energy to influence them more than what's done in the reading itself."

As before, I stare at the deck and the card I'm meant to pick practically vibrates on a frequency that sings to me. "I'm not sure if the magic is coming through stronger this time because I know what to expect or maybe I'm tapping into the fae juju better this time, but yeah, I know exactly which cards I'm supposed to pick."

"That's a good sign," Dora says. "Lead the way."

I point at the first card, then rinse and repeat from my second through to the ninth. In my mind's eye, a warm glow comes off the card each time I'm supposed to select one. I move through the deck, focused on Myra, and indicate which card I'm supposed to choose one by one.

When I finish, Dora lays them out in the spread and turns over the first card.

"The Chariot. The Chariot indicates a time for overcoming obstacles. It foretells challenges, tests, and crises popping up. There will be plenty of fires to put out. The environment around you may seem unstable at times. Yet, it's also a time when rising stars tend to shine. Stay on top of things. Muster your courage and know that you can do it."

"Wow, one card says all that?" Emmet asks. "How does that help us find out who and what did this to Myra?"

She smiles at him, and I'm relieved to see he's not bothering her. Emmet has a lot of energy. I liken him sometimes to a puppy who's been let out to play. He has endless exuberance and tons of curiosity. His Emmet-*ness* can be a lot for someone who's not used to it.

"It's too early to say, cookie. Each card holds a meaning, but based on position within the spread and what other cards it comes paired with, that meaning has to be interpreted as a whole. That's only card one. We'll go through one by one, and we'll pull it all together, I promise."

"Watch and see, Em. It'll all make sense in the end. Oh, and maybe write stuff down so we don't forget."

Emmet pulls his police notepad from his hip and sets up at the counter. "Okay, ready. Can you go over the Chariot's stuff again? The part about unstable times."

When we finish the reading, and my mind is filled with all the ambiguous possibilities, I file that away to study later. Under the guise of making us tea, I send Emmet to the kitchen while I fill Dora in about finding the email about the *Eochair Prana*.

At the mere mention of the book, she recoils.

"Okay, so it's as bad as Garnet thinks?"

"Oh, hon, it's so much worse. People think they know what that woman was capable of, but they don't. She's bad news. Like, the end of days bad news. If someone has the notion of using Myra to decipher how the *Eochair Prana* works, no good can come of it."

"Do you believe it's possible to summon the Morrigan?"

"When you live as long as I have in the magical world, you learn that anything is possible. But it won't happen. I promise you that. I took steps long ago to ensure the book wouldn't fall into unsavory hands. Wherever Morgana is, she can bloody well stay there."

Emmet returns with the tea tray and gets us set up.

"How do we use what we've learned so far to find the people who either have a copy of the book or are searching for one and stop them?"

Dora points at the Devil card. "I'm going to make some educated guesses here, but I think they should be fairly accurate. The Devil card is about the entrapment of being tethered as a slave to evil. It implies oppression and being bound by a masochistic sense of duty. The castle image came up several times. You see? Here, and here, and there."

As she points at the cards, I follow her long, zebra print nails and realize she's right. There is a reoccurring image in several of the cards.

"You may or may not know this but Xavier, leader of the vampires, lives with his nest beneath Casa Loma."

"You think the vampires are behind this?"

Dora shakes her head. "No. They are already immortal, in a sense, and don't fuss with magic and fae power. But I believe they're involved. You see, vampires are greedy. They can be bought, and the kinds of people behind the search for the Prana's Key will pay their minions handsomely."

"What do the cards say about the odds that my sister comes out of this alive?" Zxata asks.

I jump. *Wow.* I forgot he was even here. "Have the two of you met?" They shake their heads, so I make the introductions. "Pan Dora, this is Zxata, Myra's brother."

Dora stands, and Zxata has the grace not to look too surprised. Without heels, I'd guess she's six-foot-four, but with the boots she has on, she must be close to six-foot-ten. Still, as

Dora closes the distance between them with her arms extended, Zxata shows no sign of hesitation.

"I'm sorry for your heartache, *Nisha*," Dora says.

"I thank you for your help. Myra speaks adoringly of her friendship with you."

Dora steps back and dips her chin. "The adoration goes both ways."

There's a moment of awkward silence, then the cuckoo clock clucks off five o'clock and bursts the bubble.

"What should I do tomorrow, Zxata?" I ask. "Do you think I should come in and open the store? A few customers are coming in to pick up ordered books. Should I reschedule them and focus on what's happening? What do you think?"

He runs rough fingers through his long, blue hair and sighs. "Leave the store to me for tomorrow. I have a free day and want to be here for Leniya. I'd feel better if you and Garnet are out there working to track down the people behind this. I'll mind the store. But please, if you find anything, let me know. I may not be much of a fighter, but I love my sister, and I want to be involved in bringing her back."

"I promise. We'll keep you in the loop. If you don't mind, Emmet and I are going to try to help Mr. Tree once more before we leave."

After spending another twenty minutes with the ancient ash, Emmet and I thank Dora for her help and leave. My Dodge Hellcat SUV is parked on Queen Street, and it feels like a year since I last sat in her leather seats. "If you don't mind, we'll take the scenic route home and drive by Casa Loma."

"Fi, we're not ready to take on a nest of vampires. If that's what you're thinking—"

I snort. "No. I'm worried and frustrated, not suicidal. I simply want to drive past, and maybe Bruin can take a quick spirit check of the area."

"Is that safe? We don't know anything about vampires. Can the undead sense spirit bears?"

I get a sinking feeling in my gut and sigh. "I don't know. Okay, we'll only drive by and take a look. No recon tonight. I'll chat with Garnet and see what he thinks."

Emmet slides into the shotgun seat and nods. "I think that's wise."

I cast a sideways glance and giggle. "Since when did you become the poster boy for level-headed thinking?"

"Hey, I've matured a lot since I touched the nakey man."

I turn the key, and when the engine rumbles to life, I check my mirrors and pull away from the curb. "Yet, you still refer to it as you touching the nakey man. You're hilarious."

"Love you too, sista."

From where the emporium is on Queen, I turn north on Bathurst and go straight up to Davenport Road, then over to Dupont. Casa Loma is a Toronto landmark. I was there a couple of times as a kid on school trips, and once when I was seventeen for a summer formal when my boyfriend at the time worked for McDonald's.

It was one of those crazy fun nights that you don't appreciate until years later, and you wish you could go back and do it all over again.

"If Sloan were here, I'd point out that the castle has character, history, and after a fifteen-year restoration, all its architectural features."

"Are you still going on about him slighting our country being a baby next to Ireland?"

"No, I'm still going on about him insinuating that unless something is crumbling and smells like an old root cellar, it doesn't have character. Next time he's here, remind me to book a reservation at the castle's steakhouse restaurant."

"That's pricey, Fi. How much is Myra paying you?"

"Oh, *I'm* not paying. He still owes me, like, twenty-seven grand from the landscaping ideas he gave Bruin."

Emmet chuckles. "If only he knew that all we needed were a few Ostara magic turds, we could've saved all that money."

"Exactly."

I pull onto Austin Terrace, ease out of the traffic flow, and take advantage of there being no curb to stop on the sidewalk. From across the two-lane road, I stare at the building with new eyes. Casa Loma is a Gothic revival mansion built over a century ago and a gem in the crown of Toronto history. I have a hard time believing the Toronto nest of vampires live there.

"Listen to this." Emmet stares at his phone in his lap. "It says here that during World War II, there were extensive renovations to the stables. It was widely believed that a secret military research facility was built under the site. Station M, as it was called, was where they manufactured covert sonar devices used for U-Boat detection."

"If it was widely believed, it wasn't a very good secret."

Emmet laughs. "It was a secret at the time. It was the guy who wrote about Camp X who started researching it."

"I thought the city owns the castle."

"It says here that an entertainment company signed a long-term lease in 2014. They use it for filming movies and TV shows and weddings and stuff now."

"Where do the vampires come in?" I stare at the beautiful stone castle and the few people coming and going. They look like ordinary people to me.

"Maybe they live in the secret military facility beneath the stables. Maybe they run the steakhouse. I have no idea."

With more questions than we started with, I pull back onto the road and head home.

"As much as I want to be in the mood to celebrate Liam's

birthday, I'm not sure what kind of company I'll be tonight. If I need to head out early..."

"I'll cover you," Emmet says without missing a beat. "I got your six, Fi."

Shenanigans on a Saturday night is busy. Shenanigans on a Saturday night when the regulars know it's Liam's birthday is insanely busy. Clan Cumhaill arrives by nine as predicted, but I've only gotten to spend five minutes with the birthday boy by eleven. This is good, in a way, because it's great he has so many friends. It also stings because I used to rank first in the friend hierarchy.

"How's yer night treatin' ye, son?" Da asks as Liam makes a circuit around to our oversized table in the back. "Yer still standin', so there's that."

Liam slumps against the brick half-wall and chuckles. "Am I standing? I thought I was floating. The pub is on a slow and steady spin too."

Da laughs. "Like that, is it?"

Tall and friendly, with brunette hair and ice-blue eyes, Liam's as popular with the ladies as he is with guys hanging out at the bar. He's the whole package.

He straightens, and a tumbler gets pushed into his empty palm. He looks at the glass and flashes me a smile. "Hey Fi, I'm magical too. Any time my hand is empty, another drink suddenly appears."

I chuckle and look around. His comment is innocent enough, but it's hard having a secret identity if your drunk bestie shouts it out in a crowded bar. "You're amazing." I raise the tumbler of Redbreast I've been nursing the past half-hour. "Here's to another amazing year to come. *Slainte mhath!*"

"*Slainte mhath*," Da, Emmet, Calum, and Kevin say while raising their glasses to join me in the toast.

Liam accepts it, takes a drink of his whiskey, and sets it on our table. "Fi, come dance with me. It's my birthday wish. You like this song, don't you?"

I pause to listen to what's playing and nope, I don't think I've ever heard it before. "Yeah, love this one."

His smile is worth the lie, and I extricate myself from the back row of the table. The two of us close the distance to the dance floor and join the crush of bodies moving to the beat of the music.

The playlist here is always upbeat with lots of Celtic tunes as well as pop, southern rock, and new country. Anything that keeps people bouncing to the rhythm—and if it has a fiddle in it, even better.

Liam side-hugs me as we take the floor and kisses my head. "I've missed this."

"Yeah, me too."

His arms are loose and wild as we lose ourselves to the flute and fiddle of a rocking Irish tune. I throw the couple next to us an apologetic smile as Liam almost beans the guy in the head. Thankfully, Liam is loveable and charismatic whether drunk or sober, so they don't seem put out.

"Life's gotten too busy," I say.

"Now that you're a superhero." Liam looks at the couple next to us and smiles. "Did you know Fi's a superhero? She has a grizzly bear and fights dragons and werewolves and is friends with a leprechaun."

I bark a laugh, and the couple laughs with me. "I think our birthday boy is thoroughly banjaxed."

"No, it's true. Oh right, it's a secret." He pushes a finger over his lips. "I forgot. Don't tell. My bad."

I roll my eyes and wrap an arm around his waist. "Come on,

boyo, let's get you some fresh air." The two of us do the four-footed teeter and shuffle down the back hall.

The night air is crisp for the end of September, but Toronto weather is like that. In October, you could be wearing t-shirts and apple-picking, or you could be rummaging for your winter jackets and mitts to go to the store.

Tonight is a fleece hoodie kinda night, but coming out here straight from the dancefloor, I've got nothing but chills from sweating. *"Inner Warmth."*

The spell is low-level, and I got so used to casting it while wading into rivers and streams last week, it comes easily to me.

Holding onto Liam as we walk, I share my heat with him. "Hey, don't." He straightens and takes a wobbly step back. "You don't get to magic me without asking."

The bite in his words stings but I choke back my quip. He's drunk and still adjusting to the knowledge that mythical and magical things live in the world around him.

I take a step back and take my heat with me. "Sorry. I got the chills and wanted to be warm. I didn't mean to make you uncomfortable. I was going for the opposite of that."

He sighs and groans up at the sliver of moon overhead. "No. *I'm* sorry. That was a dick comment. You were great, and I dicked it up."

I roll my eyes. "Maybe we should head back inside."

I'm reaching for the handle of the back door when it opens and swings out at me.

I yelp and jump back. "Oh, shit."

CHAPTER EIGHT

A leather-clad man the size of a hybrid truck steps out to join us. Dark hair flows past shoulders as wide as the doorway itself, his wide palms up between us. "A moment." Mountain Man blocks our path. "We'd like a word before you head back inside."

"With me? Okay, a word about what?" My shield tingles against my back, and I take an easy sidestep to stand between the mountain of muscle and Liam.

He matches my movement, his arms and thighs bulging. His body speaks of violence, and his gaze promises it. "We were sent to take you in. Intercepting you out here eliminates the chance of causing a public scene."

I chuff and take another step back, matching the guy's shift in position yet again to keep Liam out of his line of sight. "Me? I don't do scenes. How about you tell me who you are, where you think you're taking me, and on whose authority?"

"I'm insignificant. To the Lakeshore Guild. And by the authority of the Guild Governors."

I back up, and three other skull-trimmed biker-types follow

our leather-clad roadblock. I take another couple of quick steps back and grab my phone.

I thumb through my contacts and call up Garnet.

"Have you news, Lady Druid?"

"Did you send four goons to grab me? I'm outside the back door of Shenanigans getting jumped and detained in the name of your precious Lakeshore Guild."

As I hoped, the air shifts and Garnet Grant appears at my side. He opens his mouth and draws a deep breath, smelling the air like he did earlier. "Vampires. What do you want?"

Goon One doesn't look thrilled with Garnet's arrival. Too bad. If I'm up against four vampires, I'm phoning a friend. A powerful friend who happens to turn into a lion and rules the city's empowered population. "This is private business."

"You said it was Guild business," I correct. "Make up your mind." While everyone is distracted by Garnet's arrival, I push Liam toward the back alley. "Hurry. Go back to your party before this gets ugly."

"And leave you back here in the dark with vampires? Are you nuts?"

"According to many, yes. I can handle this. Go."

Faster than my eyes can track, the three latecomers blur into motion and have us penned us in. The biggest of the four—let's call him Moose—looks down at us like we're bugs he's about to squash. "No one leaves."

Goon One frowns. "Just come with us, little girl, and your human friend will be left unharmed."

My human friend seems offended by the comment, and I see his Irish ire flare.

"Leave it alone, Liam. It's in the handbook of don't be stupid. Never piss off the undead." I place a firm hand on Liam's chest so I can track him while my focus is on Goon One. "Tell me who sent you and what they want."

"I did. The Guild requests your presence."

Garnet's smile is cruel and cold. "I am the Grand Governor of the Lakeshore Guild, and I don't know you."

Busted.

Goon One casts a glance at his boys and the air snaps with the outbreak of violence. The first punch rockets toward Garnet's head and the standoff bursts into a chaotic explosion of fists and fury.

I push Liam back and raise my hands to defend. *"Bestial Strength."* The flood of power to my muscles is a boon, but even so, vampires are stronger.

"This didn't have to be difficult." Goon One grunts and pushes me up against the dumpster.

We're too close together to call Birga, and I realize too late that I should carry a melee weapon.

"Women are allowed to be difficult." I duck his white-knuckled fist. The tight collection of fingers whizzes past my ear and punches a hole in the side of the dumpster.

I call my Tough as Bark armor, and my skin transforms from pasty white with freckles to steel-strong and covered in badass tats of trees flowing up my arms, roots reaching down over my fingers, branches spreading up over my shoulders.

There's a deep, throaty growl, and I don't need to see him to know Garnet shifted to his lion form. The man fights like an alpha predator. I'm not surprised to see one decapitated vampire body on the ground and a head sailing through the air toward the dumpster.

Three against three. That's better.

With my skin hardened, I barely feel the hit to my shoulder. If the impact didn't knock me, I wouldn't have known.

"Stop." Moose lifts Liam by the throat.

I freeze as the threat rings in the air and watch my best friend's feet dangle a foot off the ground.

"Resist us, and he dies," Goon One says. "Move one inch, and he dies."

I lock my knees to keep from lunging and getting Liam killed. Violence burns hot in my veins and twists in my guts. "Get away from him. Let him go."

"Come with us, and there won't be a problem."

"Don't listen, Fi." Liam struggles against the solid hold of the vampire who's got him locked down. "You don't go anywhere with these undead douches. I'll take my chances."

Garnet's growl rumbles deep and low behind me. I cast a glance back to see he has Vamp Two pinned to the ground with his three-inch canines clamped around his neck.

Garnet and I could defeat these assholes with enough time, but we don't have it, not when they have Liam in their grasp. It's a checkmate move, and we all know it.

"Fine. Let him go, and I surrender. You have my word."

"No!" Liam snaps. "No deal."

I roll my eyes. "Liam, you're not *part* of the negotiation. You're the *point* of the negotiation. Big difference."

"Done." Moose lowers him to the ground. "Clasp your hands behind your back and stand here. I'll release him and transport you."

I do as instructed. After lacing my fingers behind my back, I move to stand beside Liam. For the bloodsucker to grab me, he'll need to release him.

I can live with that.

Liam's gaze is feral and wild. I send him all the reassurance I can. "It's cool. I've got this. What kind of BFF would I be if I let some psychotic undead kill you on your birthday?"

"Fi, don't."

"It's done.

I give the vampire a nod, and he shifts his hold from Liam to me. "Keep him safe, Garnet." The lion roars and I give my captor a nod. "Beam me up, Scottie."

I stretch my neck from side to side as energy explodes in my cells. Stupid Chariot card—yep, Fiona Cumhaill—facing one crisis popping up after another.

I'm no expert on magical transportation methods although I do have some experience. Sloan is a wayfarer, so I've portaled with him many times, been flashed by shifters, and even transported by dragon portal to the Wyrm Dragon Queen's lair. I'm accustomed to a little disorientation, some light-headed spinning, and even nausea, but the pain of Vamp Transport sears me to the bone.

Could it have something to do with the fact that vamps shouldn't be able to transport? Do they get to keep the ability if it was part of their life before transition? I'm not sure.

There are still so many things I don't know.

I drop to my hands and knees, panting and seeing double. "Dude! What the hell?"

Through the ringing in my ears, I hear a groan and someone else cursing. If I gave a fuck, I would look to see what happened. Except, I don't. Zero fucks given.

"Fi, are you okay?"

Strike that last statement.

My head comes up fast, and my heart pounds at triple time in my heaving chest. Our vampire Uber is gone, but I'm not alone. "What the hell, Liam? Why are you here? I bartered for your freedom."

"And I said no."

I groan and flop onto the plush carpet of the room we're in. "Do you know how dangerous it is to tag a ride during transport when the man in charge isn't prepared for the extra passenger?"

I do. Sloan already bitched me out about that and made it very clear it was a bad thing—a big no-no.

"It's done. I'm here. Get over it."

I close my eyes and draw a steadying breath. "You're right. You're here. We need to figure out where we are, why we're here, and who's behind it."

Liam rolls to his feet with more coordination than he had fifteen minutes ago. "You sobered up fast."

"Being taken prisoner by vampires does that."

"I suppose. It's becoming my new normal. Whatevs."

Liam chuffs. "The lion man…he's one of your new friends?"

"Calling Garnet Grant a friend might be stretching it, but we're acquaintances with some common goals and allies."

"Will he know where to come for us?"

I shrug. "I don't think we should count on that."

"You've got your bear though, right? That's why you gave yourself up? You knew he could back you up?"

"Nope. I planned a late night out drinking with family and gave him time off for good behavior. He's getting his ursine groove on with his little bear harem in the Don."

His face screws up with one heck of a sour-puss. "So, you were letting them take you with no backup plan? Fuck, Fi. You gotta be smarter than that."

I open my eyes and wait while the room stops spinning. "Don't underestimate the redhead Irish lass. I've always got an escape route up my sleeve."

He doesn't seem convinced.

The study we're in is the type of man cave where you'd expect the owner of the manse to wear a smoking jacket and use pressed tobacco in his pipe. Rich wood panels line the walls, the books on the shelves look like first editions, and the art pieces are gallery-quality Renaissance oil paintings and frescos.

"Would it kill them to have a window?" Liam grumbles.

"It would likely kill the art and books, yeah."

Liam lets out an annoyed *hmph* and twists the doorknob. "It's open. Shit—why is it open?"

He closes it again like his ass is on fire and I chuckle. "Either they know I'm a druid and a locked door won't hold me, they know we'll try to leave and are ready for it, or we're completely trapped, and they aren't worried about us getting away."

He glares at the heavy wood panel. "Geez, Fi. None of those options are comforting."

"Sorry. I'm tired, I've had a shit day, and I need to pee."

"Same. Well, my day was going pretty good there for a while, but now I'm with you for a solid three for three. What are the odds we bust out of here, take a piss, and get back before anyone notices?"

I giggle. "That's your big getaway plan? Escape our prison, pee, then run back to our cage?"

"Not the whole plan, no. It's broken into phases. Phase one, don't piss my pants. Phase two, take on angry vampires and likely piss my pants anyway. Phase three, die a horrible death wearing pee pants."

I roll to my knees and get up. "Aim higher. I won't let you die in pee pants on your birthday."

"As much as I appreciate that, I'm not hopeful." He comes over to squeeze my hand. His eyes have lost their glossy haze of happiness from his birthday buzz, and I'm sad about that. "Why do the vamps want you, anyway?"

I sit on the edge of the desk while my equilibrium recalibrates. "No idea. They might be pissed that Bruin and I killed two of their kind earlier in the summer."

"Can you really kill something that's not alive?"

"I don't know. Ended them? Expired them?"

He tilts his way this way and that. "Either works."

"Okay, either it's because Bruin and I expired two of the members of their nest, or someone paid them a lot of cash, or its new business and has something to do with the book Myra was attacked over this morning."

"Your boss was attacked? Were you there? Why didn't you tell me?"

I stand and run my fingers over the spines of the books. Reaching out with my magic, I search for anything that makes my senses sit up and take notice. "I spent the day working with Garnet and Da, trying to figure out the identity of two dead guys in the shop and what kind of poison they used to drug my friend."

"They poisoned your friend, *and* you found two dead bodies? Why don't I know any of this?"

"It's not something you bring up with your bestie at his birthday bash."

Liam shakes his head and exhales. "Dammit, Fi. I'm sorry. I've been so annoyed about being left behind on the *normal* plane of things I haven't wanted to hear what's going on with you. Some bestie I am."

I shift from the bookshelves to the walls and run my palm across the darkly stained wood. "I honestly don't blame you for that. It's a lot. I get it."

"Yeah, but it's a lot for you too. Then I mucked things up by blurring the lines. I'm sorry."

I shrug. "I've blurred that line a time or two myself. I don't blame you for that either."

"Well good, because me snubbing your druid problems is over. I may not be able to turn into a lion, but bartenders have superpowers too. We're damned good listeners. Tell me, what's going on with your boss?"

I fill Liam in on everything I know and think I know and by the time I finish, my magical search of the room brings me right back to the door.

"All this is really about a book?" he asks.

"A rare, old book that has powerful dark magic spells and people who want to find it at all cost. Maybe. Or maybe vampires just don't like me. As usual, I'm clueless."

I leave out the part about Morgan le Fey and the book being

ensorcelled for resurrection and the ability to call the fabled witch queen back from whatever end she currently serves.

Why ruin a good story with too much tension?

I grab the doorknob and check that Liam's with me. "Okay, first we pee, then we—holy crapballs. *Duuude.*"

Moose fills the doorframe and blocks our view of the building beyond the mountain of his leather-clad muscles.

I pound my chest and wait for my heart to start pumping once again. "Lady tip number one, scaring a girl with a full bladder is bad form. You made me squirt."

Liam laughs and shakes his head. "Only you would overshare with our vampire kidnapper."

"Cause and effect, man. It's important to be aware—even if you're a hired-muscle vampire." I set my hand on Moose's chest, and with a gentle shove, back him up enough to gain freedom into the corridor. "Lead the way. We need a short side trip to the washroom first. Not sure how many human captives you entertain, but it's imperative. You are free to loom and glower as you wish. I have brothers. I'm not shy."

I'm not sure if Moose means to comply or he's not sure what's going on, but we get our pitstop before he marches us through the high-end estate home.

We end our Metropolitan Homes tour in a small antechamber with an entrance to the hall and another that I assume leads into the main meeting room.

Moose comes inside with us and closes the door. Male voices argue in the next room, but they're too muffled to hear what they're saying. It's not rude to eavesdrop if it's you people are talking about, is it?

Liam and I sit on the sofa, and I close my eyes and reach out with my gifts. *Wind Whispers.*

"My master paid for the bookshop owner, not her assistant. This won't do. It won't do at all."

"The tree nymph is gone and under the protection of the

Grand Governor. There's no way to get her now that she's secured within the alpha's compound. The assistant is the next best thing. She works in the shop and can help you find what you're looking for."

"No, she can't. That's not what was agreed upon, and you've forfeited the agreement. You'll have to dispose of her. She knows too much."

"What about the money you owe us?"

"The money was to be paid at the time when you brought Myra D'anys here, not the girl."

"Then our business is concluded."

I let out a heavy breath and sigh. "Well, shit."

"Well, shit, what?"

Before I can answer, Goon One opens the door and nods at Moose. "Our business here is done. Good thing we have another buyer."

"Wait? What?" My mind stalls out on that one, but before I can find out what that means, Moose grabs us and we're portaled again.

We're back on our knees, coughing and groaning, this time with a concrete pad as our floor.

"What's happen—" Liam gags and unloads a night of drinking onto the hard, cold floor.

I look away, or I'm going to hurl too. "Serves them right. Moose, you gotta work on your transport skills, dude."

Rough hands dig into my arms, and the world tilts in a blur. I'm dragged to my feet and swallow, my head still spinning from Mr. Moose's Wild Rides.

"Liam?"

"Yeah."

Goon One has Liam, and they're right behind us.

As we round a corner, I clue into the surroundings.

Moose nods at two men in blue leather armor guarding a set of metal doors. As we cross the threshold, we're in a wide corridor with tiled walls and floors and fluorescent lighting humming over our heads.

My hamster runs NASCAR fast in my head, trying to put the pieces together. This place is cold and sterile and feels like a subway station—"Oh, crap."

CHAPTER NINE

Liam's ice-blue gaze shoots me a sideways glance. "Oh, crap, what, Fi? I hate it when you say shit like that."

I study the space, surer of things with each second that ticks past. "I don't know who the high bidder for my head was, but I have a bad feeling I know who the runner up is."

"Yeah? Who?"

"I'll bet my balls we're prisoners of Kartak of the Narrows and his hobgoblin dickwad army."

Liam frowns. "He's one of your new friends who wants to catch up on the gossip? Her bestie asks with a fleeting shred of hope lacing his otherwise sexy tone."

I'd laugh, but there's nothing funny about any of this. "Nope. He's a vengeful asshole out to make me pay for showing him up and making him look redonkulous in front of the mighty Lakeshore Guild."

"Awesome. You do have a way with people."

"Don't I? I'm expecting to be named Miss Congeniality Toronto any day now."

"It's a lock."

Moose takes us into a long, open throne room filled with a

couple of hundred men. If this were still a working subway line, we'd be standing on a crowded platform. What was once the track has been built up as a raised platform with a run of five thrones.

Emperor Kartak sits in the center in the highest and largest of them, with two women to his left and two men on his right.

He swapped his fancy gold and blue tunic for a gold top that stretches across his chest's banded muscles and what looks like a black flak vest. Unlike in the luncheon cruise's dining room, I have no doubt he has weapons available to him should he choose to pull one out and impale me.

The crowd parts for us as we make our way forward and the buzz of male voices hushes to an expectant silence.

Moose stops our approach, and I keep my hands loose at my sides, ready for anything. "Take one step toward the Emperor, and you die."

"Rude. Seriously, Moose, I thought we were past all the judgy snark. We had a moment, remember? At the washroom? We both reached for the doorknob at the same time, and our fingers brushed. I giggled, and you blushed. It was like something straight out of a Rom-Com."

He stares at me stone-faced.

Liam shakes his head. "I don't think he remembers."

"Oh, he remembers. He's just playing it cool because we're not alone. He's shy like that, my Moose."

The mammoth vampire reaches behind his back. When he straightens, he rests his hand against his tree-trunk thigh with a gun in full view. After widening his stance, he clasps his hand over his wrist and pegs me with a glare. "Not. One. Step."

"Fine, then. We are so over. You screwed the pooch on our budding relationship." I flash Moose a look and focus on the man of the moment. "Emperor Kartak. I didn't expect to meet with you again so soon."

"That was your miscalculation, female. Did you think I would let your impudence stand unchallenged?"

Impudence stand unchallenged?

I bite back a dozen quips. As much as I enjoy tough odds, I'm outmatched here at two hundred to one. Even if Liam were trained and could hold his own against hobgoblin goons, it would still be a hundred to one.

And he can't. So, it's not.

"Look, what happened with the Vow of Vengeance doesn't have to be a thing between us. I realize that Droghun put you up to it. When it got revoked, you didn't get the update. Garnet explained that to me, and I accept it. Accidents happen, amirite?"

I hope he'll take that lie as an opening not to declare war on one another. "As far as my family and I are concerned, it was all a big misunderstanding. We're good."

Kartak throws his head back and barks a laugh. "We are far from good, female, but depending on what happens here and now, perhaps I'll allow your father and brothers to live."

The threat rankles every bit of patience in me. I want to lunge, to call Birga for her to drink Kartak's blood, to level everyone who thinks it's okay to threaten my family.

I can't. It's a death sentence for both Liam and me if I let my temper get the best of me.

"Killing me might give you some personal satisfaction, but it won't raise your standing with the Guild. Garnet already looked into Barghest's charges about me threatening them. He knows they're bullshit. He knows you jumped on their bandwagon. Don't get jammed up because of their hostility."

Kartak laughs again, and the crowd around me erupts into a roar of amusement. "I don't wish you dead because of what Droghun and their druid scum say. I have my own reasons."

"Well good, as long as everyone's goals are clear. So...this is a death to Fiona shakedown?"

"Unless you can prove yourself more useful to me alive."

"How do I do that?"

"I heard you're searching for the true copy of the *Eochair Prana*. If you have a lead on where it's been held the past centuries, that would be worth telling me."

"I only learned about the book twelve hours ago. I have no idea who has it or where it is. I can't help you."

"Then you're no use to me." Kartak tilts his head, and I follow the telegraphing of his gaze.

Moose nods and raises his gun.

I'm staring at the barrel when—*bang, bang.*

I scream as the vampire's gun goes off and I hit the tile floor. The shots echo against the hard surfaces of the underground tunnel, and the world slips into slow motion.

Liam is heavy on top of me. I bring my bloody hands up from between us. My ears pound with the thunder of blood pulsing through my veins and my hearing fritzes.

Liam chokes, and blood splatters out of his mouth.

"Liam!" I roll him off me and kneel beside him, my vision growing wavy behind tears of equal parts terror and fury.

Moose moves behind me, and my warrior side bursts forward. I call Birga to my palm. With a two-handed swing, I roll back and slice through the air.

No normal weapon would have the bite to decapitate a vampire in one swipe, but Birga's no ordinary weapon. I catch Moose's neck and his head clunks to the floor.

The crowd erupts, and I scream and swing to hold them back. Two hundred to one is impossible. They won't part the way and let me leave with Liam, and he doesn't have time for me to negotiate.

We need to leave.

I swing Birga once more to back off the hobgoblin horde, then sheath her, drop over Liam, and grip my upper arm.

I told Liam I have an escape plan up my sleeve.

With everything in me, I focus on being in the lair of the Queen of Wyrm Dragons.

A split-second later, I materialize on the rough-hewn stone of the Queen's lair and breathe a sigh of relief. My hands are bloody and trembling, and I look up at the startled and concerned gaze of Patty and the dragon queen herself. "Pardon the intrusion, Majesty. I hate to pop in and out, but I must get my friend to a doctor. I'll return as soon as I can to explain."

As far as I know, my dragon portal trumps all other transportation modes, but I also know there is always a cost for doing magic. With that in mind, I don't try to leap back to Toronto into a hospital. Instead, I focus on the one place I'm sure Liam can get the help he needs.

When I open my eyes this time, I'm crouched on the polished stone floor of the Mackenzie family's Stonecrest Castle. "It's okay, Liam. I've got you. Wallace can patch you right up. I know it."

I sit back on my heels and look around the clinic. "*Help!* Wallace? Sloan? I need you."

There's no one here. I launch to my feet and swing open the stainless-steel doors to Mr. Mackenzie's supply cupboard. I grab a couple of towels and race back to Liam. I press a towel onto both entry and exit wounds and wince when he cries out. "I'm so sorry. I have to slow the bleeding."

"Fiona?" The gray lynx pads toward me, his fluffy paws silent on the stone. His bright green eyes take in the heap that is my bestie, and his lips curl back over his canines. "You smell like vampire."

"I'll explain later. I need Wallace and Sloan. Hurry."

"Right away." Sloan's animal companion turns tail and races off.

"Okay." I swipe my hair out of my face with the back of my wrist. "Help is coming. Wallace is the best healer in the Order. He'll fix you right up."

Liam's breathing is scary enough, but there's a weird *click* rattling deep in his throat, and it makes my stomach squirrel. "You're going to be fine. Hang in there."

Tears clog my words, and I can't seem to swallow past the lump in my throat.

I hear the thundering of approaching footsteps at the same time Sloan appears at my side. "Fiona, are ye hurt?"

I shake my head. "Liam's shot. I need your dad."

"I'm here." Wallace rushes through the door. "Get him on the table and expose the wound."

"This will hurt, *sham*. I'm sorry about that." Sloan scoops Liam off the floor and sets him on the steel surgery table. His pain sears me, and I match his strangled cry.

With steady hands and the same efficiency he shows in all situations, Sloan cuts away Liam's shirt and exposes his chest. "I have an entry wound left side upper quadrant, no exit, and a second entry wound in his back, also no exit."

My legs threaten to fold beneath me, so I sit before I fall. The room spins so I lay flat on my back. From my place on the floor, I watch the two Mackenzie men trying to save my best friend. "It's his birthday," I hear myself say. "He can't die on his birthday."

Another man and a woman rush in and take Sloan's place. The moment Sloan's relieved, he kneels beside me. He brushes his hands over my shirt and looks frantic. "Are ye hurt, Fi? Did ye suffer any wounds yerself?"

I shake my head, my gaze locked on the chaos at the operating table. "Liam jumped in front of me. The hobgoblins did it... No, a vampire did... The hobgoblin king ordered it."

Sloan scoops me up off the stone and a blink later, we're in his room.

"No. Take me back." I fight against his hold, but he's strong, and I'm trembling so badly I can't make my arms work.

He carries me into his ensuite and sits me on the vanity beside his sink. "Da has things in hand. Yer no help to them hoverin' and cryin'. Let me get ye cleaned up, and we'll check on him right after."

I blink at Sloan, and I'm numb. "I don't... They shot him."

Sloan wets a facecloth and runs the moist heat over my face. "They did, but ye got him help, and he'll be fine. Ye'll see. Da works miracles every day in that clinic."

I hope so. I have to believe Sloan because a world without Liam isn't a world I want to be in. It's already bad enough that I lost Brenny. "I hate guns so much."

He finishes washing my face and rinses the cloth in the sink. I blink at the swirling pink water and don't understand. "How... Why am I bleeding?"

"It's not yer blood. Let's not think about it. Tell me what happened. Ye said it's Liam's birthday, before. Were ye out on the town celebrating?"

"We were all at Shenanigans. Liam was feeling the buzz, so I took him out back to get some air."

"Gettin' jumped out the back of Shenanigans is a bad habit of yers."

"It seems to be a favorite spot for disreputable men. Maybe I should avoid going back there."

"Might be a good idea." He finishes wiping my hands and upper arms and rinses the cloth again. "So, yer gettin' some fresh air. Then what? May I take off yer shirt? It's soaked through and yer shiverin'."

I lift my arms, and he eases my blouse over my head, and it falls to the vanity with a wet *plop*. While he continues his male nurse routine, I go on to explain the night's events beginning with Goon One coming out to detain us in the name of the Guild and ending with Liam bleeding on his castle floor.

"So, yer Da and the boys, they know the vampires got ye, but that's all they know?"

I blink. "Oh…they'll be frantic." I reach for my pockets, but my hands shake too much to retrieve my phone.

Sloan squeezes my trembling grasp and smiles. "It's fine, Fi. I'll call them. Here, let me get you a clean shirt, and ye can change while I let them know yer safe."

Sloan comes back with a long-sleeved jersey a moment later and leaves me to change and pull myself together. I splash some water on my face and by the time I've taken off my bloody bra and pulled on his shirt, I feel a little more myself.

"Howeyah?" he says as I emerge from the bathroom. "Anything I can get ye?"

I glance at the digital clock beside his bed and groan. "No wonder I'm ready to drop. It's three in the morning back home."

"Then look no further for a place to lay yer head. Climb up and close yer eyes. I'll check in on Liam and will wake ye if yer needed."

I stare at the crisply made bed and smile at how disciplined he is. I must boggle his mind in every direction.

"I should wait with Liam."

"Da will work on him and knock him out cold with painkillers. You might as well both get some rest."

"You promise to come get me if he needs me?"

He presses his hand over his heart. "I swear it."

Giving in to exhaustion, I head over and climb in. "When we were kids, Mam made us attempt to make our beds. She said it was important to start the day by making a good impression. After she died, we all kinda lost interest. Da always said our bedrooms were our personal spaces and were for self-expression, not good impressions."

Sloan smiles and helps pull the coverlet out from under me to tuck me in. "My Da always said, no one likes a slovenly soul. If ye expect food on the table, we expect ye to earn it."

I sigh. "It doesn't rhyme."

"No. It doesn't. Close yer eyes, Fi. Ye've had a night. Ye'll feel better after a few hours' sleep."

He moves to step away, and I catch his wrist. His arm is warm, and I squeeze it, feeling grounded for the first time in hours. "Thank you."

He winks and strikes off for the door, catching the light switch on the way out. "Sweet dreams, Fi. And don't worry about a thing. I'll fend off the world for ye for a little."

I wake later lost in one of those moments where you're unsure where you are or what day it is or how you even got there. It's the smell that grounds me. With my face in the pillow, the musky male scent that is unique to Sloan fills my senses. *Right.* It all floods back in a horrific rush.

"Liam." I bolt upright and smile at the gray lynx stretched out on the bed beside me.

"Is our naptime over?"

I exhale and flop back to the mattress. "I need to check on my friend."

"He's well enough." Manx wriggles on his back.

"Thanks for getting help earlier."

He rolls onto his stomach and gives me a hopeful look. "You could repay me by giving me a back scratch. There's a spot right between my shoulder blades that I can never get."

"How could a lady say no?" I scrub my fingers through his fur and marvel. "Gawd, you are so soft."

"I do try to take care of my coat. Healthy diet, exercise, and regular grooming. Thank you for noticing."

I finish with his shoulder blades and give him a couple of long strokes from head to tail. The black tufts at the tips of his ears are adorable, and I'm humbled, as always, that as a druid I get to share this type of bond with an animal.

"Where's Sloan?"

"In the recovery suite, I suppose. He said the only way you'd rest is if he made sure you didn't miss anything important with yer friend."

"Smart man. Do you know how it went?"

"From what he said, Wallace thinks the outcome is a solid success. Yer friend is resting comfortably—or at least as comfortably as he can having been shot."

I let out a long breath, and the room spins. "Good. I'm so thankful."

I stretch, give Manx another scrub, and roll to sit on the edge of the bed, which, if I'm not mistaken is an antique King Henry bed. The four posts rise to a wooden frame and a paneled ceiling. Heavy burgundy drapes are tied back but could be drawn for complete privacy, and I guess total blackout darkness when hanging freely.

It's like something out of *The Tudors*.

I don't know many men who could pull it off and have it seem in line with their personality, but the carved shields and grapes and forest creatures adorning the headboard and footboard walls make me think it's pretty much a perfect bed for Sloan Mackenzie.

I wonder how many women before me have thought the same thing? While pushing that thought out of my head, I roll off the edge and drop to the area rug on the floor.

"Do you think he'd mind if I take a quick shower to wake up and bring myself back to life?"

"At yer leisure, lass. I think he wants ye to take all the time ye need. He left ye some toiletries and such."

"Really?" I take that as my cue and shut myself into Sloan's private bath. He *has* left me some things. There's a change of clothes—ladies, my size, the brand tags still on them—and a little woven basket by the sink with a few homemade soaps, a new toothbrush, and some Colgate. I smile. He even got the maxi-fresh blue kind I like with breath strips.

He's a Crest man. There's no accounting for taste.

And yep, a small selection of female toiletries, which is odd and slightly awkward but very thoughtful.

I lift a couple of Wallace's homemade soaps to my nose, select one that smells like molasses cookies, and shuck off Sloan's shirt. The hot spray feels glorious on my skin, and I groan when it's time to get out. Soon enough though, I'm dried and dressed and hanging up my towels.

After taking a look at myself in the mirror, I shake my head. I've never worn this color of cornflower blue before, but it looks lovely with my hair, and I don't think for a moment that's a coincidence. Sloan has more style and class than anyone I've ever known. More money too.

Not that I care a lick about that. I don't.

I take a last look around the bathroom before I leave and make sure I'm a good houseguest.

Manx is sitting in the middle of the bedroom floor when I exit. "Shall I escort ye through the passageways, Fiona?"

"I would love that, thank you."

The two of us walk side-by-side through the castle's stone corridors, and I try to imagine growing up the only child in this home. Both Janet and Wallace Mackenzie are even-tempered, well-respected, driven people—they're simply not very nurturing.

I told Sloan once that I thought it was perfect that he found my grandparents at a young age and adopted them as his. Or maybe they adopted him, I'm not sure, but I'm glad the three of them had each other.

"May I ask something?" Manx says as we turn a corner.

"Sure, what is it?"

"How is it yer always on the receiving end of every chaotic situation? Are ye a reckless person by nature?"

I chuckle. "No. Da always says I've never been a lucky girl, but I've always been fortunate. Things have always happened to me or close to me, but most things work out in the end. And since Sloan triggered the Fianna mark on my back, it's been even more chaotic—"

"Are ye still goin' on about that, woman?" Sloan meets us at the next corner. "I've told ye a hundred times that I had nothin' to do with the druid shield appearin' on yer back. That was all Fionn. Fer whatever reason, he picked ye to be his heir apparent. He's the one who magnetized ye fer all things dark and dangerous."

I giggle at his pique and walk straight up to him and hug him. "Hey, tall, dark, and surly. Thank you for everything. You never let me down."

He wraps his arms around me, and I admit, it feels good in his embrace. After a squeeze, he rests his cheek on the top of my head and draws a deep breath. "Hey, Cumhaill. Yer welcome for everything. I'll try never to let you down."

I pull back and smile. "Manx says Liam's okay?"

Sloan nods. "He is. Come, he was askin' for ye. I told him I'd fetch ye back to him."

"Lead the way."

Liam is sitting up in a twin bed when I push through the door, and I rush to his bedside. He's pale and his hair sticks up on one side of his head, but he's alive and well, and my tears flow unbidden. "Hey, now." He pulls me in for a hug. "I'm all right."

"I'm sorry. Gawd…you have to know I never wanted to drag you into any of my druid drama."

He presses his cheek to the top of my head. "You don't need to say that to me. I know you, Fi. This was a crazy thing that happened *to* you, not *because* of you."

"So I'll still get an invite to your birthday party next year?"

He pulls back and arches a brow. "I didn't say that."

We both chuckle, and I sit up and swipe away my tears. "Are you in pain? Are you fully healed? How's things?"

He lifts his shirt and shows me his chest. It's muscled and smooth and beautifully unmarred.

"Oh, dayam, I know Wallace is good, but there's not even a mark."

"I know, right?" Liam leans over to his bedside table and sits up with his hand closed. "Check these babies out." He flips his palm up and uncurls his fingers to show me two copper slugs.

"Are those the ones Wallace took out of you?"

He nods. "This one's kinda mangled, but I'm thinking of making this one into a pendant. Like a good luck charm."

"Or a horrific reminder that I almost got you killed."

He waves that away. "No. It's a reminder that life is short and when shit gets real, I can always count on you."

I press my fingers over his forehead. "Are you delusional? I got you shot, then flashed you halfway around the world so Sloan's father could save you. I'm not the hero in this story —he is."

"Hells yes you are. Fi, whether we're kids and you make me a piece of sugar toast when I'm sad or adults and you dragon portal me to Ireland to have a druid healer save my life, you'll always be my hero."

"Whatever these drugs are, I'll talk to Wallace to get you a to-go pack. Loopy Liam is fun."

Liam chuckles and looks over my shoulder at Sloan. "Hey. Thanks for letting us crash into your life. I appreciate all your family did for me."

Sloan nods. "I spoke to Niall earlier. Yer mam needs a call when yer up to it. She's in a bit of a state."

"I have no doubt. It's the only child thing. She tends to put all her hopes and dreams on me. You probably get the same thing with your parents, right?"

Sloan smiles and nods.

I see the truth, and it hurts my heart.

"I told Niall I'll take ye both to Lugh's and Lara's when yer up and about. They're anxious to see Fi and want to talk to her about the poisoned tree she was askin' about."

"When do you think he'll be up and about?" I ask.

"By tomorrow, I expect. Magic healing can bring him back from the brink, but he still suffered a shock to the system. His body needs time to heal and recalibrate."

I nod. "Okay, perfect. I need to go to the dragon's lair and check in. I kinda breezed through there but didn't explain. I don't want to seem ungrateful or disrespectful, so I'll pop in for a quick visit."

Sloan frowns. "I'm not a fan of ye goin' there. What seems a few minutes in yer estimation is hours and days in ours. It's hard on those worryin' over ye."

"Or months," Liam says and shares the same look of concern as Sloan.

"Or months," Sloan agrees.

It hurts me that it hurt them so much when I was missing that first time. I hate to put them through it again, but at least now they know where I am. "It's important. I promise I'll try to be quick. When I get back, I have to talk to you and Granda about something important too."

Sloan lifts his chin in question. "And what is that?"

"I need to learn everything I can about the *Eochair Prana*. Think about that, and I'll be back." I raise my hand to grip the infinity dragon tattoo above my left elbow and focus on traveling to the Wyrm Queen's lair. "Laters."

CHAPTER TEN

I materialize in the main chamber of the dragon's lair and wave at Patty. "Hey, there. Sorry I rushed through before."

My leprechaun friend is in his usual spot, lounging in his La-Z-Boy recliner with Elvis Presley playing on the old-fashioned gramophone and his video game controller in his hand. When I step farther into the cavern, he pauses his game, hops out of his chair, and rushes over to the wet bar. "After the bloody scene earlier, I take it you could use a drink."

"Yes, please. Make mine a double." I plunk down on the barstool and unload all the gritty details of the murder and mayhem of my night.

I tip back my drink and finish it with a burning gulp.

Patty and the Queen understand my haste rushing through here earlier and don't seem put out in the slightest. Good. I'm relieved.

"I don't think the Toronto empowered ones know what to think of me, so they either hate me on principle, pretend I don't exist, or assign me a personality that suits them."

"Some humans are best chomped hard and swallowed quickly, regardless of the heartburn," the queen says.

"Uh...thanks. I'll remember that, Your Graciousness."

The slither and scrape of scales on stone precedes the influx of dragon wyrmlets. The horde of baby slugs has changed since I saw them less than a month ago. "Wow, they're losing their baby chub and really slimming out."

"Och, they're growing up too fast." Patty strokes a red girl's head. "They'll be strikin' off to start their own lives in no time."

I glance across the writhing floor, the scaly bodies of blue, scarlet, gold, and green wriggling and wiggling to see who's dropped in. They were likely hoping to eat me and are disappointed to find that I'm a friend, not food.

"Hi guys." I stroke and pat as many as I can reach. "I missed you all too. Look how big you've grown."

Crazy as it is, I used to have to pretend to be interested in the serpentine monsters. Now they've grown on me, and I genuinely care.

The whole time I'm chatting up the brood, I search for my blue boy. I know you're supposed to love all your children the same, but that firstborn boy stole a piece of my heart.

Love is funny like that. "Where's my blue dude?"

Patty looks around and frowns. "He should be here. Dartamont, where are ye, *sham?*"

"Dartamont? Is that his name now?"

Patty nods. "Wyrm dragons get named on their first birthday based on their personalities. In the language of the wyrm dragons, it means brave-hearted blue."

"Oh, I love that. It's perfect." I search the cavern again. "Dartamont, where are you, sweet boy?"

When he doesn't come to me, I wade past the others and head for the nursery. It's easier to navigate around them now that they're slimmer and more coordinated. Things were awkward and clumsy when they were in their chubby slug stage.

Some of them stay out with their dragon mother in the main chamber while others follow me deeper into the cavern. I'm glad for the company. I may only be their mam in a token status, but I wish I could spend more time with the little guys.

I find Dartamont alone in the nursery and looking sad. "Hey, dude. What are you doing here all alone? Are you sick? I thought you'd—oh wow! Look at you."

I sit on the floor next to him and marvel at how much he's changed. "You have legs...and wings!"

"He does. Dartamont is a Western."

I pull his head into my lap. While leaning forward to see him face-to-face, I rub the three horns on his nose. "You grew into a different dragon since I saw you. How exciting."

"The early days of a dragon's development are filled with milestones," Patty says. "As the oldest, he's the first to grow into his true form. I think he feels a little out of sorts with all the changes."

I shake my head. "I thought he was a wyrm dragon like his mam?"

"No. Basilisk seed holds the base gene for all dragons. While the dragon queen is a wyrm dragon herself, that doesn't mean all her young will be. Many offspring will grow to be other forms of dragons: a wyvern, a drake, a lung, a sea serpent, a Western dragon, or the like. The father's part in this brood is only beginning to take hold. Dartamont is the first to have his species traits make themselves known."

I look at my little Western dragon, and my mind is officially blown. "I didn't realize he'd hit puberty and take his form. Wow, buddy. Congrats. You're rockin' the new look."

Dart lets out a soft sigh and blinks up at me.

"Why are you so sad? I was surprised you didn't come out with the others to see me."

"Och, there's nothing to worry about." Patty waves away my concern. "Dart's been in a bit of a funk since his transition. It seems he has yer zest fer life beyond the world we live in and sees himself out and about on grand adventures now that he's taken his adolescent form."

"Is that it, dude? Are you suffering from wanderlust?"

I stare into those glossy opal eyes, and my heart goes out to him. "Is he old enough to leave the cavern now?"

Patty nods. "That's when the trouble began. The Queen takes them on hunting trips three and four at a time. As the oldest, Dart's enjoyed those expeditions from the very beginning. He enjoys them even more now that he can run and stretch his wings."

"Can he fly?"

"Och, not yet. He'll be a baby still for years to come. The problem is, he's not content to be in the cavern with us much anymore."

Poor dude. I look at Patty and wonder... "I'm staying at my Gran's and Granda's for the day, maybe until tomorrow. Do you think he'd be allowed to have a sleepover at the Cumhaill household? It won't be much of an adventure, but it'll be something different to occupy him."

"Och, I think that's a grand idea. Let me pass it by Her Most Benevolent. One moment."

Patty shuffles off, and I worry about what I've done. I have no idea how to entertain a baby dragon, but I can't take it back. Dart's looking up at me with what I think is excitement in his eyes. It's hard to tell. I'm not the best at reading dragon body cues.

A moment later, Patty comes back grinning from ear to ear. "It's all set. Dartamont can spend some time with ye up top. When yer ready to leave, send me a wish and I'll fetch him to bring him home."

Okay. I have to admit that I'm excited about this. "Perfect. What do I do? Where does he sleep? What do I feed him?"

"He's a carnivore, so feed him meat. He's not fussy about much else. He'll sleep indoors or out. He'll let you know what he wants and when he wants it. He's a strong-willed little fella. With dragons, it pretty much all revolves around a full tummy. Everything else is immaterial."

"Perfect. Fed and happy, got it. I'll let you know when I'm set to go home, and we'll get him back here."

"Oh, it'll be a grand adventure, Dart. Behave and mind yer mother of dragons."

Dart climbs into my lap and lays his head over my shoulder. Dragon hug. How cute. "Okay, buddy." I wrap my arms around him. "Are we ready to roll?"

He dips his chin, and I take that as a yes.

"All right, here we go."

I focus on seeing myself on the back lawn of Gran's and Granda's house, and a moment later there we are. I let go of Dart, and he takes in his surroundings. After a quick look around, he starts running wild zig-zags and rolls in the grass.

While he's playing, I pull out my phone and text Sloan. *Back from the lair and at Gran's.*

Be there in a jiffy.

I laugh. *A jiffy. What are you? Fifty?*

Whoopsie-daisy, did I say jiffy?

I laugh harder and put my phone away.

"Fiona, luv. Yer here!" Gran comes out of the grove with her woven basket hung over her elbow and her sixties-style dress flowing in the breeze. "Och, and ye brought a friend."

I smile at my happy little blue dragon and wave him over. "Dart, come meet Gran."

Dart trots on all fours like a prize pony, his head and chest lifted, his wings up behind him. The difference in his mood from a moment ago until now is a complete one-eighty-degree turn.

When he gets to us, he arches up, and if I didn't know any better, I'd swear he's smiling.

"Dartamont, this is my Gran. We love her. Don't bite her or try to eat her, okay?"

Dart makes a cooing sound, which I hope is him understanding my point.

"Och, isn't he the most beautiful boy? May I have the honor of touchin' ye with my gift?"

Dart looks at me.

"It's okay. Gran's special. You can trust her."

Gran sets her wee basket onto the ground and reaches up to stroke Dart's cheeks. After he relaxes into her touch, I feel Gran's magic build in the air around us. "Such a smart boy."

I grin, puffed up like the proud mam I am. "Right? Has been since the moment he hatched."

Dart's mouth drops open, and his forked tongue extends and tickles my cheek.

"Mmm, dragon spit, thanks, dude." I fight the urge to wipe his kiss away and wait until his attention is focused on Gran again. They seem to be having a private conversation on a mental wavelength I don't share yet.

"If you can, you might want to explain to him what he can and can't eat, Gran. I wouldn't want him to munch down any of your animal friends, even Dax. The old grouch would probably give him a bellyache."

Gran smiles and strokes Dart's scaly cheek. "My connection works with him much the same way as it does with other animals. His thought patterns are different but based on instinct and survival the same as all animals. He loves you."

"I love him too. He's my boy."

"Your boy is hungry. He hasn't wanted to complain, but sharing with his brood mates is getting less and less comfortable for him since his transition."

"Oh, no. What can we feed him?"

Gran picks up her basket and smiles. "Jimmy and Terry O'Rourke next door work for the road works department. They often clear dead deer or cattle off the road. I'll call them and see if there's been anything today."

"Mmm, a whole deer would fill your tummy, wouldn't it?" I rub my knuckles between his horns, and he lets out another purr. "Thanks, Gran. I hate the idea of him being hungry."

"I'll call right now. Be back in a jiffy."

My smile widens, and my heart melts. "Perfect. Thanks. Is Granda home? I need to ask him about something I'm dealing with back home."

"He's down at the rings."

"Okay. I'll check in with him. Oh, and Sloan is coming with Liam, my best friend from home. I'm not sure how spry Liam will be. He's had a rough couple of days."

Gran pulls a patch of windblown hair from her face and pegs me with a knowing look. "Sloan mentioned that when he called us this morning. Fash not, luv. When they arrive, I'll pamper him up a little. Yer friend will be in good hands."

"The best hands. Thanks, Gran."

I head across the lawn and wave for Dart to come with me. He's keen to follow and prances and rolls and plays all the way there. When we crest the edge of the amphitheater's sunken rings, I point down at my grandfather working out with a staff against a wooden dummy. Well, dummy is generous. It's a wooden post with thick poles sticking out of it in every direction. "That's Granda. Don't eat him either, 'kay?"

Dart dips his chin.

"That's my boy. So smart."

The two of us descend the three tiers of steps cut into the valley. I take the stairs and Dart runs off each tier and flaps his wings as he falls the three feet to the level below. Granda is engrossed in his workout, but when we get close, I call out and wave. "Hellooo, Granda!"

Granda's look of affection morphs to wide-eyed surprise. "Fi, *mo chroi*, who have ye here?"

After we complete the introductions and I warn Granda that Gran says my boy is quite hungry, I get to why I needed to visit. "And so, now Toronto's buzzing with dark and greedy people seeking the *Eochair Prana*. They dragged Myra into it, and me by extension."

Granda wraps a towel around his neck and pulls a sweatshirt over his workout shirt. "It's too cold to chat about it out here when I'm covered in sweat. Let me get changed, and we'll see what we can figure out."

By the time we get back to the house, Sloan and Liam have arrived, and my bestie is getting the royal Gran treatment of tea and sweets inside. I ask Dart if he wants to come in, but he's having too much fun rolling in the grass. "Okay, but don't go anywhere. Stay within the line of the trees, okay?"

I'm fairly sure he understood that, but figure I can watch him from the window, to be certain.

"—the winter when she was ten, we went tobogganing on what the local kids called Murder Mountain. While all the neighborhood tough guys stood at the top daring everyone else to go down, Fi grabbed Calum's Thunder Tube and ran over the ridge."

Gran chuckles. "Och, and she showed the boys who was the bravest of them all."

"Ha!" I laugh. "Nothing as inspirational as that, Gran. Sorry to disappoint."

"It didn't end well?"

"I'll let Liam finish his story."

They all turn to him, and he continues, "Being the youngest, she'd been a passenger on the tube many times but hadn't gotten to steer it. After an unlucky bounce, the innertube went off the side of the hill and over a rise. When the tube fell away beneath her, she flew headfirst at the trunk of a tree. She crossed her arms in front of her head to break the impact, and that's exactly what happened."

Sloan makes a face. "How broken did you get?"

"Two broken arms and one exposed bone."

Gran winces. "Oh, luv. That must've been excruciating."

I pull my sleeve up my arm and show them the scar where the bone came out. "The bright side was John-David Hurst, the cutest, toughest boy at school, heard what happened and came to sign my cast. He kissed me and said I was brave."

Liam laughs. "Yeah. Then Aiden, Brendan, and I tackled him into the snowbank around the corner and gave him a beatdown for putting the moves on her."

Sloan chuckles. "Poor John-David. He likely couldn't help himself. And what's good oul John-David up to now?"

"I think he sells carpets."

Liam leans back and snatches another pastry off the sweets plate. "He wasn't good enough for her then or now."

I frown at him and shake my head. "And you're still stepping in and trying to protect me. It almost got you killed this time. It can't happen again."

The two of us stare at one another for a long time before Granda clears his throat. "Weel, if I get an opinion, I'm grateful yer not dead, Fi. And although I've never officially met the boy yet, anyone who spent his life as one of yer brothers, watching out for ye and protecting ye is family in my book."

Liam shifts to get up and Granda waves him back down. "Don't get up, son. I heard Wallace pulled two bullets out of ye yesterday."

He nods. "True story. Although I'm sore, I feel much better than I should in such a short time."

"That's healing magic for ye, son. And we're thrilled it all turned out—"

111

A shrill screech at the side of the house has me running for the door and the household clamoring behind me.

The scene out on the driveway takes a moment to figure out. A screaming woman is hiding behind the stone half-wall that lines the walkway, Dart's in the back of a dusty red pickup truck, and blood and fur are flying in the air.

"Sweet mercies." Granda rushes out to the woman. "Terry, are ye all right?"

"That... That... What is... It jumped in..."

"Och, the poor dear was famished." Gran sends Dart a look of utter adoration. "Have ye more than one deer, Terry? A cow, maybe?"

The woman looks from Gran to Dart, and her eyes roll back in her head.

"Well, now." Gran's eyebrows arch with amusement. "Fi, take yer wee man and his dinner around back. Sloan, darlin' can ye take care of our traumatized neighbor? Lugh, ye'll need to clean up this mess."

"Yes, Gran," I say as the three of us rush forward. "Come on, Dart. We'll bring your deer with us. Don't worry."

Dart rises with half a deer sticking out of his mouth.

I grab the two front hooves and pull it down and out of the pickup. "You get to keep it, just bring it around the back so the nice lady doesn't freak out."

The two of us get around the house before Terry O'Rourke revives. Granda is in the back of her truck with the hose. And Sloan's bending over the collapsed neighbor.

"I take it that not everyone here knows about the druid and dragon stuff?" Liam chuckles and follows me onto the back lawn.

"No. Very few, actually."

"What happens now? With her, I mean?"

"Nothing. Sloan will take care of her memory and ease her anxiety. She'll be fine."

"Another fire put out."

"That's life these days—" my phone rings, and I wince. Damn. No phone plan. I check the number but accept the call anyway. "Garnet, hey, did you get the message that I'm okay?"

"I did. Your father called me last night. You must have some feline in you Lady Druid because I'm quite sure you have nine lives."

"Yeah, well, my survival wasn't my doing. Liam jumped in front of the firing gun. He's the hero this time around."

"That's why I called. Did you by chance put out a retaliatory strike on Kartak and the hobgoblins?"

"Me? No. Why? Has something happened?"

"You might say that. It seems Kartak and his warriors have all spontaneously died a violent and bloody death. Shredded to bits is the best way to describe it."

I hit the button for speakerphone so Liam can hear. "I can't say I'll mourn them, but it wasn't me. I escaped with Liam using the portal to the dragon lair. I'm in Ireland, and Liam's just coming around."

"And would your bear be there with you?"

Dread rushes over me in a hot wave and I ass-plant on the grass. "Oh, no... Is that what you think happened?"

"Officially, I asked you, and you knew nothing about it. I'm satisfied with that. Between friends, I'd say your bear is very unforgiving of brutes targeting you. I won't look too closely at this because I don't want to find what I think I'll find, but I thought you should know."

"Thank you. Garnet, I honestly had no idea... I never would've—"

"Enough said on that. Now, to the next point. You told me that if you knew the magical sect of the dead spellcaster in the bookshop, your Gran could likely help Leniya. The man was an Evening Shade Wizard."

"Okay, thanks, I'll tell her. What about Myra? Any change there?"

"Nothing new. She's comfortable and stable."

I draw a deep breath and take comfort in that much at least. "Okay, good. I'll let you go and text you when I'm back home."

"Safe travels...and I'm very pleased you're not dead."

I hang up and smile. My baby dragon has finished eating and taken what's left into the nest he made for himself in Gran's weed garden. He's lying with his head on his front legs, his eyes heavy, and is purring.

"Is your tummy all filled up, buddy? Are you good?" I scrub his nose horns and lay my head against his. "Sweet dreams, baby boy. Remember, don't go anywhere and I'll see you in the morning."

CHAPTER ELEVEN

"How's yer wee dragonborn, luv?" Gran asks as Liam and I step inside.

"Quite content. His belly is full, and he's curled up and drifting off to sleep in your weed bed. Sorry, all your weeds will be crushed flat when he's finished out there."

"That's all right. If that's where he wants to nest for the night, my weed bed is honored to be his dragon bed. It's better than having him decide to sleep in the house. I'd allow it, of course, but I'd worry about things."

I can't even imagine that. "Not to worry. Until he's fully housebroken, outside in the garden is fine." I feel the round of the teapot and smile when my hand warms against the ceramic spout. Grabbing an oversized mug from the cupboard, I pour myself a heaping huge tea. "Oh, and I'm supposed to tell you that the spellcaster who harmed Myra's home tree was an Evening Shade Wizard."

"Och, that's good to know. I'll get to work researching what spell could've been used based on the tree's reaction and work on a remedy straight away. You head into the living room. Yer men are waitin' to talk to ye about the Morrigan's spellbook."

My men. I don't comment on that. Instead, I push the thought of men out of my head and focus on the business at hand: the *Eochair Prana*, the people who threatened Myra, the antidote to wake her, and the remedy to help her ancient ash recover from the dark magic spell poisoning.

I find Liam lying on the couch in the living room with his eyes closed and a blanket pulled over his legs. I raise my cell-phone and take a picture of him looking peaceful.

He cracks an eye open and smiles. "Is there a reason you're taking pictures of me?"

"I didn't think a mental snapshot would do you justice. As sick as it makes me to say it, I almost lost you last night. You mean a lot to a lot of people. It would've killed me to be responsible for that. I feel extremely fortunate right now."

"I love you too, Fi. Now go away. I'm tired."

"Consider me gone. Sleep well."

I leave Liam to his recovery and find Granda and Sloan in the office with their heads together over a pile of texts and scrolls. More than once, I've wondered if the two of them bonded because of their shared love of history or if Sloan loves history because it connected them.

It's a chicken and the egg question.

It works for them, whichever way it started.

"Fi, come in." Granda coaxes me farther into the study. "Come see what we've pulled together for you so far."

The two of them are standing on the working side of the desk, so I stay on the opposite side and look across. With my palms planted on the wide, wooden surface, I glance over several of the open books. "What language is that?"

Granda points in turn to three different sources. "This one is Latin of the Renaissance era, this one is Old Irish, and this one is a coded text that Arthur and his knights used to keep from letting enemies read their encrypted messages."

"You both can read them?"

Sloan shrugs. "I'm competent with Latin and Common Brittonic. Lugh was explaining the cipher for the Arthurian script to me."

The way he says it, it's as if he's embarrassed he's not proficient in all three. "You amaze me, Mackenzie. Here you are all chiseled and polished in all things druid, and I'm clunking along in the dark. You must think I'm a total chunk of unsculptured rock weighing everyone down."

Sloan frowns. "Not even close. Michaelangelo said he saw the angel in the raw marble before he began to sculpt. He simply worked to set it free. To me, you are the blossom of a rare and unique flower. When you fully bloom, you'll take everyone's breath away."

The reverence in his tone is way too real. I draw a deep breath. "You really can lay on the charm when you want to, can't you?"

"It's easy when it's the truth."

I swallow, waaaay too aware that this convo is getting very personal in the company of my grandfather. I look at Granda and scrub a hand over my heated cheeks. "Okay, tell me what you found. What do we know for sure?"

Granda rescues me from the awkwardness of the moment by diving headfirst into the research. You gotta love a scholar. He gets so excited about the facts he finds in books. "Let's start with what we know for sure. Legend states that there is only one true *Eochair Prana*—which Morgan le Fey penned in the days of her declining morality."

"And the copies?"

"It's said the original book circulated for a very short time before it disappeared and was copied by the manservant of the sorcerer who had it last. While he captured the knowledge, the copies didn't possess the enchantment of the original."

"Which is probably a good thing," I observe. "Garnet described it as a tell-all info dump of all things fae magic."

"That it is. Some believe that Morgana's need for power and control sent her into the clutches of using darker and darker magic, blood payments, soul siphoning, and necromancy. The taint of those sources, in turn, infected her with the darkness that began to consume her."

"So, she's going batshit. She's super powerful, and she writes a book. What happened to her then?"

"That's the stuff of legends and theories. Did she incur the wrath of the fae gods? There is mention of her being imprisoned in a dark hell. Some people believe she went mad and chose to disappear and seclude herself from the rise of Christianity. Some think she challenged the Lady of the Lake and was never seen again."

"And her book lived on as her legacy."

Sloan flips the page to show me a faded pen and ink sketch of a book cover. "It's believed she gave it a simple leather cover so it wouldn't draw attention."

"So, how did she supposedly enchant it to allow practitioners the ability to call her from the beyond?"

"She put a piece of herself into it."

I frown. "Like Voldemort's Horcrux?"

Sloan chuckles. "For lack of a better example, sure. The Morrigan is believed to have penned the tome with her blood and attached a fragment of her soul to it as well."

"The fragmenting of her soul couldn't have done her any favors in the batshit category. It probably fueled her crazy-train to chug faster down the tracks."

Granda nods. "It might well have done that. There's no way to know for sure."

"So, how does this help us? Garnet said a friend of his owned one of the copies and tried to summon her for immortality, but he died anyway."

Granda flips a few more pages and shows me a picture of —Ohmygosh.

"I had much the same reaction," Sloan says.

I lean closer to examine the picture. It's not entirely clear, and it's only a rendering...but there's no mistaking it. "That's the amulet you and I retrieved for Pan Dora from the graveyard."

Granda's brow creases and he straightens. "All right, how about you start that from the beginning of that story?"

"I'll tell you Granda, but I need you to promise it stays between us. Pan Dora is a friend, and unless she's done something incredibly wrong in her past life, she has the right to her privacy and her current secrets."

Granda's scowl reminds me so much of my father it's crazy. "I promise to honor your friend's privacy as long as it's within our power and doesn't put anyone at risk."

I check with Sloan to see what he thinks, and he nods. "That sounds fair to me, but it's yer call. She's yer friend."

I mull that over and decide to give Granda the full story. "Okay, a few weeks ago when we were working on the grove, I went to my druid ink master Pan Dora for some advice."

"That's your friend that is or was a man, but lives and performs as a woman?"

"A drag queen, yes. She's trans—to oversimplify for the sake of time, she was born a male but chooses to live as a woman." Granda's look of confusion makes me smile. "I suppose that might sound strange to you living here in a quiet little Irish countryside and insulated in the druid community, but it's not so strange in the city."

Granda shrugs. "To each their own. I don't fully understand it, but I believe in life choices."

"That's okay. You don't have to. The point is, Dora took us upstairs to give me a Tarot reading. I've known since I met her that she carries a deep connection and a lot of fae power, but I didn't know who or what she was."

"But you found out?"

"It turns out Bruin knew her in another time...an Arthurian

time. When she lived as a man, a powerful druid magician who was an advisor to the kings of the time."

"Yer friend is Merlin?"

"She goes by Pan Dora now, but that's what Bruin led us to believe."

Sloan nods. "I believe she is. I've done some research over the past weeks, and the physical descriptions all match. Plus, I found this."

He shuffles through the heaped texts and pulls out a book on Arthurian lore. The inside cover is a detailed picture of Merlin in a flowing green cape riding on a horse with a magical staff in his hand.

I take a closer look at the picture and nod. "Yeah, put a fuchsia wig and an animal print sheath dress on him, and that's Dora."

Granda flops into his seat. "All right, so tell me about this amulet she had ye fetch."

"It was a favor for a favor sort of thing. We needed someone to go to the Lakeshore Guild on our behalf and stall them while we fixed the ambient magic shortage, and she wanted her medallion back from where she hid it in a graveyard years ago."

"Why couldn't she get it herself?"

"We didn't ask," Sloan says.

"Honestly, Granda, we were in a bind, and it didn't seem like a big deal. For whatever reason, she needed us to fetch her medallion, so we did."

He leans forward and taps his finger on the picture on the page. "And yer sure this is the amulet here?"

I nod. "Positive. What is it?"

"It's the Morrigan's brooch. It's said to be enchanted as the catalyst to bring her back to the living realm. The person who possesses the *Eochair Prana* won't get anywhere without holding the brooch as he casts the summoning spell."

That won't happen. I've taken steps to ensure it.

Pan Dora's words come back to me now, and I wonder what

that means exactly. What has she done to ensure it? "Do you think she destroyed the brooch?"

Granda shakes his head. "I doubt that's possible. A cursed or enchanted object of that age and power would be resistant to destruction. Trying might well activate the summoning and bring about the end yer trying to prevent."

"Okay, so how widely known is it that they'd need the book and the brooch?"

"Is that what they need, though?" Granda asks. "We know nothing fer certain and can't take the chance of making assumptions."

I rub my forehead and squint. "You're hurting my head, Granda. We're still guessing."

"Weel, that's the truth of a great many things in the research world, *mo chroi*. Educated guessing is often the only way for us to move forward."

I yawn and scrub my fingers through my hair. "Okay, I'm done for the night. Do you mind if we pick this up in the morning? I need to crash."

Granda nods. "Sweet dreams, luv. Until the morning."

I smile at Sloan on my way out. "I didn't ask, and I should have. I'm sorry to have assumed. Will you be able to take us home tomorrow? Can you spare a few days being trapped in Toronto with us?"

He dips his chin. "I'll be back in the morning. We can leave at your leisure."

———

The morning comes all too soon, and I take my coffee and oatmeal out on the patio to spend my last moments with Dart before Patty comes to bring him back to the lair. "Before you go, little dude," I say. "Granda has a surprise for you."

I gesture to where Granda rounds the side of the house,

pushing a wheelbarrow. In the bucket of the wheelbarrow is... "Yep, that's for you, buddy."

Dart looks at me, and his opal eyes shimmer.

As Granda dumps the dead calf on the lawn, I nod and walk him over. Dart doesn't need much encouragement. The moment he lifts his nose to the breeze, he lets out an excited squeal and runs to consume his breakfast.

"Such a happy wee thing." Gran joins us with a smile on her face and a bouquet in her hand.

I chuckle. "That wee thing will soon be the size of my SUV. I swear he grew overnight."

"He likely did."

"I hate to send him back. He's so happy here and was so sad in the cavern."

"Do ye believe bein' with his dragon siblings and the wyrm queen is the best fer him?"

"At this stage, yeah, I do."

"Then that's where he needs to be. The beauty of a mother's love means it's as unconditional as it is never-ending. Distance won't change that."

We stand there in silence as Dart eats his calf. Bones crunch. Fur flies. Blood sprays. Yum. When Granda comes around the house with a second calf, my mouth falls open. "Well, he won't go back to the lair hungry, that's for sure."

Gran chuckles. "That one is for Patty to take back for the young. There's no reason why roadkill needs to go to waste in a cleanup facility. I've arranged with the works department to bring the dead animals here for us to take them off their hands."

Granda brushes his hands against his pants and wraps an arm around Gran's hips. "Yer Gran's taken it upon herself to ensure the dragons don't go hungry."

Gran shrugs. "Waste not want not. The meat might as well be eaten."

"Agreed." I love the idea. "How did you explain that to the road works department?"

She shrugs. "I didn't have to explain. One of the head administrators is a druid. When I informed him that we have a brood of hungry dragons in the area, which is causing the sinkholes and loss of livestock across the county, he was more than happy to have me take the dead off his hands. It lends to the cycle of life quite nicely, I think."

"It does indeed." I hug Gran, thankful every moment of every day that they reached out and are now a part of my life.

By the time Sloan arrives, breakfast is long over, Patty has picked up Dart and the calf, and Gran and I have gone over the instructions for how to administer the remedy for Mr. Tree. "How long do you think it'll take before we see an improvement?"

"An improvement from the poison, within hours. He's still suffering from the state of yer friend, luv. He'll not fully heal until she is well and revived."

"Yeah, Garnet's working on that side of things. It's so sad, Gran. It's obvious that their feelings for each other are deep and genuine, yet they're apart and both living alone."

Gran smiles. "Yer a true romantic. There are a great many things that can divide a loving couple: a misstep, a loss of trust, a tragedy. There's no way for ye to fix somethin' that—from what ye said—has been broken for decades."

"Maybe not. But I can hope that this tragedy brings them closer so they realize they still care for one another, can't I?"

Gran smiles. "Och, that ye can surely do. Come. I'll even give ye a spell to help cleanse old wounds and clear their minds and hearts."

"You have a love potion?"

"No, nothing like that. All it'll do is sweep away the hurt and pain of the past and give them a clearer view of where they are now."

"I'm sure that's all they need." I follow Gran to her work area at the back of the house and tickle some of the hanging plants and roots dangling from the dirt ceiling from the hill above. "Oh, another thing I wanted to ask you about. My fae are cold. How do I keep them warm through a Canadian winter? Toronto is downright uninhabitable at times, and they're already chilled."

Gran goes over to her bookshelf and pulls out a slender book about as big as a third-grade reader. She hands it to me, and I read the cover. "Caring for your Grove Inhabitants."

"If I knew when ye left last time that ye'd have fae taggin' along with ye, I would've sent it with ye then. Better late than never, I suppose."

I flip open the pages and frown. "It's empty. Is it written in magic ink or something? Do I need a decoder ring?" I hold the book up to the light and move it this way and that. Still, no writing appears.

Gran chuckles and closes the book in my hands. "Ask it what ye asked me."

I blink at her but do as she says. "How do I keep the fae in my grove warm through a Canadian winter?"

I open the book again and smile. The pages are now filled with spells and instructions and all kinds of ideas on different ways to approach my problem. "All I do is focus on what I need for my grove fae, and the book will tell me?"

"That's how it works. Focus your intention, and the magic will do the rest."

I hug her tight and breathe her deep into my lungs. "Thanks, Gran. I love you."

CHAPTER TWELVE

S loan *poofs* Liam and me into my house. Although I've only been gone two or three days, it's good to be home. "There's no sense for you to sleep down on the pullout," I say as Sloan heads for the basement stairs. "You and Calum were roomies last time and it went well enough. You might as well take Brenny's bed. No one will mind."

Sloan gauges my sincerity, and I know he's hesitant. We're all still a little sensitive about Brendan's things. "I'm fine in the basement too. It's not a bother."

"No. The weather is turning, and you'll be warmer upstairs. Come up, and I'll get you settled. Let's be quiet though because Da's probably sleeping. He's on nights while everyone else is on days or afternoons."

I tug Liam as I head up the stairs. "I have a couple of ideas for how to make that bullet into a pendant. Come up, and I'll get out my jewelry wrapping kit to hook you up before you go. Did you tell your mom we're on the way?"

"No, I thought we'd surprise her."

The three of us jog up the steps, and I balk at the top of the stairs. Auntie Shannon is stepping out of the bathroom in a towel, sees us, and screeches.

While I'm trying to figure out what she's doing here, Da rushes out of his room naked. "What's *wrong*?"

Well, *allll righty* then. "I think we surprised her."

"What. The. Fuck?" Liam says.

Poof. Sloan's gone.

"Wow." My eyes bug. "So, this happened."

Da curses and ducks back into his room. Shannon normally shares my pasty, pale complexion but her cheeks have blotched up as red as two beets. "You're home. Liam... I'm so glad you're all right."

I look over at Liam and pat his cheek. "Breathe. You look like you're going to pass out."

"I might. So, you and Niall? How long has this been going on?"

Scenarios spin in my mind, and I come up with a plausible answer. "Liam got shot. You were distraught, and Da was there for you. Right?"

Da comes back, and thankfully he has his man bits in a pair of track pants so my retinas can stop burning. Naked isn't anything new in a house of all men, but a naked father when there's a naked Auntie Shannon in the mix is too much.

"Shannon and I are grown adults," Da snaps, "and we're the heads of yer households. We don't answer to either of ye."

Liam seems frozen in some form of paralyzed torture. "I...wow, okay. I'm just thrown. That's all. I get it. Fi's right. I was shot. You were upset and lonely. The two of you have been tag-teaming our patchwork family for a decade together. I suppose it makes perfect sense. It just happened."

Auntie Shannon looks like she might crumble, and my heart goes out to her.

"Don't cry, Shannon. You and Da both lost your other halves

in life, and you've both been alone raising kids for over a decade. S'all good. It caught us by surprise. That's all."

"It isn't because Liam was shot," Shannon admits. "Niall and I have been seeing one another for a while now."

Liam frowns. "Define a while now. Since Brendan was shot?"

Da steps in beside Shannon and puts his arm around her. "Go get dressed, *a mhuirnin*. Ye'll catch yer death."

She takes the opportunity to get outta Dodge, and Da straightens. He meets us with a hard scowl and raises a finger. "This is none of yer business. Whether we're in love or find comfort in one another on occasion or succumb to drunken booty calls, it's not yer concern."

I palm thrust my face trying to get those images out of my cranium. That my father even said *drunken booty call* when talking about him and Auntie Shannon blows my world. While he's right, he's also *soooo* very wrong.

"Then I should be upfront and tell you that Liam and I have been doing the naked tango on the drunken occasion too. Nothing serious. Just frivolous sex when we want to rip our clothes off and get it on."

Da's brow comes down in a dark scowl, and Liam chokes. "She's totally fucking with you, Niall. Never happened. Not once. Not ever. She's throwing me under the bus to make a point."

Da looks at me, and I throw my hands up. "Well, don't give me that bullshit about us not getting to have an opinion. By your face just now, you definitely had one when you thought Liam and I were boinking."

"It's not the same at all."

I wave that away. "I agree you're adults and I think it's natural that you two ended up here, but don't tell me we don't get to have feelings about it. We get to be curious. We get to worry. And we get to weigh in."

Da *harumphs* and rolls his eyes. "Fine. Over the years, there have been a few isolated moments when we've turned to each other. Very rare and only as friends with shared lives. When ye went missin' this summer, and we lost Brendan, it became more. Shannon isn't yer mam, but she loves ye both like her own, and we shared those fears and losses."

"I get that." I wrap an arm around Liam's hip. I'm not sure if I need to hold him up or if he's holding me up, but it feels necessary. "And it 'becoming more' is nice. We're happy for you, aren't we Liam?"

Liam runs a hand over his face and exhales. "Well, yeah, of course. Niall, you've been my father figure since I was in grade school. There's no man who I respect more. This is good. I'm glad the two of you are happy."

"Do you mean that, son?" Auntie Shannon comes out from behind Da. "There's been so much going on... I didn't want to add to the strain of our lives. We weren't exactly hiding our feelings, only seeing where things went first before dragging you kids into it."

I nod. "Okay, that's fair. Liam and I will go into my room, and I'll get him the chain we came up for. When we come downstairs, we'll all be reset, and everything will be normal."

Da chuckles. "Will it now. Yer sure?"

"I'm sure. S'all good. We're happy for you both."

I close Liam and me in my room, and he crosses my floor and flops on my bed. "Did Sloan pop us into an alternate timeline? Because holy hell, I did not see that coming."

I laugh and text Sloan. *You are such a scaredy-chicken, Mackenzie.*

Cluck. Cluck. Not my circus, not my naked monkeys.

I open my closet door and pull out the plastic organizer with my jewelry wrapping supplies in it. I take it back to the bed, climb up beside Liam, and cross my legs. "Give me your bullet."

He hands it to me, and I wrap it in a twenty gauge black dead soft wire. The groove near the base gives barely enough depth to secure a couple of laps around the cylinder before creating a loop to hang it from. After clipping off the excess, I wrap the ends with my pliers and make sure everything is twisted tight. I pull out a length of gold chain and a length of black leather. "Preference?"

"The leather."

"Okeedokee." I string the leather through the little loop and —"Voila."

He smiles, and the panic and confusion of finding out our parents are sexing it up has seemed to pass. "Awesome. Thanks, Fi."

"My pleasure. Now, are we ready to head down?"

"Is hiding in your bedroom for the rest of my natural life an option?"

"Nope."

Liam sighs and loops his "I-was-shot-and-this-slug-proves-it" pendant over his head. "All right, then. If you won't let me hide and wallow, I suppose I've got to pull up my big boy pants and get over the awkwardness of knowing my mother has sex."

I snort. "*That's* what's bothering you?"

He makes a face and shivers. "Yeah. What else would it be? Mothers aren't supposed to have sex. That's just wrong."

I chuckle and put away my supplies. "If you say so."

To Liam's relief, Shannon has her coat on and is ready to head home when we go downstairs.

I hug him before he heads out the door. "I'm glad you're not dead, but if you step in front of bullets meant for me again, I'll kill you myself."

He chuckles. "Love you too, Fi."

I giggle and push him toward the door. When they leave, Da follows me into the kitchen. He leans back on the kitchen counter while I pull out the fixings to make Sloan and I some lunch—wait, it's almost dinner here.

Time change. It's hell on your tummy.

Fine. I switch gears and grab the Swiss Chalet takeout menu from the basket on the fridge. "Are you game for takeout, Da?"

He looks at the mailer and nods. "If ye like. That's fine with me."

I grab my phone and open the app, choosing the family special I always order, same sides, delivery, and paid with the credit card on file. I hit send and smile. "Supper is in the oven. It'll be on the table in twenty-five minutes."

Moving over to the table, I set three placemats out and head to the cupboard for glasses.

"That's it?" Da asks, his eyebrows raised high enough to disappear behind his russet bangs.

"Is what it? Dinner? Yeah. It's as easy as that. We live in the age of convenience."

"Fiona Kacee Cumhaill, ye know full well what I'm askin' ye. Have ye nothin' ye want to get off yer chest about my involvement with Shannon? Because I figured the moment we were alone ye'd be bustin' at the seams."

I set the three glasses in place and turn to face him straight on. "Da, I'm honestly good. I love both you and Auntie Shannon with my whole heart whether you're together or not. I know how good the two of you have been for our families and you're right. The dating details are none of our business. I'm a little afraid that if it goes south it might impact our family, but that's about it. You do you. If you're happy, I'm happy."

His gaze narrows and he leans closer. "Yer sure?"

I move in and hug him, wrapping my arms around his waist and across his back. "Positive."

He grips the hair at the back of my neck and kisses the side of my head. "How did I ever manage to raise a woman of such wisdom and character as my darlin' girl?"

I shrug. "I am pretty incredible, I know. So, on to the next question. Do I get to tell the boys? Or do you want to?"

He eases back and shakes his head. "I have a feeling yer lookin' forward to it. Have at it, but please make sure no one upsets Shannon. She loves the lot of ye like yer her own. If there are any cross words to be spoken, make sure they come to me and not her, understood?"

"I don't think there will be, but yeah, I can do that."

I leave Da in the kitchen, and when I don't find Sloan in the basement, I check upstairs in Calum's room. "Oh, so this is where you're hiding."

He flashes me a guilty grin and turns from his computer. "I have a rule about not getting involved in the fallout of interrupting naked family members of the girl I'm courting."

I snort. "Really? And what rule is that?"

"Don't do it."

"Oh, that complex is it?"

"Yep."

"Well, the coast is clear. Everyone has clothes on now, and dinner will arrive in a few minutes. Come down, and you can help me fill Da in on what he missed."

He stands and points at the mason jar on the bed next to his duffle bag. "After dinner, should we head over to the bookstore with Emmet and see if we can get the ancient ash on the road to recovery?"

"Yeah. I'll text Zxata and tell him. Maybe he'll want to join the party."

"Ye told that Garnet fellow ye'd text him as well when ye returned."

"Right, thanks." I pull my phone out and send both of those texts. The responses come back quickly. "Zxata will meet us there. Garnet says for us to swing by his compound when we finish. There's something he wants to talk to me about."

His brow pinches. "Ye know where the man lives?"

"No, but Zxata does, and he was heading over there to visit his sister."

"How is Myra?"

I shrug. "Still unresponsive, as far as I know."

"I'm sorry, Fi. We'll figure it out. I promise."

"Thanks for coming, Emmet." I hug my brother outside the front door to the Emporium and notice he hangs on a little longer than usual. I ease back and pull my keys out of my purse. Once I unlock the doors, I step inside to release the wards and turn off the security system, then the three of us go inside. "How was your shift?"

"Uneventful. More importantly, how are you?"

As the three of us head into the back room, I fill him in on what happened from the time Liam and I left the table to go dance until now—except for the part about Da and Shannon. I'm saving that for the right moment.

"Liam's okay?"

"Yep. I wrapped the slug, and he's wearing it as a badge of honor—a symbol of survival."

"Well, kudos to you and your Da for saving him, my man." Emmet bumps fists with Sloan. "Looks like we owe you yet another life-saving win."

Sloan waves that away. "Lugh and Lara are my family. That means yer my family as well, and Liam and Shannon by extension. I'm happy it all worked out."

"I hear you."

"Now, to the next patient." I turn on the lights to the back room and lead the way. Mr. Tree, a.k.a. Leniya, looks as sickly now as he did three days ago. Thankfully, he doesn't look much worse, but he certainly doesn't look any better.

"Hey there, Mr. Tree. I promise we'll get you fixed up in no time. I brought you some medicine as well as a druid healer and a booster cable to give you a jump start."

Emmet chuckles. "Thanks for that."

I wink at him and press my hand on the tree's trunk. "It won't be long now, buddy. Once Zxata gets here, we'll be—"

"Zxata is here." He strides through the doorway from the front of the store. "I brought a friend as well."

I smile as Dora follows him in and wow, yeah, now I'm excited. If Pan Dora is willing to help us, I can't even imagine what kind of druid chops she's got. "Welcome, Dora. Thank you for coming."

Dora steps close to the tree and brushes her fingers over his crumbling bark. "I'm not sure how much help I'll be. I'm more than a little rusty."

Sloan's eyes are wide, and I know he's thinking along the same lines of awe-inspiring wonder as me. "I have no doubt ye'll bring us nothing but successful results. It's an honor to work at yer side."

Emmet's confused, but honestly, that's not an uncommon expression for him. "Oh, do you possess nature magic, Dora?"

She offers him an adoring smile and dips her cleft chin. "In another lifetime, I did, yes. I might have a bit of magic left in me somewhere. Shall we give it a try and see?"

"Sure. I'm a buffer. Do you want me to boost you?"

She shakes her head, and her bright purple hair flows loosely around her broad shoulders. "Boost Mocha Manliness over there. He's got the most focused healing abilities in the group."

Before Emmet asks how Dora could know that, I interrupt. "Gran created a remedy to counteract the base magic of the Evening Shade Wizards. With that and our combined efforts, I have faith we'll have Mr. Tree lush and blooming in no time."

"How would ye like to do this?" Sloan asks Dora.

She seems embarrassed by the attention, but I can't blame Sloan for handing over the torch. There's no way I'm going to lead this band of merry men.

Not with her here to take charge.

"We'll kneel around the trunk and pour the remedy as we pass the jar withershins from one to the next. If you have a spell to cast, that is your time. Then, we'll plant our palms flat against the earth. I'll speak a formal healing incantation, and the four of you can call upon your Guardian of Nature bonds to infuse the healing."

Dora kneels directly beneath the weeping gash in Leniya's bark. The burn mark from the dark magic makes my heart ache. Zxata kneels next. I take my position, then Sloan, and Emmet.

Sloan uncaps the remedy and pours a sweeping arch of the deep, mulberry mixture in front of him. As the liquid soaks into the ground along the base of the tree, he says,

As the tincture pours
So, yer health restores
Remove and banish
Dark magic vanish
Radiant health is yours.

He hands me the jar, and I repeat his actions and words before giving the remedy to Zxata. We go around the tree withershins—the pagan way of saying counter-clockwise—until Emmet finishes and hands the empty jar back to Sloan. He sets it aside and presses his palms to the earth.

We all follow his example, and I close my eyes.

"Guardian of Nature," I say, then focus on my connection with Myra's home tree. I remember Gran's teachings from that first day in her garden.

Empty yer mind of the noise that buzzes inside yer head, no questions, no expectations, no turmoil.

Like then, the connection builds beneath my palms. It starts deep in the soil beneath us and arcs up into the palms of my hands, through my wrists, and into my body's core. The energy isn't strong and warm like I'm used to.

It's sluggish and cold.

Poor Mr. Tree.

I reset my focus as Dora starts the incantation. Her words are harmonic and roll off her tongue as if she speaks them every day. The language is strange to my ears, but something ancient and instinctual inside me recognizes it.

My shield warms against the flesh on my back, and I feel Dora's energy signature radiate through our connections. Her power snaps in the air and makes my lips tingle. Even with my eyes closed, I'm aware of the living force that is nature.

I sense the rich nutrients of Gran's remedy soaking into the earth beneath my fingertips. It sinks deep, burrowing into the darkness to find Leniya's roots. The healing moisture seeps, drop-by-drop, into the pores of the home tree's root system. It carries restorative energy and healing sustenance. It cleanses the destruction of the dark spell.

Dora's voice has a strength to it that makes my ears pop.

Rusty, my ass. She's incredible.

I send all the healing energy I can into Leniya's roots and farther still into the tree's connection with Myra. I embrace the link with the source energy, and it surges from my arms, into the ground, and out into the natural world.

Druids are the conduits of earthly power, Gran told me. *It will never harm ye as long as ye hold it in yer heart with reverence.*

I do. I am a conduit of our Divine Lady's gifts. She ignites in my cells and, through me, rights the damage done to this ancient ash.

I listen to Dora and her words spin in my mind, painting scenes of forgotten times. I swallow. It's disorienting. My stomach tightens, and my breathing picks up.

Wait. I don't like this—

A jolt of power shoots up my arm like a rocket and throws me into the air. Distantly, I hear Sloan and Emmet shout.

I am weightless.

I fly backward until I ass-plant hard on a patch of mossy scrub and come to a violent, crashing stop. My breath leaves my lungs in a *whoosh*, and I lay on my back, gasping to get reacquainted with oxygen. A cool breeze blows over my face, and I open my eyes to the champagne sky of twilight.

As suddenly as the power surge hit me, I remember having this exact sensation once before...

I gasp as my heart hammers behind my ribs.

"Oh, crap."

CHAPTER THIRTEEN

"We meet again, fair Fiona," my great-great-great-who knows how many greats-grandfather says. I stare at the ruddy face of my ancestor, his messy, blond braids swishing beside his face as he bends to help me up.

He clasps my wrist and hauls me to my feet with an easy smile and unstrained strength. "Fiona mac Cumhaill, blood of my blood, my heart sings to be in yer company once again."

"Good to see you too, Fionn." I brush off the bits of nature smudging my butt and shake off the timewarp trippiness spinning in my head. It's a warm, autumn evening, and I'm staring up at a massive gray and red stone castle with soaring spires and flag-tipped towers. "Where are we this time?"

"The Castle of Carlisle."

"When are we?"

He places his arm against his navel and bows while sweeping his other arm out to the side. "Fiona, welcome to the final days of the fifth century."

As his words hang in the air, I blink at the smell of farmyard, the sight of peasants with oxen, and the sound of horse hooves clomping on hard-packed ground. This isn't the first time he's sucked me back in time for a bonding moment, but it's no less disorienting.

"Why am I here?"

"For a quest of critical importance. Here, cover yourself with this."

Fionn hands me a heavy green traveling cloak with oak leaves embroidered in gold around the hood's edge and down both sides of the lapel. I swing it around my shoulders, and he stands before me. After tucking my hair back behind my head, he latches the bronze broach at my throat and lifts my hood to cover me.

"Why am I hiding?"

"I need hardly tell you the passage of time changes practices of what is common and acceptable. Here, in the now, a female wearing breeks inside the castle walls would draw us undue attention and likely unwanted scrutiny."

I roll my eyes and pull the two sides of the cloak closed at my navel. It drapes to the dirt ground at my feet and hides my inappropriate femaleness from view.

"Why are they staring?"

"Merely curiosity. You are quite visibly a Celt, yet you have the flawless, porcelain skin of royalty and wear the clothes of a manservant. It's only natural you draw notice."

We round the back of a wall made out of bound bunches of collected twigs and join the common folk's movement. Even with the cloak on and the hood up, people seem curious about me. I drop my gaze and try to blend.

"How proficient is your Celtic Brittonic?"

Fionn casts me a sideways glance. "Your understanding of ancient tongues. Celtic Brittonic, it's what was generally spoken in this part of the world from the sixth century B.C. to the sixth century A.D."

"Oh, yeah, not good. I didn't even know what it was."

Fionn frowns. "What have ye been doin' with yer time? I thought ye'd be further along by now."

The comment stings and I straighten and lift my chin. "Since you ignited your mark on me and threw me to the whacked and weird wolves, you mean? Well, let's think about how I've spent my time. I've been kidnapped countless times, poisoned, hexed, stabbed, and shot at. I've been held captive and impaled on the altar for blood sacrifice. In between all that, I returned to Ireland, retrieved your precious Fianna heirlooms, built a fae grove, stopped a necromancer massacre, and freed the ley lines of Toronto so ambient magic can now flow freely. It may not tilt your scale, but for me, it's been a busy four months."

"Four months?" Fionn's bushy blonde brow rises like a startled caterpillar. "Apologies. Time moves differently in the Nether. I didn't realize ye'd still be at the infancy of yer journey."

I stand down a little and uncross my arms. "All right, I know how time warps mess with things. Apology accepted."

Fionn's expression relaxes, and his full lips turn up at the corners. "A lass as gracious as she is beautiful. Now, ye said ye retrieved the Fianna treasures. Do ye have my precious girl with ye, then?"

I push my arm out of the cape and pull back my sleeve.

He brushes a gentle caress along the inked replica of Birga tattooed on the inside of my right forearm. "Och, there she is. I can't tell ye how relieved I am my trove is back in the hands of my clan."

"All good on that front. My brothers, father, and I have accepted the weapons and taken up the mantle of bringing the Fianna into the modern age."

Fionn places his closed fist over his chest. "Ye make an oul man proud, lass."

As crazy as it sounds, it fills me close to bursting to hear him say so. I really do want to honor him and the Fianna of old. "So, tell me about this quest of critical importance. Why am I here?"

"Have ye not guessed yet?"

I look around and draw a blank. History was never my strongest subject, but maybe I can pull a rabbit out of my ass. Or hat, I guess. Pull a rabbit out of my hat.

"So, end of the fifth century, we're inside the Carlisle Castle... which I've never heard of..."

I examine the simple folk coming through the open gates, carrying bundles of wheat on their backs and lumpy and heavy sacks in their arms. Filthy dogs run between dirty kids playing with sticks and rocks.

"Yeah no, sorry, I've got nothing."

He points at the red flags with the golden dragon. It's a Western dragon with four legs and wings. I chuckle at myself. Before becoming a mother of dragons, I never would've known the difference between a wyrm, a drake, or a wyvern.

I stare at the tunics of the guards standing at either side of the open city gate. They're wearing chainmail head coverings and cowls and red tunics with the same golden dragon.

"The crest looks familiar, but I'm not sure—*Oh!* I recognize it. Sloan and Granda showed me ink sketches from the time of Arthurian lore when we looked up where the *Eochair Prana* could've gone. That crest was on the flags in the back of one of the pictures."

"Where do ye think the dark book went?"

I shrug. "I have no idea. A couple of copies surfaced over time, but from what we learned, the original one—the one scribed in the blood of Morgan la Fey that had all the best resurrection spells—disappeared around the start of the sixth century and was never found."

He blinks at me. "It seems unlikely, does it not, that a tome as powerful and coveted as the *Eochair Prana* could remain hidden for fifteen hundred years?"

I nod. "Lucky for the people of those times. From what my

friend Dora said, it could've brought about the ruination of the balance of all power."

Fionn *tonks* my head with his staff.

I groan. "Hey! What the hell? What did you do that for?"

"Checking that ye've got working cogs in there and not a vast space."

"My cogs are working fine, thanks. Or at least they were until you beaned me one."

Fionn sighs, takes my arm, and hooks it under his elbow. Together we walk away from the gates and up toward the castle proper. "Ye know the dark book came from this time and ye know the dark book disappeared from this time never to be seen or spoken of for at least the next fifteen centuries. What do ye suppose happened to it?"

I hear the thread of expectation weaving through his words. Then it dawns on me. "*Me?* I have it? You're saying the reason it disappeared was that I traveled back and took it?"

He looks at me, and I'm sure if he knew the term 'bingo,' he'd be saying it right now. "Druids are the keepers of nature and the guardians of fae prana, yes?"

"Yes. Of course... It's a little mind-bendy to think that current me in Toronto was searching for the book that disappeared when I took it fifteen hundred years earlier but didn't have it yet. Cray-cray, amirite?"

Fionn chuckles. "I do so enjoy how ye tend to think in queer circles."

"Um...thanks?" My cells tingle with the excitement of it. I'm going to safeguard humanity and remove the *Eochair Prana* from temptation for the next fifteen hundred years. Yay me! "Okay, so how do I do it? Where do I get it?"

Fionn pulls us to the side of the sloped walkway as the worn dirt ground gives way to a cobbled road. The higher up we go, the more polished the surroundings get. The castle proper is still quite a climb into the city.

"We must gain the confidence of someone within the royal hierarchy and learn who might possess a book tethered to Morgana's very soul."

"Right. No biggie."

Lost in the paradigm shift of my place in the history of fae magic and humanity's well-being, I don't notice the man backing his mule out of its harness.

The jack and I collide, and the beast of burden brays and fights against the farmer's hold. I dodge and slide. Fionn catches my arm and saves me from skidding out on a steaming heap of mule shit. The farmer yanks the mule sideways, and his muscled hindquarters knock me as the beast stomps his hoofed feet.

The man yells, and even without a formal understanding of Celtic Brittonic, I get that he's cussing me out.

I flip him off and give it right back. "Screw you too, you mangy ass—and I mean *you,* not the mule—you ass."

Fionn places a firm hand at my back and escorts me away from the street scuffle. His eyes are alight with laughter, and I'm glad he's amused because I'm fuming and have mule crap on my fabulous new boots.

"Asshole," I grumble.

Fionn chuckles. "While it seems certain languages are universal, I'm not sure foul-mouthing the locals will achieve our goals. The viler ye are, the more enemies ye make."

"Yeah, well, he started it. I couldn't even understand what he said, but I knew what he was saying."

Fionn takes me behind a wooden guardhouse and grips both my wrists. "Let us address the language barrier. Connect with yer source power and repeat after me."

Ancient tongues of pasts long gone
Fill the air like Babylon.
Charm my ears and bless my words
To sing their tune like sweet songbirds.

I close my eyes, breathe the ambient magic in the air into my lungs, and pull from the earth below my boots. When the connection is firm, I repeat his spell.

When I open my eyes, he's there watching me with warm reverence. "Well done, *a leanbh*. Four months only, and yer further along than I was as a young man. I was wrong to think ye'd be as good as my father's sister, Bodhmall. Yer gearin' up to stand in a class all yer own."

That's high praise from a master mentor.

I stick that feather in my cap, and the two of us stroll into the main courtyard at the front of the castle. The wide-open area is paved in gray, interlocking stones and seems to stand as a social and political meeting place of the people of Carlisle Castle.

There is a teenaged boy locked in the stocks with children pelting him with rotten produce. Everyone seems to think this is hilarious, including the teen.

A group of lovely gowned ladies giggle and watch two knights practice their swordplay.

On the far side of the courtyard, a mason pieces together the last blocks of a huge stone fountain.

Fionn and I climb the six polished steps and stop in front of the oversized wooden double doors. Fionn bows his head to the guards at the main entrance and offers them a charming smile. "Fionn mac Cumhaill and family."

"State your business."

"My niece and I bring gathered herbs, tinctures, and remedies for yer court physician. Could ye direct us to where we might find him?"

"Will you be staying for the Feast of the Last Harvest tomorrow night?"

"If our business isn't concluded, we would be honored to attend."

The guard looks me over, then Fionn. "Are you armed? No weapons are permitted within the castle walls in the hands of the common."

Fionn holds out his arms and does a runway turn. He's wearing hide pants and a thick navy blue tunic with a wide leather belt. Over that, he has a vest made out of the fur of some unfortunate beast who once had a very long, brown coat.

Other than the walking stick he holds in his right hand, he's unarmed. Having seen what my father can do with a staff, I well know how dangerously armed Fionn truly is.

The guard opens Fionn's satchel, peers inside, and squeezes it from the bottom. When he's satisfied with that, he looks me over once again.

I hold out my arms and open my cloak to show him that I too am unarmed.

"Very well. You will find Davant in the apothecary on the lower level most days until the dinner gong. After which, he'll be too gone with drink to be of much use to you. "

Fionn nods. "I thank you, sir."

The two of us move inside when the second guard on the other side of the door opens our way. I step onto the polished stone floor and breathe in the scent of—oh, it doesn't smell like a crumbly old castle at all.

Oh, yeah. That makes sense. It's not old yet.

I cast an assessing glance around the pristine space and think of Sloan. He's going to have a crap and a half when I tell him about this.

Oh, I have my phone. I'll take pictures.

"What puts that devilish smile on yer face, *a leanbh?* Have ye a suitor on yer mind? A betrothed, perhaps?"

Granda and Da call me *mo chroí,* their heart, while Fionn calls me *a leanbh,* my child. It's sweet. "I was thinking of a guy, yes, but Sloan's only a friend."

"I recognize a look of feminine affection, and the smile ye had on yer face a moment ago had little to do with mere friendship."

I tilt my head back and forth, and my hood flops onto my

shoulders. I pull it back into place and shrug. "How about a friend who is lobbying to be my suitor?"

Fionn nods. "Yer smile suggests yer taken with him."

"Maybe a little."

"What is yer objection to the match? Is he uncomely, of meager means, or perhaps indifferent to yer sensibilities?"

I chuckle. Are those the only reasons a woman of his time would hesitate to jump into a relationship? "No. He's very hand-some, quite wealthy, and more attentive and understanding of my queer sensibilities than I likely deserve."

"And yet, ye rebuff his advance?"

Why am I having this conversation with my ancient ancestor? "Not rebuff so much as ask his patience. I mentioned earlier that a lot has happened in four months. I need a moment to steady my footing."

"Wouldn't having a husband be the quickest way to ensure yer life's stability?"

"*Husband?* Slow your roll, Fionn." I say it a little louder than I meant to. "I live in a time when a woman is looked on as an equal to a man...in most cases. I don't need a husband to stand on my own. I'm a force in my own right."

Fionn chuckles. "Then perhaps yer the one who should court him. If he's comely, of fortunate means, and of kind tempera-ment, he sounds like a rare prospect."

I laugh. "Enough about my love life. Can we get back to our quest? Tell me more about this part of history. Morgana's book is here, but she isn't, right?"

"Aye, there are theories as to what befell her, but theories they remain."

"And she was Arthur's sister?"

"There are different interpretations. A ward to Uther Pendragon, Arthur's father, raised within the halls of the royal family is the one most commonly believed."

"But no relation?"

"Not beyond a commitment to the obligation of rearing and sheltering her."

Fionn and I saunter through the castle's main entrance, and I'm surprised how bright it is. Windows aren't a thing on its main floors so yeah, I figured it would be dark. Second and third story windows peaked with Gothic arches allow light into the grand entrance.

"So, our cover is that we're here to track down Davant, the court physician, but who are we really looking for?"

Fionn shrugs. "Someone who knows about the book."

"In a castle filled with people and more flooding in by the hour to attend the big Harvest Feast tomorrow, how will we find that someone?"

"By the will of the gods, I suppose."

I frown. "That's not comforting. How much time have we got to getter done?"

Fionn's expression gives me no confidence. "I have never held travel for longer than a day. I expect this will be no different."

I reach into my pocket under my cloak, pull out my phone, and face the wall. While keeping my cell hidden under the folds of my mantle, I set an alarm for twenty-four hours.

"That's not a lot of time."

He shrugs again. "It's time to sup now. I'll find the head of the house and arrange lodging and a late sitting for us for tonight. We've surely missed our opportunity to speak to Davant until morning. We'll eat and get our bearings tonight."

"Will a day here be like last time when I went back, and it was the same moment I left?"

Fionn nods. "If all transpires as it should."

Okay, cool. "Then it's cake and eat it too time. I get to focus on our task in the past and not worry about my posse in the present shitting kittens."

"What kind of magic is that?"

"Is what?"

"Shitting kittens." His face screws up. "I have never heard of a spell to defecate felines and what would be the purpose?"

"Oh, not literally. No, it's a saying. It means they'll be beside themselves with alarm."

"If they are passing animals they *should* be alarmed."

I'm about to explain more of that when I see—"Holy-freaking-schmoly, no way."

CHAPTER FOURTEEN

"Dora!" I rush over to the six-foot-four male and realize my mistake too late. "Oh, sorry, we haven't met yet."

In royal velvet garb, with long, dark brown hair and a drunken glaze to his gaze, Merlin of old rakes me with a blank look. "Are you the boy to wash my feet?"

I drop my hood and smile. "No. I'm the girl who becomes your friend in about fifteen hundred years. We live in Toronto. You're my ink spell artist."

I tug the neck of my shirt down my shoulder a little to expose a recent concealment sigil. With all the trouble I've stumbled into, we thought it would be a wise addition to my repertoire.

He stiffens, pulls my cloak to cover me, and shoves me back. He casts a glance around us before looming forward. "How dare you openly flaunt a sigil? Have you a wish to kneel in the gallows? Out of my sight, wench, before you get us both sentenced to death."

With the back of his arm, he knocks me aside and stomps off, his cloak billowing in the wake of his fury.

Thankfully, there's no one around except Fionn to catch the

full exchange between us. The few that saw him shove me and stomp off seem quite accustomed to such scenes and pay no attention.

I frown and return to Fionn. "That could've gone better."

Fionn sweeps a hand through the air and gestures for us to take our leave. "Failures lay the foundation from which to build a new level of understanding."

"Ha, if that's true, I've lain more foundation than the crew who built the Great Wall of China."

He smiles at me with the blank look he gets when he has no idea what I'm talking about. "Come. Let's secure our lodgings, and I'll arrange for a proper gown for you so we can attend dinner."

"A gown? Seriously?"

He throws me a look, and it's as familiar as any could be. The Cumhaill scowl has inarguably passed down through the generations. "Aye, a gown. In yer time, if ye choose to dress as a male, there's naught to be said about it. In this place, it's liable to get us arrested and burned on a pyre. There are appearances to be kept, and consequences for those who raise the disapproval of the gentry."

Well, la dee da. "Fine. I'll wear a gown, but I've seen the movies. I'm not gripping a bedpost while some sadistic maidservant yanks on the lacings of my corset until I can't breathe. I don't play the body image game. Like it or lump it."

Fionn snorts. "What makes ye think ye rank a maidservant? Ye'll dress yerself. Like it or lump it."

Our lodgings are modest but perfectly acceptable. Fionn says I get the bed, and he's fine with a straw pallet on the floor in front of the fire. I'm not about to argue. The fact that we scored a fireplace at all is a boon. I think that has more to do with Fionn whispering a few private words to the girl making the arrangements than two snake oil peddlers ranking an upgrade.

I hadn't thought about it, but we have no coin.

Fionn pointed out that there are many currencies beyond gold, and he considered himself a wealthy man.

'Nuff said. Do what you gotta do.

I don't think the payment owed is much of a hardship on either side. Fionn has a weathered, worldly way about him and is in peak physical shape while the room assignment girl was plain, but seemed nice and filled her dress out to Fionn's liking. Live and let live.

My clothing arrives, and I step behind the dressing screen to figure out how to put it on. Man, there are so many layers. "Women must get up an hour early to put these on."

"Thus the privilege of having a maidservant."

I see the allure. "Okay, which is first?" I hold up two layers. One is a gown with sleeves, and the other looks like a sleeveless toga-type thing but the shoulders aren't sewn together. "More importantly, how does this one stay on?"

"The white one with sleeves first. That's yer undergown. Then the blue. There should be a brooch front and back to fasten the shoulders. If not on the garment, the lass should've brought them as well fer ye to use."

"Why do it that way?"

"How should I know?"

"What's this?" I hold up a swatch of dark blue cloth with silver piping. "It looks like a lopsided poncho."

"It goes over the top and covers one shoulder and arm."

"Why have a one-armed poncho?"

"Why do ye think I can answer these questions? I have no notion of how to dress a female."

"Well, you get them undressed, don't you?"

"Occasionally. But far more often, it's a case of finding a dark corner and lifting skirts."

"Such a romantic. And you're lecturing me on settling down and getting betrothed."

Fionn harrumphs. "It's not the same thing at all."

"Dream on, gigolo. It's exactly the same thing."

"Has anyone ever told ye that yer a frustratingly outspoken female?"

"It may have been mentioned on occasion." I pull the peacock blue toga layer over my head and find the brooches in a cloth bag. "Okay, you'll have to do this part."

I come around the screen, and Fionn throws me a flustered look. "Have ye no sense of modesty?"

I laugh. "I'm covered from chin to toes. What am I flashing that's making you uncomfortable?"

"Well, yer underthings. Yer my granddaughter, for goddess sake."

"Trust me. This isn't indecent. Just brooch me up, then I'll get my poncho on, and my virtue will be safe."

"Ye have the wicked sass of a concubine and the forked tongue of a woman living in the lower town."

I laugh. "True story."

"Ye'll have to put on airs for this to work, Fiona."

"Trust me. Once we leave this room, I'll act the part of a perfect lady of the gentry, I promise."

He eyes me, and the tension in his face softens. "I look forward to witnessin' the show. Very well. Come here, and I'll see what I can do about yer brooches."

The dinner is an experience I'll never forget. As travelers arriving after the dinner gong, we don't get to eat in the hall with the royals and palace guests. Fionn and I join the middle class at the second sitting. We have a traveling minstrel, a few squires, a couple of lower-level clergymen, a Roman actor intent on gaining an audience for his monologue, and the entertainment arriving for the festivities tomorrow.

In other words, I'm with the band—my peeps.

"How was your dinner, milady?" the flutist asks and flashes me a coy smile.

The chicken was greasy, the bread hard and grainy, the wine filled with filament floaties. "Delicious, thank you." I flash Fionn a smug grin. If he knew how many hours I played princess to my brothers' brash knights routine, he wouldn't be so surprised.

"Will you be staying in the castle long?" he asks while sidling near.

"Only tonight." I turn to face him so he can't get much closer. "Then my uncle will take me to reunite with my betrothed."

"Betrothed, ye say?"

I nod. "Oh, yes. A brawny male with shoulders as broad as a door and muscles that rise like the rolling Irish hills. He's a warrior, fiercely loyal to his cause, and wildly protective of those he loves. I pity anyone at the wrong end of his sword."

My flutist dips his chin and eases back. "If you'll excuse me, milady. I must make inquiries about the arrangements for tomorrow night's performance."

"Of course. I look forward to seeing you."

"Until then." He rises from the bench and makes a hasty exit.

Fionn chuckles beside me. "Shall I escort ye back to our chamber or do ye wish to stay and torment some other poor fool with bright ideas?"

I sip a little more of my wine before leaving the sediment at the bottom. "I'll leave with you, but I think I'll explore the castle a little."

He raises his brow. "A lady wandering the halls of a castle

alone after nightfall is generally askin' fer one of two outcomes. Neither will be to yer likin'."

I rise from the table and hold out my hand for his elbow. As we strike off, I tap the inside of my forearm and smile. "Birga is never far. We two ladies will be fine."

"As ye wish, but do try to remember we're not here to cause trouble."

I walk with Fionn until we get back to the main juncture of where the staff quarters open up to the east wing. The girl from the lodging assignments is there, standing with a girlfriend. The two of them look quite excited. *Oh, like that, is it?*

Fionn waggles his brow. "Duty calls."

I snort and wave him off.

Alone in a castle of hundreds, I breathe it all in and wish, not for the first time, that Sloan was here. He would die to see this.

I have to record a little of it for him.

Exploring unpopulated corridors, I take a selfie with a bronze dog, film a bit of drunken strip-and-shuffle as a couple disappear into one of the curtained alcoves, and take a panoramic of the torchlight lining the streets of the town below from a balcony off the fifth floor.

After slipping my phone back into the cloth brooch bag that came with my dress, I draw a last breath of the night air and move to continue my exploration.

I stop with my hand on the latch of the door.

A heated scuffle inside has me stepping back into the shadows. When my back presses against the stone of the castle, I fall still and envision the shade around me intensifying.

Shadowed Darkness. The darkness grows denser and wraps around me, concealing me completely. I slide my hands under the flap of my poncho and take a calming breath.

The argument spills out onto the balcony and cuts off my exit.

"—a cheat and a liar," one man says. "Do you think because you live in the tower and have the king's ear you get to swindle the hard-working folk out of their coin with impunity? You don't. Give me back what's mine, or I'll report what you've done."

"Who do you think the guard will believe, a trusted royal advisor or the boy who paid me to cast a love spell on the stable-master's daughter?"

I recognize the deep timbre of Merlin's voice, and my heart quickens. He's a legendary druid. Surely he'll sense me.

I'm so busted.

Shit. I close my eyes and focus on my concealment spell.

"Knowing who and what I am, is it wise to threaten me? I warned you that love spells are fickle, but there are a great many other spells I could perform to silence a boy who chose to become my adversary."

It doesn't take long for the argument to fizzle out after that. The door opens again, and the balcony falls quiet.

Thank you, baby Yoda.

I hold my position and draw a few deep breaths as my heart gears down from total panic to racing like a rabbit. I'm surprised Merlin didn't hear the pounding and discover me lurking in the shadows.

"You can come out now."

Annnd we're right back up to panic. I flex my fingers and shake out my sweaty palms. As I step out from my stony nook, I release my concealment spell. "Hello again."

"Are you following me?"

I chuckle. "I was here first."

He throws me a look and his gaze narrows. "It's dangerous to spy on powerful people. Especially for a woman."

I raise my palms. "I have no interest in whatever that was, but I'm glad to see you again. I know it sounds crazy, but I told you the truth before. You and I are to become friends in the far-distant future."

He moves to leave, and I throw out my hand.

"*Wood Wall.*" The wood of the door seals to a solid sheet and the hinges and latch disappear.

Merlin turns and pegs me with a scathing glare. "Do you not understand how dangerous it is to cast here?"

"No. Not really. I thought in the days of Merlin and Arthur in Camelot, magic and dragons abound."

He makes a pinched face. "Magic and dragons abounded at one time, but the age of the One God is upon us. Now, all magic is viewed as evil sorcery, and casters are drowned or burned alive."

I remove the spell, and the door is a door once again. "Then I'm glad I don't live in this time because I'd be fried extra crispy before you know it. It sucks that you aren't able to live your authentic life yet—but it's coming."

He eyes me and arches a brow. "How and why would we ever be friends?"

"Ouch. Harsh. Because you agree to ink the spells for my brothers and me."

"That doesn't sound like me."

I shrug. "You're very different. In my time, you're happy and authentic and flamboyant, and you sing."

He huffs and turns for the door.

"Wait! I can prove it. Give me two minutes…please."

I pull out my phone and scroll through saved messages. "In the time I come from, we can send messages through devices like these. They're like magical carrier pigeons. This is a message you sent me before I came to this time. Just listen."

I call up the message and play it.

"Hey, cookie. I don't want you wasting time searching for the *Eochair Prana.* Focus on Myra and her home tree. No one will find the original of Morgana's book. Trust me when I say we took care of it. You'll understand soon enough and when you do, know that I'm sorry I was such a drunken prat. Chin up, Fi. And good luck."

The call ends, and I see the first glimpse of the person I know in those eyes.

"In my time, you shed your life as Merlin and live as a night-club entertainer named Pan Dora. May I show you? I sat in on one of your practice sessions a few weeks ago and recorded it."

He's glaring at me but doesn't say no, so I push forward and press play. When the video of Pan Dora comes on, and she's singing *Burlesque*, I feel the shift in the force.

"You're really good. You live above your nightclub, and you decorated it in wild colors and sexy pictures of naked men. You read my Tarot, and you're friends with my spirit bear—Killer Clawbearer—do you know him yet?"

He staggers back a pace.

I'm getting through to him, so I press on. "Your club is called Queens on Queen, and you throw outrageous theme nights and parties."

He scrubs a hand over his face and his rings catch the light of the moon. "I'm lost to drink. It's some kind of bafflement magic I don't understand, and you're ensnaring me."

I shake my head and put my phone away. "No. We're friends. You're a good person. Hell, you run a soup kitchen and feed the homeless and the hungry in your spare time."

He holds up his finger. "In that message, I speak of the *Eochair Prana*. What is it and why would I say we took care of it?"

I spend the next twenty minutes explaining everything that happened over the past week and end with us standing here. "I think you're supposed to help me steal the book so I can take it with me back to my time so no one can use it."

His face twists in horror. "I'm not the man you think I am. Maybe at one time I was—or maybe even will be—but that's not who I am now."

"I get that. You told me a little about your past, and I don't care. That's not who you are to me."

"What did I tell you?" His eyes filled with equal parts of hope and fear.

"You said over time, you wore many titles, some you were proud of and others you weren't. Wizard. Prophet. Drunk. Confidant. King's advisor. Mentor. And while you believe we learn from the past, you don't enjoy looking back."

"That's true. I don't." He points at where I put away my phone. "Show me again."

I play him both the video and the message a second time. If he doesn't yet believe me fully, that's okay. He's not dismissing me altogether.

"What do you know about Morgana's book?" I ask.

"Rumors stir—whispers really—that the witch did something vile and dangerous. No one has seen her for years. She's mad, that one. Darkness always dwelled inside her, but it took root and festered. The kind of magic she embraces is evil and gnarled. It will get the rest of us killed by association."

"So, you didn't know there is a book?"

"A week ago, I was in another part of the country attending to another matter. I dreamed of a sleek, black raven riding the wave of a violent storm cloud. She covered a great distance, calling darkness to feed the storm. When she finally landed, she perched on a balcony of this castle."

He raises a pointed finger and frowns. "A cloaked man stepped out of one of the upper levels and called the storm. He welcomed the raven. It ended there, but I knew if that great storm entered the castle, it would darken the days to come."

"So you came to stop it?"

He shrugs. "Whether a prophecy or a warning, I saw it for a reason. I'm not so lost to the ways of the goddess that I would ignore something like that."

"So, you think she's here?"

"Morgana? No. I would feel her presence. But if what you say about this book is true, it would take a very powerful sorcerer to wield the summoning and bring her back from the clutches of the dark forces that claimed her."

"Any idea who that powerful sorcerer would be?"

"Now that I know more, yes. The only magician in the castle with that kind of fixation on power is Bathalt of Anglia. It's said he had a dalliance with the she-devil herself. Perhaps he thinks himself her chosen one. Those of us who know the witch better might consider him her unwitting fool."

"So, you think he would release her from her prison?"

"Men do a great many stupid things for power and love."

"And does this Bathalt have the goods to deliver? Do you think he could do it?"

"He has the skills as a practitioner. I don't question that. The lusty lure of immortality and the reward of Morgana's favor might blind him to being her pawn. And tomorrow is the equinox. If I wished to attempt something momentous, I would time it to line up with the wheel of the year."

"So, we take the book from him before he has a chance to complete the spell and make sure he doesn't call her back to the living plane."

"We'll need to do more than steal the book. We'll need to resist its charms ourselves."

"What do you mean?"

"I know how Morgana thinks. If you say the book is ensorcelled, it will desire to be used. It will collect power by having its spells cast. Temptation and seduction will be part of her plan, to ensure if one practitioner fails, it will draw another to take up the task."

"So, we steal it, seal it shut, and ensure no one uses it."

By the arch of his brows, he's not convinced.

I look out at the flickering light of the town below and the stars above and wish I could talk to Granda or Da or Sloan. They always know how to tackle an impossible situation. Unfortunately, the past only got me. "Another question. If and when we get it, how do I take it back with me?"

Merlin lifts a shoulder and frowns. "If you truly come from days yet to happen, shouldn't you know?"

CHAPTER FIFTEEN

Fionn and I get to breakfast late because I'm lost in layers of dresses, but that's fine. I'm a toast and coffee girl most mornings, and since neither is offered, I make do with a rock-hard chunk of stale bread from last night and a swig of warm wine. Yum.

Fionn watches me with amusement in his eyes but says nothing. When he's finished eating his fill, the two of us head off to meet with Davant in the apothecary. Although it was only our cover to justify being in the castle during the harvest festival celebration, we follow through.

The devil is in the details, right?

"Davant, I am Fionn mac Cumhaill." He lays the brogue on thicker than usual. "I come bearing herbs, dried plants, and poultice ingredients you might find useful here in the castle."

Davant, a slim, pale man with shoulder-length white hair looks over the wares Fionn has set out and seems unimpressed. "Why would your offerings interest me, Celt?"

Rude much?

Fionn winks at me but doesn't seem put out. "Because ye seem like a wise man and ye know that as the leaves turn and the trees go dormant, yer halls will fill with all manner of aches and ailments. What does that mean, Fiona?"

I blink and say the first thing that pops into my head. "Winter is coming."

I almost can't keep a straight face, but since no one here heard that in the voice of Kit Harington except me, what's the point of giggling?

They do however sense my mirth and look at me funny.

"Excuse the child." Fionn looks somber. "She's a beauty, but she does come off addle-minded at times."

"Hey. Be nice."

The physician looks me over like I've suddenly become his patient. "Have you tried wormwood tea?"

"I shall do that."

I roll my eyes and wander around the room while positioning my phone in front of me so I can take pictures of the apothecary for Sloan and Wallace. I bet they'll get a kick out of seeing a medieval healer's clinic.

Nothing sterile about this place though. There is no stainless steel, and I'm quite sure the stench coming from the closed cabinet at the back of the room is decomp.

I continue out to the hall to let them insult me in private. Even here, in the lower levels of the castle, the excitement of tonight's banquet is building. Little do they know that there's a powerful sorcerer among them who's planning on raising a psycho-powerful dark priestess.

Oh, to live in the unburdened bliss of the ill-informed.

I used to. Hanging out at Shenanigans and drinking with Liam and my brothers, I thought I knew more than most because of what Da and the boys dealt with on the daily.

Ha! I was in "tip of the iceberg" territory.

I wander to the end of the corridor, and my shield tingles against my back. While looking around, I search the smooth, stone corridor for any sign of what might be triggering my survival instincts.

It isn't the burning itch of Moira's illusion and ill intent. There's no gut-twisting nausea like the time I was hexed. And it doesn't feel like a million tiny spider feet racing across my back like when a breeze catches your hair, and you shiver from the tickle.

It's a warning tingle.

Fionn finishes with the court physician and joins me in the hall. "What is it?"

I shake my head and look up and down the long hallway again. "Not sure. My Spidey-senses are tingling."

He doesn't understand, but he gets the gist. "Yer instincts ye mean? Like the fairies ticklin' the little hairs on the back of yer neck?"

I nod. "Yep. Like that. You too?"

Fionn takes a firm hold on my elbow and turns us toward the stone staircase that curves up the tower to the main floor. "Aye, me too. Perhaps a breath of clean air and a bit of time under the rays of the sun will do us both some good."

I feel better as the two of us descend the stone steps of the castle entrance. The stone courtyard is busier today than it was yesterday. The fountain is filled, and all around it are little carts and stalls with merchants selling their wares and making crafts and —"Juggling."

I tug on Fionn's arm and go over to where two men in velvety costumes and striped tights are amusing the crowd. They are very good. "I signed up for juggling in a summer camp elective once. It's not as easy as it looks."

Fionn studies the men who have set aside the balls and fruit and are now juggling daggers. "Those blades must be well-crafted and weighted with precision for them to be able to manipulate them like that."

"I bet they practice for hours every day." A gentle push of the wind hits my face, and I turn to see what it was.

Merlin is across the courtyard and lifts his chin in acknowledgment before turning and heading toward the stables.

"I think we're being called to a meeting."

Fionn glances around, but Merlin is gone. "Lead on."

We find Merlin in a small alleyway behind the stables. He greets Fionn with a nod, then looks at me. "I've done some investigating. Do you see the manservant in the brown tunic there by the blacksmith's door?"

I cast a subtle glance. "Yes. Who is he?"

"He's the manservant to Sir Bathalt of Anglia, the sorcerer I spoke to you about last night. It seems he's asked the stableman to have his master's horses saddled and ready to leave tonight at midnight."

I take another cautious look, but there's no need for my discretion. Everyone has their attention set on the festivities, and we're far enough out of the stream of excitement that we're practically invisible.

Or maybe…

"Did you cast a spell to keep us from notice?"

Merlin smiles. "Would you prefer we announce ourselves to the boy and have him mention it to his master that strangers were staring at him in the courtyard?"

"No. Okay, so why are they leaving at midnight and not staying until morning?"

"Why indeed? I assume the man expects his business here at the castle to be complete. We were right about him using the power of the autumn solstice tonight. He plans to use the turn of the wheel of the year to increase his power."

"All right, what's our play?"

Merlin smiles at me. "The pretty girl goes and makes nice

with the servant boy so he leads us to his master's chamber and the evil grimoire."

Fionn frowns. "Your plan hinges on her charming the boy into betraying his master?"

I prop my hands on my hips. "You could at least try to hide your skepticism. I can be charming. I've got game."

Fionn chuckles. "You have a charm unlike any other I've known. I simply meant the boy might not have the sophistication to appreciate your particular graces."

I snort. "Yeah, yeah. Watch and learn, oul man. I've got this. The best way to find out what I can do is to tell me what I can't do."

"That's obstinance, not skill."

"Some would disagree."

"Aye, and that would be you. Point made."

I roll my eyes and leave him in the background with a flick of my hand. Charming, eh? I can do charming. With my gaze firmly locked on my prey, I assess my surroundings and notice the stablemaster's daughter also has her eye on my manservant.

She has other problems. She needs to worry about the guy trying to love potion her into liking him.

Bathalt's servant finishes speaking with the stablemaster and peels away to head back into the castle.

The daughter gives him a little wave, but by then, I'm drawing his attention away from her.

"Hello there." I match his stride. "I am Fiona. Are you here for the Harvest Festival?"

"In a fashion, although it is Christians that changed the name to call it a Harvest Festival. For all of time before, people have called it Mabon, or my people call it Albon Elfed."

"Och, yer a druid then," I say in a thick Irish accent. No idea why I started channeling my grandparents, but hell, maybe it'll make me seem more Celtic and mysterious. "Grand. I'm a druid as well. It's nice to meet ye."

He looks at me and stops on the stairs leading up to the main entrance. His smirk is far too condescending for his good. "Truly? A druid?"

His dismissal rankles, but the heat of Fionn's gaze has me tamping down my knee-jerk reaction to throat punch him. "Believe me or don't. That's not my concern. I simply thought ye looked like an interestin' fellow. My mistake."

I quicken my stride and leave him at my back.

Within five paces, his fingers close on my elbow, and he tugs me to a stop. "My apologies. You can't blame me for being skeptical. Look at you."

I hold out my arms and glance down. "What about me?"

His cheeks flush. "I've offended you."

Needing a bit of distance, I continue up the stairs. "Ye'd have to matter to offend me. I'm not the delicate flower type that maybe yer used to. No harm done. Go on about yer business, and forget I even said hello."

I continue through the grand entranceway, and he catches my wrist. "Lady Fiona, I apologize. My mind and manners were occupied elsewhere. Let me start again. I am Oswald Avant. I'm pleased to meet you."

I exhale. "Fiona mac Cumhaill."

He looks over his shoulder, and something he sees makes him stiffen. His hand shifts off my wrist and pushes back his sheepskin cloak, and I notice the coin purse hanging from his belt. "I'd like to talk more, but my master is expecting me back with his purse."

I shrug. "I'll walk with ye a bit if ye like. I've nothin' much to do until the celebrations begin."

He nods and gestures across the great hall. "We're in the west wing."

I follow and fall into step.

We walk in silence for a little and only after he casts a glance over his shoulder a few times more does he relax. "So, a female druid. In truth, I have never heard of such a thing."

I chuckle. "Weel, it's not that uncommon. Where I come from, there have been female druids over the centuries."

"Where is that? I've never heard of one."

Huh, maybe I'm dating myself. Oops. "Have ye ever stretched yer legs on the Emerald Isle?"

"No."

"Och, well then, there's yer answer. A pity, really. Ye should travel a bit."

"I'm a manservant. I go where my master goes."

I shrug. "Ye never know. Perhaps he'll visit the Celtic lands one day."

The bustle of people readying for tonight's banquet fills the corridors, and we have to walk single-file in places not to be swallowed by the tide of people.

"Wow, it's gettin' busy."

Oswald glances back at me with a teasing smile. "Have ye never stretched your legs at a castle feast before?"

"No. It's my first."

"Well then, there's your answer. They're all like this."

Touché. I appreciate the mental wordplay and give him a point for turning my comment back on me. We climb the stairs to the fourth floor and head across an open room.

It has bookshelves and seating around the perimeter but in a pinch, could pass as a ballroom. On the far wall, a set of double doors leads out to a balcony very much like the one where I met up with Merlin last night.

"So, will ye be at the banquet then?" I attempt nonchalance. "I overheard yer conversation with the stablemaster. Ye mentioned yer master wants the horses ready after the celebration. Are ye leaving right after the festivities or just going out fer a moonlight ride?"

Oswald turns, and his gaze narrows on me. "Where were you that you heard that?"

"Oh, passing by. Apologies, I don't mean to pry. I wondered is all."

He seems to relax, and we carry on. "Well, I'm not certain to tell you the truth. Sir Bathalt doesn't confide his plans in me. I do as he bids and leave it at that."

I nod. "Well, I hope to see ye later then. How about that?"

His smile is warm, and I feel bad that I'm using him for information. "If I'm able, I shall try to—"

The scuffle of footsteps behind us has us both turning to defend.

"Tough as Bark." My skin transforms from flesh to armor in time to block the strike of a wooden staff. Three brutes are setting in, and the beauty of being the female in the fight is that they've already discounted me as a threat.

"Gust of Wind." I sweep my arm through the air and knock the third man in on his back. After ripping the staff from his hand, I spin it and thrust a sharp jab into the belly of the man I'm facing off with.

"Bestial Strength." As my muscles sing with power, I spin and clock my attacker in the side of the head. He falls over his buddy, and they tangle in a heap.

I turn to help Oswald, but he's finished his guy off. He looks at me, and his eyes flare wide.

I release my natural armor, and the tattoo of branches and roots that cover my skin recedes to leave me pale and soft.

"You truly are a druid."

I chuckle. "I said I was. Why would I lie?"

He shrugs. "Again, I apologize."

One of my guys groans and struggles to sit up. I use the staff to sweep his arm out from underneath him, and he faceplants on the stone.

"Maybe we should talk about this somewhere else. May I escort ye back to yer chambers?"

He laughs and tilts his head. "This way."

I only get moderately lost making my way back to my chamber to meet Fionn. The important part is that I made notes on my phone so I can find my way back to Sir Bathalt's room should I need to. Which, I'm sure I will.

We dress and get to the dining hall early so we get a good seat. Tonight, everyone eats in the Grand Hall, so when Bathalt arrives, we want a seat near the door to slip out unnoticed so we can search his room.

We arrive at the Grand Hall along with the first fifty guests, and I scan the crowd. Merlin is at the front. He wears a long, fur-trimmed cloak and looks every bit as wealthy and sophisticated as the royals who surround him.

I meet his eyes from across the room, and he glances casually at a man with long, raven-black hair speaking to Oswald on the far side of the room. After pointing at a place on the table quite close to the royals, he slides his cloak off his shoulders and hands it to his manservant.

"He looks like Professor Snape," I comment to Fionn, which, of course, he ignores. "The good news is, as long as we can see them, we know they aren't performing any clandestine rituals. Should we go up and search his room?"

"Aye, we should."

"Fiona!" someone calls from over my shoulder. It's the flute flirter from last night. "You're here. Have you come to watch me perform?"

Awesomesauce. "I did, but unfortunately, my uncle feels unwell. I'm going to take him back to our room. Once I get him settled, if there's time, I'll try to get back."

He nods. "I wish you good health, sir."

Fionn nods. "That's kind of ye, lad. I'm sure ye'll captivate the crowd."

With our excuses made, the two of us head off to fight the traffic flow as everyone heads into the banquet hall.

"How much time do we have?"

I pull my phone out of my silky cloth bag and check the timer. "An hour and forty-two minutes. Give or take."

"If luck be in our favor."

I frown. "Yeah, luck has been a fickle friend with me these days. I'll adjust the timer for one hour. It would suck large to get this close, then return to my timeline empty-handed."

Fionn nods. "Agreed."

I slow to walk behind him for two reasons. First, he's a brawny warrior, and people get out of his way faster than they get out of mine. Second, we cut through the crowd quicker with me following him than when we walk two abreast.

Once we're free of the press of bodies pushing into the Grand Hall, we make our way to the front entrance, and I take the lead. "We came this way and up this corridor into the west wing." It's only been a few hours, so there's no reason any of it should be foggy, but foggy it is.

When we were kids, Aiden said I could get lost in a cereal box. Sadly, he wasn't wrong.

"One moment." I press my hand to my chest and step close to the stone wall. "Allow a lady a moment to catch her breath." I smile at the group of courtiers passing, and when the coast is clear, I take up my phone and tap on my notes. Once I've oriented myself, I slide my phone under my wonky, one-armed poncho and off we go.

"Yep. We're good. These steps. Fourth floor."

We climb the stairs together, and I fight the urge to fist pump the air. "This is the ballroom space where we got jumped. We're doing well."

I point at the corridor ahead, and we march on. "End of the corridor turn right. Third door on the left. Bathalt's emblem is an antlered stag beside the door."

Fionn's in the lead, and when he stops at the door, he taps a finger on the signage. "Here it is. I've never been happier to see such a full rack."

I blink up at him, and I'm not sure if he meant that as a joke. "So-many-comments. Brain. Hurts."

He frowns at me, but before I start cracking wise someone's coming down the hall.

"You there. You're not from this floor. What business have you here?"

"Oh, crap."

CHAPTER SIXTEEN

At the sound of the guard's voice, Fionn straightens, eases me tight into the doorway, and turns. He leans against the wall to block the entrance with his broad shoulders, and I do my best to shrink back into the inset of what can't be more than ten inches from the hall.

Fionn taps his finger on the stag plaque.

"This isn't a griffon…it's a deer," He slurs his words. "I'm lookin' fer the griffon plaque. Have ye seen a griffon? Do you know where my chambers are?"

My gallant escort raises his arms, and I watch his shadow gesture willy-nilly as he staggers up to the guard playing hall monitor and blocking any line of sight to expose my hiding place. "Och, I need to take a piss."

"Not here, you don't."

"Aye, I do. And it needs to be now."

The guard curses and the quick shuffle of footsteps leave me alone in the corridor.

"*Open Sesame.*" I pass my hand over the latch plate of Bathalt's chambers. The real spell is *Access Granted,* but mine is more fun.

A slide of the latch grants me entrance. The moment I step over the threshold, my shield tingles.

"Cat crap on a cracker."

I wait to see if it was a ward of protection I tripped, but when nothing comes at me to fry my ass, I wonder if maybe the book's magic set off my warning bells.

"Tough as Bark."

What can I say? I'm a safety girl. If fireballs are about to strike me down, I want some protection. Then again, if Bathalt has half a brain, he probably wouldn't ward a magical book with fire. That could end badly for him.

Nothing overtly threatening comes at me, so I take another step and close the door.

"Fiona?"

Crap. I close my eyes and wish with all my might that when I turn around, I'm not staring into the eyes of... "Oswald, you're here. Perfect."

He steps out from behind the heavy door of the armoire and frowns. "I am. Why are you here?"

"I... was looking for you, silly." I go with that and rush closer. "I honestly had such a nice time this afternoon. I thought we connected. When you left the banquet to,"—I spot the black cloak hanging in the armoire—"bring your master's cloak back upstairs, I thought I'd take advantage of the opportunity to get you alone and surprise you. Surprise!"

He frowns and looks at the door. "You're not allowed—Wait. How did you get in here?"

"The door was open."

"No. Sir Bathalt spelled the door to close, lock, and set a Ward of Warning on the chamber entrance. He'll know someone other than me came through that door. He'll be coming."

Shit. "We'll explain it to him. I'm sure it'll be fine."

"And you've lost your accent.

Double shit. I roll my eyes and hold up my palms.

"Exhaustive Slumber." As Oswald collapses and crumples toward the stone floor, I grab hold of his shoulders and push him back into the armoire's depths. "I'm so sorry, Oswald. You're a good guy. I totes suck."

I lift his feet, bend his knees, and pretzel him into the tall, wooden wardrobe. When I close the doors, I make sure nothing catches in them, and no one will find him before I want them to.

If I tripped a warning to Sir Bathalt, time is ticking faster than ever. When I reach out with my senses, my shield fires to life, and there's no doubt in my mind the book is behind the door to my right.

I hurry over, press a palm to the door, and feel for any other spells of protection. Nothing obvious comes back to me, so I raise the latch and swing it open a crack.

"Detect Magic." I ease the door open more, searching for any arcane designs in the air.

Everything looks good.

I open the door, shuffle inside, and am drawn immediately to the wooden chest behind the door. Merlin is right. I feel the lure. The book is there, and it wants to be used...and I need to get to it.

The chest is a heavy, oak monstrosity with black, iron hinges and locks. My shield fires to life and burns hot against my back. I feel the thrall of the *Eochair Prana* drawing me into its confidence.

It has so much it wants to show me.

I'm practically a blank slate next to the knowledge this book holds. It's an honor simply to be nominated.

"Open Sesame." The trunk latch succumbs to my need for access, and I fling the top up and back.

A bolt of power explodes from the chest and hits me with a force that throws me back on the floor. I blink and fight to scramble to my feet.

I don't move. I'm locked in my body, and my muscles don't respond. *Shitshitshit.*

The Ward of Paralyzation has me in its grip.

In the long moments that follow, I struggle to breathe. My chest won't inflate, so I can only draw minute amounts of air into my lungs. My panic shifts from not getting the book in time, to not getting caught, to not suffocating while I wait for a powerful sorcerer to come find me robbing him of his "Precious."

"What's this?" a smug male voice mutters above me.

My eyes are locked straight ahead when my waiting ends. I see nothing but fabric boots and a cast shadow darkening the space between me and the chest.

"A woman thief? A seductress come to take what is mine?" The shadow shifts and the *snick* of steel pulling free from a sheath cuts the air.

I'm rolled onto my back, and Sir Bathalt looms over me. He holds a dagger above my chest and smiles. "It's too bad I'm in a hurry. There are other ways I would rather teach you the penalty of crossing me."

My heart races, and as hard as I pull at the base of my throat for breath, oxygen refuses to fill my lungs. I'm starved for air. My vision swims as blackness closes in.

Hot tears singe my temples, but I'm helpless to defend, to retreat, or even to close my eyes.

Steel glints in the torchlight and the dagger plunges hard and fast. The blade pierces my dress...

It takes a moment for reality to set in. I'm not impaled.

My mind flickers. Right.

Tough as Bark for the win.

Bathalt pulls back his dagger and frowns at the bent tip. "You are a mysterious one." He draws the blade from the soft hollow of my throat down to my navel and splits the layers of my dress. "What magic is it that makes your flesh impenetrable to my blade?"

His dark brows pinch tight as he flips the fabric back and sees the inked bark of the armor across my chest and torso. He rises with his gaze fixed on me. "That's a mystery for later. More pressing matters await at the moment, I'm afraid. You wait here, and I'll get back to you as soon as I can."

He shifts to the storage trunk, grabs the book from its belly, and cradles it in his arms like a beloved child. "Think of me while I'm gone, lady thief. I look forward to unraveling your many mysteries."

I track the shuffle of footsteps as he leaves, and I'm both relieved and anguished. I'm thankful for the distance between us, but he has the book. My book.

Left to myself, I focus on breaking the spell's hold. It's not that different from when Sloan paralyzed me in Ireland and made me feel like a fool.

"Focus, Fi. Control yer temper and come at me with a clear plan." I slow my panic and focus on my breathing. Passing out isn't an option. To break free and go after the book, I need to be conscious. *"If yer not in control of yer offense, yer out of control and no good to yerself or the others."*

I hear Sloan's words so clearly now. At the time, I was hurt and angry about being made to look like a fool in front of my family, so I missed the whole point.

I have to be ready for anything at all times and know how to handle adversity when it hits.

"Better she learns the lesson here than at the hands of the enemy," Da had said.

And here I am.

"Fiona, *a leanbh.*" Fionn kneels over me and places his rough palm heavy on my chest. The rush of power is immediate, and I'm free from the hold of paralysis.

Rolling to the side, I grip his hand and swallow air in huge gulps. He squeezes my grip and anchors me. I feel his strength and power and absorb a little of it until my panic subsides enough that I can breathe.

"Bathalt has the book. We have to go."

Fionn looks at me and frowns. He grabs a plain muslin tunic and tosses it to me. I shrug out of the tatters of my dresses and pull it on.

"Damn, I miss pockets." I shove my phone against my belly in my underwear and flatten my tunic. The poncho survived unscathed, so I pull that on over the top. "And today's guest on TLC's *What Not To Wear*, Fiona Cumhaill."

"Where's the manservant lad?"

"In the armoire."

"Why is he in the armoire?"

"It was a moment of crisis. That's where he ended up."

"Did ye kill him?"

"What kind of girl do you think I am? He's sleeping."

We're about to run out the door when I spot a parchment and quill set out on a little desk.

A convo with Garnet smacks me in the face. *"It's said the original book circulated for a very short time before it disappeared and was copied by the manservant of the sorcerer who had it last."*

"Oswald is the one who makes the copies." I scan the pages and frown. "Will it screw up the timeline if I destroy these?"

"It'll change it. I can't say whether that's good or bad."

I think about it for a minute and gather the pages. Destroying dark magic spells and demented ramblings of evil can't be a bad thing.

I run them over to the fireplace and drop them inside.

Bonfire.

As the parchment goes up in flames, Fionn arches a brow. I wave away his concern. "It'll be fine. Trust me."

The two of us rush out of Bathalt's chambers and up the hall. When we round the corner, we practically crash bodily into Merlin as he strides toward us. "Have you got the book?"

I shake my head. "No, Bathalt took it and bolted."

"Where'd he go?"

"I have no idea—" The *crack* of a lightning strike makes the three of us wince and duck. "The sudden, freak lightning storm could be a hint."

Fionn nods, and we race off. We weave through the corridors of castle chambers until we come to the open ballroom space where Oswald and I were attacked this afternoon.

The charge of energy in the air makes the hair on my arms stand on end, and I look out onto the balcony. "There!"

I point and launch into a run.

Bathalt stands at the end of the balcony, arms raised, the amulet in his right hand glowing against the night sky. The book sits on a stone podium before him and pulses with golden light.

I point at the scene ahead of us. "There's your dream of the raven in the storm."

It's exactly as Merlin described it to me last night. Bathalt reaching up to the dark storm, the malevolence in the air churning with ill intent.

"I'll handle the sorcerer," Fionn says. "You two get the book and get clear of here."

"What? Why?" My heart races. "We should all get the sorcerer."

Fionn shakes that off. "Which one of the three of us is already dead?"

I meet Merlin's confusion and shrug. "Long story. But no, I need you to get back. You're my Tardis."

Merlin steps forward. "Yer uncle and I will take on Bathalt. You get the book."

I sigh. "Okay, I'm on book retrieval...but if the sorcerer proves too much, it's Musketeer time."

Both of them look at me blank-faced.

I roll my eyes. "All for one and one for all."

Without waiting for the looks of billowing fog to clear, I call

Birga and stride into the mix. Merlin and Fionn each have much longer legs so although I'm the first to start, they pass me a split-second later.

Fionn raises his hands at the same time Merlin does, and the fight is on. The moment the first spell hits the protective bubble, Bathalt turns, and we're busted.

He laughs, and the dome strikes back, countering their hit.

The two of them are suddenly defending, and I wait for the incoming hit on me. It doesn't come.

The storm intensifies, and whatever he's muttering in tongues makes my skin itch. And that stink. Ugh...it's like maggoty trash that's been sitting in the July sun.

Dark magic is so nasty.

Merlin and Fionn attack the protective field surrounding Bathalt, and with each hit, the dome lights up against the darkness of his workings and retaliates.

That's it. The dome *is* retaliating. If I throw in with them, we'll all be defending instead of moving in for the attack.

The howling *cuckaaaws* of a demented raven rend the air.

The bird wasn't a placeholder of symbolism in Merlin's prophetic dream. It's here, and even a noob like me can guess that's Morgana or the essence of her somehow.

Another couple of massive hits from Fionn and Merlin and the dome looks as solid and as pissed off as ever.

"It's not working," I say.

Merlin casts me what might be the all-time first "Well duh" look in history.

The baleful screams of wind seem to mock my distress. I corral my hair and flip it out of my face.

Lighting strikes again.

It cuts a jagged line through the void of violence and hits the book. Fae magic sings in my blood as the book swells and glows gold with power.

Bathalt shouts his spell, reading the words as our last chance to stop him quickly circles the drain.

Merlin and Fionn bombard the ward, but it's no use. Every strike comes back at them three-fold. Except...

When the shield lights up this time, I notice it's not actually a dome. It's more like a clamshell protecting him from the sides and behind. The beast's belly is exposed so he can work his magic and cast out to the sky.

"We need to attack him from the front," I shout.

Merlin looks at me, and I cup my hand and gesture with the tip of Birga's spear that we need to attack the open side.

Damn, I wish Sloan was here.

Any chance Merlin's a wayfarer?

When he doesn't immediately *poof* to the balcony's open side and attack head-on, I assume not.

From the front...from the front...

Oh, shit.

The book swells, and its glow magnifies. It levitates off the podium, and the raven spreads her wings, embracing the chaos of the storm that holds her suspended in the air.

The hair on my arms prickles again and I feel the lightning build. This strike will seal the deal. I don't know how I know that for sure, but I do.

I can't let that happen, but how do I...

When the sky explodes, I flash Birga away and raise my hands. After gripping onto the lightning's energy, I call the power of the bolt with everything I have.

"*Command Lighting.*" I pull against the instinct of the strike. The sorcerer may have conjured it, but a druid has dominion over nature. I scream as the power vibrates in my cells and rattles in my bones.

Instead of striking the book, I retarget the lightning and —"Bam! Nothing but smoking boots."

Bathalt goes up in a fiery explosion of magic, and the raven shrieks a shrill promise of vengeance.

"Booyah! Drop the mic. Good guys get the book."

Without the sorcerer fueling the storm, the raven shrieks and is pulled back into the darkness. The skies clear and the stars in the night sky shine through. I wait until the book stops glowing, then approach the makeshift altar Balthar used with extreme caution.

Fionn scowls. "Be of care, lass."

No kidding.

Deciding to give the book a timeout and let it cool down, I retrieve the broach from the ground. "I think you're supposed to take care of this, my friend. You still have it in our time. Although, when you need a good hiding spot in 1817, the grave of John Ridout will do you well."

Merlin pockets the broach and nods. "I won't forget."

"Now for the book." I inch closer, my hand extended, my attention focused on the shield on my back. When nothing comes back at me besides a general tingle of warning, I figure the worst is over.

I'm about to touch it when—"Ah! Holy-crapamoly!"

I jump up and down and smack my chest as my heart punches at the base of my throat.

"What is it?" Fionn's gaze skitters in every direction.

Merlin is tense and searching for danger.

The vibrate phone alarm went off in my underwear. TMI. Wicked TMI.

"Never mind. S'all good. I...uh, had a moment. Fionn, our time is up. It's time to get this evil baby home. Have you figured out how we're doing that yet?"

He shakes his head. "The trouble is, ye'll reappear there back in yer body. Yer physical form never left the bookshop. Yer still there."

"Right, but there has to be a way. Otherwise, why are we here and what have we been doing?"

"Aye, there's a way. I simply don't like it."

"Lay it on me, dude, 'cause it's now or never."

"You need her to take it into her body." Merlin frowns. He points at Birga lying in wait in the tattoo on my arm. "It's the same principle as this."

I draw a deep breath and nod. "Okay, then do it. I'll accept it. Then, when we get home, I'll cast it out, and we'll figure out what to do with it there."

"What if the tie remains, *a leanbh?* Accepting an enchanted object into your body creates a bond. You can't take magical ties that bind lightly."

"I'm not taking it lightly. If there were another way, I'd be all ears for hearing it, but you've thought about this for days, maybe longer. We're not going to come up with a better idea in the next ten minutes. So, we go with what we've got."

"Fi, I admire yer commitment, but ye have to understand that tempering power as dark and seductive as this will be a great burden. What if ye succumb to the allure? What if ye become the next dark druid of Toronto people need to stop?"

I shake that off. "Won't happen. I can do this."

Merlin frowns. "I swear to you, Fiona. I will dedicate the next fifteen hundred years to figuring out how to remove it, but understand there may not be a way."

"Okay, let's say I'm stuck with it? Give me a best to worst-case scenario here."

Merlin pegs me with a serious gaze. "If we can't free you of the burden, the best case is that you'll fight the pull of dark power the rest of your life and you go mad for not succumbing to Morgana's call. The worst is that you access the book, turn to the seduction of evil, and release the dark witch from her prison to destroy the world as you know it."

Allll righty then. "An A-plus to you for capturing the drama of the stakes." I think about it, and my mind spins. As sucky as it sounds, I don't see another answer. "Okay, do it. We'll handle that disaster when it blows up in my face on the other end of the line."

Merlin shakes his head. "There's a saying that on the field of combat is when you truly learn a knight's true nature. It's in the face of destruction the world sees if he is a warrior or a coward. You, Fiona mac Cumhaill, are a warrior."

I smile. "You say the nicest things, my friend. Now, curse me with the evil book and send me back through time."

He chuckles. "Release your natural armor and sit. You won't want to be standing when I do this."

I release Tough as Bark and sit on the stone balcony, my back against the wall.

Merlin places one hand on the ensorcelled book and the other on my bare thigh. The darkness of the power taints the air. He tenses and winces under the strain. With his eyes closed, he speaks in tongues, his lips moving too fast and his voice too low for me to follow his enchantment.

I close my eyes as nausea builds in the pit of my belly, and I'm pretty sure I'm going to puke on my friends. I press my fingers over my mouth and try to ignore the burn of indigestion aching at the bottom of my throat.

I swallow to push down the fire, but it's like I've eaten an entire bag of spicy jalapeno bombers from Church's Chicken, and I didn't tamp down the fire with three of those delicious honey biscuits.

"How do you fare?" Merlin asks.

"Two thumbs up. I'm not possessed by evil, and I am very glad we skipped dinner tonight. I'll see you at Myra's Mystical Emporium in a minute."

"I'll be there with you, Fiona. I won't let her take you."

I nod, more worried about the darkness taking him in the meantime. "Keep your chin up. The time for Pan Dora to shine is coming. Life is good in the twenty-first century, my friend. Queens on Queen, remember that."

Merlin finishes, and I look down. The skin of my leg consumed the book.

Awesome. Yet another tattoo I never wanted.

"Thank you."

He rises and helps me to my feet. "Go now. I'm waiting for you on the other side."

I smile at the face of my friend, and whether it's a man with stubble and long brown hair or powdered and wearing a fabulous navy blue wig and leopard sheath dress, a true friend is all I see. "See you soon. Yeah, I hope you've figured out how to exorcise me."

I nod at Fionn and feel the building energy as he accesses whatever tricks he has in his Nether bag to take me home. My head spins, and Fionn's power builds inside me.

I gasp and throw my hands out as the world rights itself.

I stare up into Sloan's mint-green eyes, and I know I'm home. "Hey, Mackenzie."

"Thank the powers. Yer back. What the hell happened?"

Before I can answer, Dora pushes Sloan out of the way. "Welcome back, cookie. I hope this works." Dora hands me a glass vial with a brilliant red liquid inside. "Every drop. Down it goes."

I do what I'm told without question and feel the book wriggling inside me. It burns, and the heartburn of earlier doesn't begin to cover the fire of the magma burning inside me.

I pop the button of my pants and wriggle them off my hips. "Get it out of me, Dora. I won't be able to hold it for long."

CHAPTER SEVENTEEN

The liquid Dora gives me burns down my esophagus and tastes like gloopy, black licorice. I gag on the aftertaste, but amazingly, I swallow and keep it down.

"Lift your hips, Fi." I arch my back and groan at the onslaught of clawing darkness spreading through me. "Emmet and Sloan, help her with her pants. I need access to the tattoo on her thigh."

I cry out as they jostle me but try to hold still as my pants get tugged down my thighs. Cold air hits my heated flesh, and I shiver.

"What the fuck?" Emmet says. "What's happening to her, and where'd that come from?"

Sloan clasps my hand and leans in. "What can I do?"

I can't speak. If I open my mouth, I'll either puke Dora's remedy or scream like a mindless banshee. I refuse to do either. Instead, I dive into those mint-green eyes.

Sloan seems to understand and locks down. "I've got ye. Whatever this is, I'll not leave ye." A rush of healing energy tingles from our joined hands, and the pain ebbs into the background. It's not gone so much as held at bay. "Focus on me, and it'll be over soon."

"Fi, I'm ready. Release the book," Dora instructs.

I do as she says, but the darkness doesn't relent. My leg is on fire, and the moment the book is gone, the agony of withdrawal replaces the pain of the bond.

It's excruciating. I want it back.

I bite my bottom lip to keep from losing my mind and begging for it back. Another wave of shivers racks me.

The trembling isn't from the cold air this time. My entire body vibrates with a mean dose of the quakes. I want to see what's happening, but I'll lose my grip if I look away from Sloan.

"Emmet. I'll take that buffer now." Dora's voice sounds strained. "I have to sever the enchantment's bond."

My brother lets go of my other hand, and Sloan collects it and brings it to his lips. "I take it ye had another one of yer astral time jumps with Fionn?"

Such a smart guy.

He gathers both of my hands in one of his and brushes away the tears streaming down my cheeks. "The brave and beautiful Fiona Cumhaill. Life's set ye on a tough path, hasn't it?"

I don't feel brave or beautiful at the moment.

"That should help," Dora says. "Any better?"

I gasp and suck in a breath. My murderous desire to level everyone in the room and reclaim the book has subsided.

I still feel out of control, though.

"A little."

"Give it a moment."

Sloan smiles, the worry in his eyes held at bay. I focus on loosening my grip on his hand, but he doesn't let go completely. "Take another minute. Catch yer breath. The world can wait until you're ready."

Another pulse of his healing energy seeps up my arms and into the core of my chest. It chases away the fire in my veins, and I feel more myself. When the shakes downgrade from convulsions to an occasional tremble, I unclench my jaw. "Help me up?"

Upright, I steady my footing and catch my breath. Before I pull up my pants, I bend to look—

"No, Fi." Sloan lifts my chin with a gentle finger. "Look at that later. It's raw and reeling from the book at the moment. Give my healing some time to work its magic."

I see the worry in his eyes. "It must be awful if you don't want me to see it."

"Yer as beautiful inside and out as ye've always been. Isn't she, Emmet?"

I ease back and tug up my pants.

"Always." Emmet looks wrecked. "Are you okay? What the hell happened?"

I hug my brother and hang on while I force a factory reset. "I'll be fine. Where's the book?"

"I put it in here." Dora points at what looks like a metal book bag. It's a sealed lead box with a leather strap. "I've worked on perfecting this as a containment vessel since the day you left me at Carlisle Castle."

I leave Emmet's hold to hug Dora. "We meet again, my friend. Thanks for being you and also for being ready."

"I am me because of you. If you hadn't given me a glimpse of who I was to become, things would've ended very differently for me. I was not on a good path back then."

I nod at Zxata. Myra's brother runs a hand over his face and looks shakier than me. I feel bad for the guy. He seems wholly unsettled by all of this.

I step back from Dora and offer him a sympathetic smile. "Sorry. You don't know me well yet, but this is kinda what happens around me. I'd rather it not, but...yeah, it does."

"Myra said you are a wonder. Can I get you anything?"

I swallow, and all I taste is Dora's remedy coating my tongue. "Could I bother you for a glass of water?"

"No bother." He flips into gear. "I'm relieved to have something to do finally."

Sloan scoops a hand around my hip and turns me toward the sofas. "Take a seat and tell us what happened."

I accept the glass of water from Zxata when he returns, then Dora and I recount the tale of our first encounter.

"Unbelievable." Sloan rakes his fingers through his dark hair. "Ye never cease to amaze me, Cumhaill."

"Oh, speaking of unbelievable, I took pictures for you. I thought you'd enjoy seeing my adventure this time." I pull out my phone and open things up to the gallery. "Yeah, start there and swipe through. Wait, where are they?"

Sloan takes possession of the phone and flips through a couple of pictures forward and back. "There's nothin' here."

"Well, I see that, but I took them. I wanted to show you the castle, the village, the architecture, the healer's clinic… Where are they?"

Sloan closes the gallery and sets the phone back in my lap. "I think I see what happened. How much do ye know about astral projection?"

"It's a strength in your Spiritual discipline."

He blinks at me. "That's it?"

"How much do you know about priming a beer line during a Saturday night rush? We all have our skills, Mackenzie."

He chuckles. "Totally not the same thing. I ask because when yer whisked away in time and space, yer physical body stays put. Yer consciousness may have done things elsewhere, but yer body and yer phone were still here in the bookstore. Back then, yer phone and yer normal clothes were the manifestation of yerself and what ye know, but in reality, they weren't there and ye didn't take pictures. Do ye understand?"

"You hurt my brain sometimes. You know that?"

Sloan chuckles again. "Then I suppose we're even. How about I take you and Emmet home?"

I look at the box and shake that off. "No. I have to figure out what to do with the book, and I'm supposed to check on Myra, and we still have to figure out who did this to her."

"That can wait until tomorrow."

"No. I'm fine." I hand Emmet my glass, and he shuffles off to put it in the kitchen. "It always looks scarier to the people watching one of these crazy Fiona-freak-fest events than it is. I do best if I keep moving."

Sloan's lips narrow into a tight line. "Yer not fine, and no one here will judge ye for it if ye need a feckin' moment."

It dawns on me then. It's him that needs a moment.

I squeeze his hand. "Okay, surly. You win. We'll take five and regroup. Dora? Are you good if I take control of the book and stash it somewhere?"

"It's your destiny, girlfriend." Dora gestures at the lead box. "Do with it as you will. I want you to come to see me every couple of days though. I'll need to cleanse any of the book's lingering aftereffects from your system."

"For how long?" I ask.

"As long as it takes until we know you're healed," Sloan snaps. He holds his hand out and squeezes Dora's fingers. "I thank the goddess fer yer help tonight, and the millennia and a half ye took to get ready to be here. Yer an absolute blessing."

Dora flutters her long lashes and winks. "Careful, Abercrombie. Talk like that will get us both into trouble."

I chuckle and pick up the box. "I don't want to drive around town with this all night. Zxata, can you email me Garnet's address and we'll meet you there in a while?"

"Of course," he agrees. "Your man's not wrong. If you need to take tonight for yourself, you've earned it. No one would think less of you for taking a moment to recover."

I wave that off. "No. I'm sure. Once I get this put somewhere safe for the short-term, we'll join you. I may be out of my hell, but Myra's not."

Sloan *poofs* me and Emmet home, and I've barely taken a step in the front hall when the boys get knocked flying, and my bear rears up on his hind legs. He pulls me in with his mighty paws and squeezes my breath out of my lungs. "Are ye all right, Red? I wanted to go with ye, believe me, but Fionn said I might alter yer path if I interfered in yer quest."

"What?" Sloan snaps. "Ye knew Fionn was takin' her back to get the book and ye didn't warn her or us or anyone?"

Bruin growls and lifts his lips to show his canines. "I couldn't. Timelines are tricky beasts. Ye don't fuck with them. I was living my life with the players in that part of history. Fionn said if I interfered, I could not only change her path; I could change mine. It was after she left with the book that I found out we would bond and when I needed to expect ye at the Cumhaill estate."

Oh, that hurts my head. "That's why you picked me—because I told Dora back then that we'd bonded, so you sought me out in Ireland this summer?"

"It was our destiny. Like I said. Timelines are tricky."

Sloan doesn't look appeased, but it doesn't bother me. Tough situations force tough decisions. I won't judge him for it. "You did what you thought was best for us to end up together. I get it. All's well that ends well."

Sloan hits me with a glare. "It didn't end well. Yer suffering from a toxic book being thrust into yer system and yer not clear of it yet. We have no idea what the aftereffects will be. Ye can't just dismiss it. Not everythin' in life is over with a shrug and a laugh."

I hear the worry lacing his tone, and I know this is more about him being afraid for me than anything else. I rub my face into the long, soft fur of my bear and hug him again. "We're one hundy percent good. I wouldn't risk what we have for anything. I love you, big guy."

"I love you too, Red."

I kiss his boxy cheek and scrub his fur. "Slurp up a roasting pan full of beer while I talk to Tall, Dark, and Surly. Then we'll head out. We have a night ahead of us, and it's about time you take your place. I miss you."

"I miss you too." Bruin dips his chin. "I'll be in the basement when yer ready to roll. Calum, can ye play the part of my bartender? Emmet, maybe ye can join us and fill us in on what happened?"

"Yep. I could use a drink myself."

I nod and take Sloan's hand. "Come upstairs with me for a minute, will you?"

"Noice!" Emmet waggles his brows. "Have fun, kids. Don't do anything I wouldn't do."

I laugh. "There's nothing you wouldn't do."

"Fair point. So, I guess that means have fun."

I roll my eyes and pull Sloan along. When we get into my room, I shut the door and set the lead box on my desk. He moves to my window, the tension in his shoulders making him look impossibly tall and rigid. He looks at the grove in the back yard as his fingers grip the window frame.

I hate to see him so twisted up. It's dissolving my resolve to stand firmly independent. Stepping in behind him, I touch his shoulder and turn him to face me. "I'm all right. I need you to look at me and believe that. I'm all right."

"No. Yer not. Ye can put on the 'Fi is invincible' show fer the others if ye think ye must, but I see more."

"It's not a show. Yeah, it sucked. I'm not one hundy percent, and I won't lie and say I am, but tying yourself in knots over what happened and who could've done what differently doesn't make anything better. Don't be mad at Bruin."

The muscle in the side of his jaw clenches. "I'm sorry."

I soften my approach and press my hand flat against his chest. "This isn't me giving you shit. This is me saying I understand you're scared, and you hurt because I'm hurt, and I appreciate it. I appreciate *you*."

He draws a deep breath. "I hate that there are times I'm left behind and can't help ye. It guts me when ye suffer and yer forced to face things on yer own."

"I get that, but I'm never truly alone. I had Birga and Fionn, and Dora was there. Even if I didn't, I'm Fiona-freakin'-Cumhaill, remember? You can knock me down, but you can't keep me down. I'll get a grip on this. Give me a chance to show you."

He groans and stares up at the ceiling, then sighs. "Yer so cock-sure. I think that scares me more."

"Nah, don't believe the hype. I lose my shit all the time. I just do it privately. My poor pillow has absorbed more than its share of screams and tears. The point is, we can't both be shaky at the same time. I need you to fake it and pretend we have things under control until we make that our reality."

He hooks his thumbs in the belt loops of his designer jeans and drops his chin. After a few deep breaths, he raises his gaze and nods. "Fine. Whatever ye need. I'll fake it until we make it if that's what ye want."

"When we're out in the world it's what I *need*, but the reason I brought you up here is that when we're alone together, we get to be real. You can be scared and angry, and I get to fall apart if I need to, and that's okay."

He looks at me, and I'm pretty sure he wants to be the one to fall apart.

"I learned something about myself during my time at Carlisle Castle."

"Yeah? What was that?"

I offer him an unguarded smile. "I wished you were there with me. I wanted to show you the things I thought were cool. I looked at the architecture and the clinic and the villagers in the courtyard and wished you were there to share it with me."

"We make a good team."

"We do, but that wasn't it."

"No? Then what?"

I close the inches between us and look up into those eyes. He's much taller than I am, so I palm his cheeks and pull his mouth down as I rise on my tiptoes. His lips are stiff and hesitant at first, but it doesn't take long before he gives in and kisses me like I know he's wanted to.

He's got skills. My shield tingles warm, and I'm not sure if it's a warning that I should take things slow and guard my heart or if my cells are simply bursting to life.

I go with door number two.

I'm breathless as I end the kiss. "That was perfect."

He gives me a cocky smile. "It was rather memorable."

I press my forehead against his chest and settle my racing pulse. When I look up at him again, his gaze is nothing but smug satisfaction. He's got me, and he knows it.

"No need to gloat. I still need to be me and figure out who I am in the druid world, but you're right—there's something here. No rush. No expectations. That's what you said."

He dips his chin. "That's what I said."

"Then, good. This was a nice way to reset our balance."

"Agreed. Ye wouldn't happen to need more of the same, would ye? I could stand you using me for a little more resetting."

I giggle and step back. "Not right now. Places to go. People to save. You know how it is."

"Where do we go from here?"

I point at the lead box. "We gotta stash that."

It's not ideal, but for the short term, I have Sloan *poof* us to the back of the St. James Cemetery. It lies within spitting distance from my house, and we've been there, so he can portal us quickly and without being followed. Assuming someone might follow us, which sounds paranoid but given my history, is a possibility. I figure this was a good enough hiding spot for Morgana's brooch to stay hidden for a century, so it'll work for the book until we have a better idea.

We sneak around in the dark and pick an old and well-used area where the groundskeepers won't dig any new graves. I explore some of the ancient mausoleums and family lots and choose one that looks full and forgotten.

I kneel on the dried grass, place my hands flat, and call my connection to *Move Earth*. I've been working on not needing to cast my spells verbally, and it's getting easier.

I send my call deep. The soil responds and creates a focused sinkhole. After doing something similar a couple of weeks ago while drilling through stone to release the ley lines' power, I assess the funnel and figure it goes down into the earth about five hundred feet.

"That should be deep enough."

Sloan closes his eyes, and the hole widens.

"What are you doing?"

"I'd rather not drop the possessed book of all evil into the big hole to knock and bounce around on its way down. While that might be a great plot twist in a cartoon, I'd rather play it smart. I'm sure Dora's lead tomb is strong, but I'd rather set it in its resting place."

Yeah, I can visualize that. As the hero and heroine walk away, a green, evil mist seeps through a crack in the casing deep beneath the ground.

"Good call. Point for you, Mackenzie."

He winks and steps to the edge of the hole. "Don't get any ideas about burying me alive."

"And give up access to those lips? Never. Be careful."

He nods, grips the box, and *poofs* off. A couple of seconds later, he's back and brushing dirt off his pants. "The book is safely squared away at the bottom. Let's hope Dora's box holds its seal and stays hidden."

"Let's hope." The two of us fill in the hole, and I repair the grass. "I want to do what Sir Bathalt did and put a ward on this site to notify us if anyone tampers with the soil. Do you know how to do that?"

He arches a dark brow. "Are ye serious? Yer Granda is a Master Shrine Keeper of the Ancient Order of Druids. Ward protection spells were something he taught me while I was still cuttin' teeth."

I laugh. "You met him when you were five."

"Semantics. Ye get my point. I'll cast it and tether it to both of us, to be safe."

"Perfect. Do your thing, oh Jedi Master."

Sloan walks over the area first north to south, then east to west as his lips move, his voice low. It only takes a few minutes. Then he gives me a cocky grin. "All set."

"Awesomesauce. Let's not forget where we put it, 'kay?"

Sloan chuckles. "I doubt that's possible, but now that ye mention it, I want to put a block in yer mind so that no one can pluck the location out of yer head."

When he finishes that, I tap his temple. "What about your noggin?"

"Och, I'm good. I have a mind like a steel trap."

"Or a head as hard as rocks."

He chuckles. "No. I truly am good. My strength in the Spiritual discipline and dream manipulation gives me the ability to erect wards in my mind. I learned how to put those up as a kid."

"Were you still teething or was it after that?"

"Funny girl."

As I extend my hand for him to *poof* us home, I wonder if that's why he feels so closed off at times. Maybe he doesn't realize. Or perhaps him being alone on an emotional island results from the emotionless druid soldiers who raised him.

We take form in the back hallway and jog down the stairs to the basement to pick up Bruin. Back upstairs, I grab my keys from the rack and my purse off the little table by the door. "We're off to Garnet's. I don't think we'll be too late."

"Have ye got Bruin?" Calum calls back. "Because you know that's the first question Da will ask when he calls to check in."

I brush a gentle circuit over my chest and smile at the flutter of pressure. My bear hasn't been in place for what now…four days? Since Liam's birthday drinks at Shenanigans. Too long. I missed him.

"Yes, I have Bruin and Sloan and Birga. Even without them, I can hold my own, thank you very much."

"Don't kill the messenger."

"Call if you need backup," Dillan reminds me.

"Is it wrong to hope she does?" Emmet asks the others.

I laugh and head to the back door. "Love you guys."

"Love you more."

The locks of my Dodge Hellcat *pop* with the click of my fob, and Sloan and I climb in. I latch my belt, smile at the beefy growl of the engine, and pull out my phone.

While Sloan taps the Hellcat's nav screen, I call up Garnet's address and read it out to him. Once we're programmed and ready to roll, I reverse out of my spot in the back lane, drive around to the front of the house, and onto my street.

Our home is the last on the street with only a dirt laneway between the fence of our side lot and an access point to the St. James Cemetery property and the Don Valley River System. The forest and creeks of the Don were our playgrounds as kids.

I suppose we were druids by blood long before we knew anything about our heritage.

I leave the sleepy streets of our neighborhood and head toward midtown. "Garnet lives in a swanky part of town."

"Are ye surprised?"

I think about the sleek, metropolitan man and shake my head. "No. I guess not. I suppose he'd have to have some money and status to be Alpha of the Moon Called *and* the Grand Governor of the Lakeshore Guild."

"I suppose yer right."

My stomach growls long and loud, and I sigh. "I might need to hit a drive-thru on the way. I feel like it's been fifteen hundred years since the last time I ate."

Sloan tenses in the shotgun seat beside me.

I chuckle. "Too soon?"

"A little, yeah. Yer hard on my heart, Fi. Honestly."

I hit my indicator and take the next lane. "I don't mean to be. Honestly."

We drive past a strip of restaurants and Sloan points. "We had that Swiss Chicken the other night. It was good. Can ye get takeout there?"

"It's Swiss *Chalet*. If you're committed to a relationship with me, you'll have to get that right. Swiss Chalet."

He laughs. "My mistake. I'll commit that to memory."

A great Thomas Rhett song comes on, and I turn it up and belt it out. I'm a halfway decent singer, and I love this one. When it's over, I turn down the volume to a polite level again and catch Sloan smiling at me.

"She can sing, too. A triple threat."

I giggle. "I don't act."

"What do you mean?"

I glance down at the lighted map on the screen and get ready for the next turn. "Usually a triple threat involving singing, is sing, dance, and act. I can hold a tune. You saw me and the boys dance at Brenny's wake, but I can't act."

"No. You can't."

I hear the amusement in his tone and cast a sideways glance. "What does that mean?"

"Not a thing. I agree with ye. Yer a straightforward lass and it's evident when ye lie. Ye have a glass face and yer every thought and emotion are there to be read."

I frown at the car ahead of me. "Says you and no one else on the planet. I'm a great bluffer. I'm spy-caliber deceptive."

He laughs. "If ye think so."

"If you don't think so, that either makes you equally skilled in the art of deception or maybe as off-center as me."

"It's likely the second one. And I'm happy to have found such alluring company off the beaten path."

We drive for another few minutes. I don't see anywhere that interests me to stop and eat so I give up the idea and decide to grab something after we finish at Garnet's.

My mind circles back around to his original comment about me being a triple threat. "So, back to the triple threat. If it's not acting, what is it? I can sing, dance, and..."

He points out the windshield. "Oh look, we're here."

The tires have barely stopped rolling when he bails out of the passenger's seat. I'm turning things off and pulling the key as he opens my door and chuckles. "This will drive you mad, won't it?"

"You give yourself too much credit, Mackenzie. You're not that complicated. I'll figure it out."

He flashes me a cocky grin. "Shall we see who caves first? I can guarantee it won't be me."

I wave the taunt away and click the locks on the truck. "I can hardly wait to see Garnet's place. I mean, what do you think the home of the Alpha of the Moon Called looks like?"

Sloan falls into step. "Never gave it a moment's thought. Then again, yer the overthinker of this couple. Always puzzling over the little mysteries in life. I'm happy to take things as they come."

I burst out laughing. "Says the guy who has his head in a textbook every spare moment and worries about everything coming at us."

"That's not overthinkin', that's common sense. Someone has to have an eye on the horizon when yer in the picture."

We walk under the brick archway that hides the house from the street, and I feel the subtle resistance of a magic barrier. My shield doesn't ignite, so I push through the bubble of the invisible wall.

My ears pop, and we emerge on the other side.

I freeze in my tracks, and my eyes widen. "Shut... Up."

Wondering about Garnet's home hasn't prepared me in the slightest. I was expecting a modern, concrete, chrome, and glass mansion with infinity pools and buff men standing at the doors —I was not expecting this.

CHAPTER EIGHTEEN

"Are we in freakin' Africa?"

Night is now day, and a hot sun beating down on us replaces the cool, late September night air. The house is built almost completely into the side of a massive savannah stone steppe. It's as if the rock holds the mansion in its gaping maw, threatening to clamp down and devour the entire place.

"I have goosebumps. Look at me. I'm covered in goosebumps."

Sloan doesn't look. His gaze is locked on the five lions glaring at us from their perch on the rocks above. "This is Garnet's pride compound, I expect."

I survey the area. Beyond the compound is a vast, golden plane with tall, dry grasses and nothing but land and trees for as far as I can see. The leaves of the sparsely spaced baobab trees wave, but the breeze is barely enough to take the singe out of the air.

The compound itself consists of the rocky steppe that encompasses the house. Over to the side, more lions lounge in a shaded oasis around a lush watering hole while others in human form wrestle and play in the water and on the green grass.

"And that's Garnet's foolish pride." I point, laughing at my joke. "Get it? Foolish pride?"

Sloan rolls his eyes.

No accounting for taste. That was a good one.

"So, is this National Geographic experience in my city, or did we portal around the globe?"

"I'm not sure. Either way, it's disorienting."

Two of the lounging lions get up from the grassy patch, stretch, and prowl over.

My fingers twitch to call Birga, but spear-hunting Garnet's lion brothers in his home compound would likely be bad form. As they draw near, they shift and continue on two feet. Dressed in black jeans and t-shirts that pull tightly over muscled chests, I recognize them as two of Garnet's men I've seen on different occasions.

"This way," one of them says. "He's expecting you."

The man who speaks has flaxen gold hair that curls over his ears, sharp cheekbones, and a square jaw. He moves with the same fluid and confident stride as Garnet and strides past us to lead the way down a fieldstone path.

The second man falls behind us, and I wonder if he's there to protect our asses from the lions or protect the lions from us. He's shorter but no less muscled than the first guy and has blond-brown hair.

"We've never officially met," our blond guide says. "I am Anyx, Second Alpha to the Moon Called, and this is Thaor."

"I'm Fiona, and this is Sloan." I figure he probably already knows who I am, but it can't hurt to return the civil gesture. "This place is incredible."

"Felines do like creature comforts." He saunters around the corner of the house, through a little cactus garden, and under the ceiling of an outdoor living room. The heat of outside cuts off the moment we step into the shade.

Anyx closes his hand around the chrome door grip and

slides back the glass wall that divides the indoor and outdoor of the house. Natural materials finish the interior: exposed rock above, wooden columns, slate floors, and granite surfaces. It exudes the elegance I've grown accustomed to expect with Garnet.

I stare at the banquet laid out on the long buffet against the kitchen island, and my stomach lets out an embarrassing growl of approval.

Anyx smiles. "Please, help yourselves. I'll let them know you've arrived."

As he strides off, I stare at the food and swallow as saliva pools in my mouth.

Thaor closes the wall and takes up position blocking our way out. He widens his stance and clasps his hands at his front, standing at attention like a good little lion soldier.

I point at the food. "Are we interrupting a get-together?"

Thaor shakes his head, his stance stiff.

"Are you expecting trouble?"

Again with the head shaking.

A quiet fellow, that Thaor.

"Lady Druid." Garnet strides into the open-concept area with a level of ease and comfort I've never seen in him before.

When he gets to me, he stops, grips my wrists, and holds out my arms as if he's checking me over. "Thank the gods you're well. You do live a life of adventure, don't you? Zxata told me of your harrowing tale."

I narrow my gaze. The last thing we agreed on before leaving the Emporium was that for everyone's safety, we wouldn't spread the word about the *Eochair Prana* being a new arrival in the neighborhood.

Then again, Garnet possesses coercion.

Would he use that on his ex-girlfriend's brother, a man he obviously considers a friend?

Was Da right about his character?

Garnet releases my wrists and steps back. "I've upset you. Why? What did I say?"

He seems genuinely disturbed by my reaction. "Sorry. I'm surprised Zxata said anything. I thought we had the under-standing to keep tonight private."

Garnet nods at his men, and they retreat outside to their sunny, summery day. "You're surprised that a Governor of the Guild reported the arrival of a potentially devastating tome to the leader of the security agency responsible for the lives of thousands of empowered ones? That he is concerned about the seduction of such an object and feels we might need to monitor our populations in case they're affected?"

"I guess if you put it that way, it makes sense. Sorry."

"It's a non-issue. As you've said before, you're unfamiliar with the workings of the Lakeshore Guild. So, tell me what worried you about Zxata confiding in me?"

"It wasn't about you. I simply don't want people to know who has the book or where it is. I'm tired of others painting targets on my family and me. It puts all of us in danger if powerful people who embrace the dark side decide they want to have a look-see and try to force me to disclose where it's stashed."

"Agreed. And again, I regret what Barghest, the hobgoblins, and by extension, the vampires put you and your family through. It was an unfortunate and regrettable start to our relationship. I, however, am no threat."

"I believe that, but can you say that about all your Guild Governors?"

He waves that away and pulls a beer from an ice bucket at the end of the buffet line. "Another non-issue. I won't report it to the others and won't tell another soul. Zxata knows me a great deal better than you, and he had the confidence to tell me the whole truth. Please, try to give me the same trust."

The ship has sailed on the "tell him everything" sea anyway.

So yeah, there's that. "I haven't had the best luck with members of the empowered community earning my trust."

"Yet." He waggles his brows. "Let's break bread and work on that right now. Please, Anyx should have offered you something to eat. You're hungry. I can smell your ravenousness, and it's making my lion prowl. I'm surprised no one pounced on you on the way in."

Ahhh... Was that what the double escort sandwich was all about? Were Anyx and Thaor flanking me from getting munched? Comforting.

I look at the food and groan. "Normally, I'd do the Irish thing and insist I'm fine, but I'm starving, and I don't want to make your lion prowl."

"Then help yourself. If not for your sake, then for mine."

I accept the offered plate. "All right, for you, I'll eat."

After I fill my belly, I take my turn and go in to sit with Myra. I tell her about my adventure with Fionn in the past and the attack from the hobgoblins and Liam getting shot. When I've exhausted the one-sided convo, I squeeze her hand and rise from my chair.

I've been sitting so long that I'm stiff.

Well, maybe it was sitting, or perhaps it was nearly being overtaken by an evil grimoire. I wish I could say the darkness was completely out of my system, but it's not.

The taint of Morgana's call and the yearning to go back and get the book still haunts me. Dora wants me to continue going back to her for clearings. By the look on her face, I'm worried. She's had a long time to consider what bonding with that book might have done to me. Who knows, I might never be truly rid of the effects.

Unbidden, images of obsessive, bug-eyed hobbits come to mine. *My Precious.*

Ohmygod, I *soooo* don't want to be Gollum.

My stomach knots and a tide of anxiety churns my buffet selections. I groan and make a hasty rush for the ensuite. I burst into the posh and polished room, hit my knees, and pray to the porcelain god as my muscles convulse and I retch.

Amazeballs.

After a couple of violent rounds of heaving, I reach with my toe and shut the door. The last thing I need is for Garnet or Sloan to see me like this. Save me from the gallantry of men.

Plunking back on my ass, I close my eyes and pull strength from the cool, slate stone beneath my palms.

Are ye all right, Red?

Peachy. I love barfing in strangers' houses.

Do ye think it was the food? Is yer shield warnin' ye about poison or anythin' of the like?

No. The food was delish. It was a shockwave from Morgana's book. I'm fine.

If yer sure.

I am. Thanks.

After another minute of telling myself to get my butt in gear, I pull my shit together and splash water on my face. As I refold the little hand towel and hang it neatly over the ring, I check the mirror and lock stares with myself.

"Nothing to see here. You've got this. You're not Gollum. You're Fiona-freakin'-Cumhaill."

I flick off the light on my way out, and a picture on the wall opposite the ensuite door catches my attention.

It's Myra, Garnet, and a young boy.

There's no looking at the three of them and not seeing that the boy is a bio-mixture of their traits. He has his father's dark, wavy hair and amethyst eyes and his mother's crackled silver skin and welcoming smile.

Then I remember Myra and I talking about Da's grief when Brenny first died.

"I know the pain of losing a son," Myra said. *"It's not something that ever truly eases. Your father may never be the same man you knew before."*

I press my hand to the tightness in my chest. *Oh, no.*

That's the loss Gran talked about.

That's the pain keeping them apart although they still love one another. I go back to my seat at Myra's bedside, take her hand, and close my eyes.

Pain of loss and wounds of old,
I set you free; you have no hold.
Your heart will heal, the burden lighter,
Your love is strong; you are a fighter.

I brush Myra's electric blue bangs to the side and smile. "Feel better. We'll talk soon. I know we will."

I find Sloan and Garnet sharing a drink in the living room. If I'm honest, the entire exchange looks strained.

Weird. I find chatting with each of them quite easy.

"Hey." I grab a chunk of smoked cheese off the tray as I pass. It has a heavy hickory flavor, and I hope it wipes out the taste of death celebrating in my mouth. "Everything okay in here? Did Zxata and Dora leave?"

Sloan stands, looking relieved at my return. "They did. How was your visit with Myra?"

"Good. I updated her on things and cast a cleansing spell to clear her system for healing. I hope with that, and the healing on Mr. Tree, she'll be on the road to recovery once Garnet's people come up with the antidote."

"You're a good friend," Garnet says. "Listen, I heard a little about what you went through since the vampires took you from the back of the bar. You've battled enough for other people. I want you to go home and take some time for yourself."

I yawn and cover my mouth. "Sorry, that was rude and had nothing to do with what you were saying."

"No. It was exactly my point. Go home, Lady Druid. Get some

rest, and spend some much-needed time in your sacred grove refilling your stores. Prana doesn't miraculously fuel us. Everyone needs to take time."

I nod. "All right, but before I go, there is one last thing I'd like to do. You asked me to trust you earlier, so now I ask the same thing. Will you trust me?"

Garnet straightens his arms and tugs on his sleeves' cuffs where they protrude from the arms of his suit jacket. "Trust you with what?"

"Trust me to help you help Myra."

Garnet's brow arches. "And what does that entail?"

"That's where the trust part comes in." I hold out my hands, palms up. "I want to give you something, and by extension, Myra. I promise it will help."

Garnet's gaze locks on me. I wait, neither advancing nor dropping my hands. In the end, he places his palms in mine and closes his fingers around my hands.

I smile, close my eyes, and send my call through my feet to the ground beneath us. After anchoring myself in the connection of nature, I repeat Gran's spell in my mind.

Pain of loss and wounds of old,
I set you free; you have no hold.
Your heart will heal, the burden lighter,
Your love is strong; you are a fighter.

Garnet gasps as I release his hands, and I wink. "Take care of her. I'll check in with you when I know more."

"What did you do?"

My skin tingles as his gaze narrows, and he pegs me with a probing stare. "Your coercion doesn't work on me, Grand Governor, so don't do that. I don't like it."

His mouth lifts in a crooked smile. "Then we're even, Lady Druid. You did something to me just now, and I don't know what and I don't like it."

I offer him a sympathetic smile. "But you will."

He waves toward the door. "Off you go. Dreamland awaits."

I'm halfway to the door when Garnet's words twang a tuning fork in my mind. "Dreamland awaits. That's it! Garnet, you're a genius. Yay, you!"

———————

I race back and burst into Myra's room. By the time Sloan and Garnet get there, I've toed off my sneakers and am climbing onto the bed. I take the outside edge and pat the velvety coverlet in the space I left between Myra and me. "Come lay with me, Sloan. I have an idea."

I give him huge credit. He doesn't question why. He unties the laces of his shoes and sets them neatly by the door. Man, he's so anal.

When he climbs up, I pat the pillow, and he lays down. I grin. "Now that I've got you right where I want you…"

He barks a nervous laugh. "Are ye havin' a stroke? Should Garnet call someone?"

I look over at the very confused Alpha lion and smile. "Trust me. This will work."

"What will?" he asks.

"One of Sloan's primary disciplines is dream manipulation, and I have this little trick where I can retreat into myself in an emotional construct sorta place. It's like Star Trek. Do you watch Star Trek? Picture it like an internal holodeck. I call it my safe place, and I've taken Sloan there before. I'm thinking, I retreat into myself, Sloan connects with Myra, and then they meet me in my safe place so she can tell us who did what and what the hell we're supposed to do about it."

Garnet frowns. "You think that will work?"

"I do." I look at Sloan and hope he agrees.

His pale-mint gaze is bright with thought, and I'm not sure if he's a yea or a nay on my plan. "If her mind is open to visitors, it might work. I'm willin' to give it a try."

I squeal and kiss his cheek. "That's the spirit." Easing down beside him, I roll onto my side and lace my fingers with his. Resting my cheek on the pillow next to his I raise my other arm over Sloan. "Sloan, you hold Myra's near hand, and Garnet, give me Myra's free hand to complete the circuit."

Garnet rounds the bed and sits at Myra's hip, lifting her hand and shifting it across so I can complete the connection.

I flash him an excited smile. "Wish us luck."

"You know I do."

I close my eyes and try to calm my mind. We can do this. Sloan will bring Myra, and I will meet them both. Deep breath in. Exhale. Another deep breath and I connect to my internal safe place.

I feel the warmth of Sloan's side against me and sink into my happy place. When Patty first taught me how to send my consciousness into the trunk of my body, he said it's like accessing the hollow in the trunk of a tree.

The tricky part is taking a visitor. I've taken Sloan before when Barghest captured us and we needed to strategize our escape with Bruin. It should be the same now.

I don't doubt Sloan can bring Myra. He's never let me down. He's the slow and steady to complement my roller-coaster of erratic. He's right. We make a great team.

When I open my eyes, I expect to be sitting in Shenanigans like always.

Hubba-wha?

Tonight, I'm not in Shenanigans. I'm in my sacred grove. Well, sort of... Brendan is still standing behind the bar of Shenanigans but in my grove. *Huh,* what does that say about me and my subconscious mind? "Hey, Brenny." I lean over the bar to kiss his cheek. "Hangin' out in the grove tonight, are you?"

"It's nice here. It feels good."

I smile at the trees and the restorative feeling they give me. I'm not sure when, but I guess my subconscious mind has been shifting my happy place. "Yeah, it does."

"Fi?" Sloan says beside me.

I turn, and he's standing there with—"Myra!"

I rush over and hug her. She looks the same as always with her electric-blue hair cropped at a severe angle, her vertically-slit eyes, and her crackled silver skin with faint darker undertones.

"We've been so worried. Are you all right? What did they do to you? We've been trying everything we can think of to counter Evening Shade magic and nothing's working. We can't wake you up."

Myra steps back and smiles at the scene around her. "You did well here, duck. Is this your grove?"

"A representation of it, yeah. When you wake up, you can come to see it in the real world. The key here is that you have to wake up. What did they do to you? How do we help you?"

She brushes her hair back and frowns. "I don't remember. Everything's foggy."

I look at Sloan. "Can you help her remember?"

He takes her hand, then takes mine. I complete the circuit and close my eyes. At first, everything is dark for a long while, then Myra's memories play back.

The wizards came. They want books about the resurrection of greater demons. Myra refuses to help them. They're torturing her when Murphy comes in and interrupts. During the distraction, she takes a piece of twisted stick and swallows it. It's bitter, and she cries out as it goes down. She falls to the floor and sees me rushing in to help her.

"You did it to yourself." My heart pounds. "That's amazing. If the thing that rendered you unconscious isn't something the wizards gave you, then you know how to undo it."

Myra stares at me, and I see she's still having trouble piecing together her memories. "When I refused to help them, they tried to force me. I took the necrosis root to induce deep hibernation. It's a long-forgotten ability of the meliae from generations past and can make it appear as if I'm dead."

"So, you're not poisoned?"

"No. Why would I poison myself? That's crazy."

"You wouldn't. So, how do we wake you up?"

"I'm pretty sure I hid the antidote right before they came...I can't remember where."

I look at Sloan. "Search back more. Maybe we'll find it."

Sloan does as I ask and we sift through her memories until —"Oh, of course, that makes perfect sense."

CHAPTER NINETEEN

I sit up with a gasp, and the room comes into focus. Garnet is there looking anxious. He grips my wrist as I roll to my feet and steadies me when the blood rushes from my head because I got up too fast.

"Well? Did it work?"

"Hells yes, it worked." I round the bed, grab my shoes, and check on Sloan. He's blinking awake, and we'll be able to *poof* in a moment. "The wizards didn't poison Myra. She took necrosis root to hibernate so they couldn't force her to help them release a demon from the hell realm."

I slide my feet into my shoes and use my finger to get my heels in. "She hid the antidote in the stacks at the Emporium. We'll *poof* over there, grab it, and *poof* back."

Sloan rolls off the bed and heads for his shoes. "No, we won't. Garnet, I'd like to take a couple of yer men with us. It may be as simple as Fi thinks, but from what I saw in Myra's memory, I don't think it will. The wizards believe Myra knows more than she's saying and are determined that their answers are in the bookshop."

Garnet follows us out to the living room and signals for Anyx and Thaor to come inside. "Have Zuzanna come in and sit with Myra. We're on the move."

Thaor flashes off and is back a moment later with an athletic blonde woman with wide cheekbones. Once Garnet sets the woman on her task of watching over Myra, we walk out of the house and around the walk to the brick archway.

"So, are we actually in Africa, or is this some kind of magic compound?"

"We're in Africa, Lady Druid, but the portal gate is in Toronto."

We leave as a group and push through the magical barrier, leaving the champagne sky of a savannah sunset in exchange for the crisp night air of Toronto in the last week of September.

When we huddle up in the driveway by my truck, I hold up my finger. "If Sloan's right, we should materialize in the alley outside the building and have Bruin go in first in his spirit mode to assess the sitch."

Anyx blinks and looks surprised. "He can do that?"

"Yeah, he can do almost anything. He's a multi-talented bear. Although shredding bad guys is his favorite pastime."

Sloan slips his hand between us and clasps his fingers around mine. "Ready?"

I test my movement in my jacket and frown. Unlocking my truck, I toss my purse and jacket into the back seat and lock it back up with my powers. "Ready and steady."

The four of us take form in the narrow alley that runs around to our delivery dock, and I shiver without my jacket. I release Bruin, and while he's gone, I tell Garnet a little about what we saw in Myra's memories.

"But she was all right?"

Sloan and I both nod. "Other than her current state, I'd say there's nothing wrong with her."

Relief flares in his eyes and I'm content to know that I had a small part to play in the imminent reunion of these two.

Yay me. A moment later, the wind picks up, but it's not cold. It tingles against the skin on my cheek, and I smile. "What did you find, Bear? Are we good to go?"

No. Not even close. Two men are searching the main store, and four more are in the back reading area. They're ransackin' the place.

"Where exactly? If we were to pick them off by the five of you *poofing* in, where am I sending everyone?"

One at the back counter. One near the doorway to the back room. One on the second-floor catwalk on the east side of the store. One on the third-floor catwalk on the west side of the store. One at the loading dock door. And the last one down by Mr. Tree sitting on a couch.

"Great job, buddy." I relay the info to the four guys who can materialize, and they coordinate their attack.

"Wait until I unlock the front door and move to take down the ward and security system. I'll pretend everything is normal and be your distraction to draw their attention to the front of the store. Good luck, boys—and don't kill all of them. We need to know what's going on."

"I vote no to that." Sloan scowls at me. "There's no need fer a decoy when we can get in there with the advantage of surprise."

Garnet nods. "Agreed. On one, men. Three. Two. One."

"Hey!" The four men and my bear disappear. I curse and run around to the front of the building. Cock-blocked from the fight that *I* coordinated. Rude.

As quickly as I can, I key the lock and let myself in. The security system doesn't beep, so I don't need to turn it off. *Huh. Did Zxata not set it?* I hustle my butt straight toward the back counter. They're focused on the men in the back. I'll take the guy in the store proper—if he's still standing by the time I get there.

With the alpha males in full offensive mode, I bet they don't leave anyone for me. Greedy men.

I call Birga to my palm and activate my body armor.

I stride up the main corridor with my footsteps swallowed by the *crash* and *clash* sounding off in the back. Sadly, the din of fighting also swallows up the sound of—

A blue bolt of magic hits me like a fizzy electric snowball. When it explodes against my shoulder, it doesn't disperse and fall like a normal snowball. It spreads and crawls across my sweater like a static-clingy electrical field.

I stiffen as the spell takes hold. It tingles over my flesh, and my body locks in place. I'm frozen and rooted to the spot.

Dammit. Not again. Sloan and I practiced shit like this. I fight down the feeling of being vulnerable and counter the spell. *Freedom to Move*.

Nothing happens, and I push down the panic rising in my gorge. A spell is only as strong as the caster's intention and my intention is firm.

Freedom to Move.

The hold breaks as the bastard flies in on the attack. I barely get my hands up before he makes a pro-wrestler move and hits me with a flying lariat. The impact knocks me off my feet, and I get air as I fly backward.

My head cracks hard against the shelving unit and the two of us tip, toppling the whole row of books. My head, shoulder, and hip take the brunt of the fall but my armor keeps me from any real damage.

A polished blade glints in the light of the window above. He pulls his arm back and jabs. He's stabbing me—or at least, he's trying to.

I curse while struggling against his hold and his advantageous position. He's heavy and strong. I'm pinned and pissed. He takes another jab at my stomach, and I exploit his confusion when the blade doesn't penetrate.

The emporium has a strong sense of nature.

The entire store is built around the love of a tree.

I connect to the energy of Mr. Tree and call for his help. A rumble deep beneath us signals his response. A moment later, tree roots break through the floorboards. They rise and writhe like the tentacles of an attacking Kraken.

They wrap around my attacker's throat and drag him backward. He's peeled off me, kicking and grabbing at the noose around his neck. The roots don't relent.

They twine and tighten with no quarter given.

I thank Mr. Tree and release my call to defend me.

The roots don't relax. Anger burns in the center of my chest, but it's not mine. Leniya the ancient ash is pissed. He wants justice—for Myra, for what he suffered, for these men breaking in and ransacking his home.

My attacker throws his fist through the empty air, and the punch lands on my cheek as if I'm standing two feet away from him instead of ten. My head snaps back, but I don't go down. I've been clocked enough times by my brothers to take a licking and keep on ticking.

I empower Mr. Tree to do what he wishes.

If he has mercy in his wooden heart, the guy might live.

I doubt it. From what I felt coming off the ash, that guy is toast. I'm about to say something to that effect when the roots recede and pull their prey into the depths of the soil below the shop. The man gasps and chokes, kicking as his feet disappear beneath the antique pegged-hardwood floor.

When everything falls quiet below, I press my palms to the floor and focus on flattening the soil and healing the wood. The planks reform and lie flat, and I brush a hand over the healed floorboards.

I'm straightening when Sloan comes out to check on me.

"Are ye all right?"

"Fine. You?"

"Same. Where's yer guy?"

I point at the floor and sigh. "Where all filthy dirtballs should be. I gave Leniya free rein on executing punishment. He's understandably upset about recent events."

Sloan arches a brow and looks at me. "Communing with trees now, are ye?"

"I don't hear him like Gran does if that's what you're asking, but yeah, I've always been able to sense his moods and intention."

I round the end of the tipped bookshelf and wonder how to get it upright. Gripping the edges, I give it a good haul.

Nothing.

Sloan shakes his head and flicks his fingers to shoo me away. "Ye'll be a druid in a class all yer own, and ye'll still be thinkin' like a civilian. Wait and see."

"Ha! I'm getting there. Sure, I'm still guessing half the time, but I'm getting more wins than trips to the clinic."

Sloan blinks. "That's yer litmus test? Yer basin' yer progress on how much damage ye suffer?"

"Why not? If I'm still standing, s'all good, amirite?"

Sloan holds his palms forward, and magic fills the air. The shelf rights itself onto its base, and he offers me a sexy smile. "Think like a druid."

"No one likes a showoff."

"I'm not showin' off. I'm tryin' to remind ye that yer the blossom of a rare flower about to bloom. All ye need is a bit of experience and some confidence and ye'll flourish."

I roll my eyes. "Don't get mushy on me, Mackenzie. I'm not that kinda girlfriend. I'm more of a punch you in the gut kinda girl."

He thumbs over his shoulder. "I'll pass on bein' yer target tonight. How about we join the interrogation?"

"We kept one alive? We did better than I thought."

I follow Sloan into the reading area, and he chuckles. "No. *We* didn't. I did. How am I the only one with enough control to fight and not kill my opponent?"

I hold up my palms in surrender. "Hey. I didn't kill my guy. Mr. Tree did. No *mea culpa*."

We cross the threshold into the reading area, and I gasp. The place is destroyed. Hundreds, possibly thousands of books have been pulled and tossed. Books from the second and third-floor shelves have been dumped over the railings and have fallen in page-bending piles below.

Suddenly, I share Leniya's rage about the intruders ransacking the store. This is horrible. Myra's life's work tossed like it means nothing.

I look around and can hardly breathe.

Anyx and Thaor are interrogating the designated survivor, and I have to fight the urge to ram Birga through his throat. They have him tied up and seated next to three dead guys flopped on the floor.

It seems neck-snapping is a favorite MO for the lions.

I scan the space for the last body.

There are a few magic scorch marks on the walls.

Some blood over by the sofas.

Oh...and one shredded heap.

"Let me guess. That one kill belongs to my beloved Killer Clawbearer?"

Bruin lumbers over, and I scrub his cheek. He lifts his lips and smiles to expose three-inch-long, white canines.

"Had fun, did you? Nothing like a good bad-guy-body-shred, is there, buddy?"

Garnet joins me and frowns. "Be warned, Lady Druid. After the mysterious death of an entire nest of hobgoblins, there are members of the Guild who don't approve of your battle bear being part of our community."

I scrub Bruin's ear and shrug. "Tough titty. He's bonded with me, and I'm not going anywhere. If people are worried, it's because they're scared about saving their asses."

Garnet nods. "Perhaps. But you can't deny your druid companion is a true and violent force."

"Why would I? He's a legendary spirit fighter. He's also very sweet and loyal. He'd only do this to bad guys or someone who comes at me and mine."

Sloan steps in behind me and rests his palm on my hip. "Would ye expect anything less from yer warriors, Governor Grant?"

Garnet cants his head and smiles. "No. I wouldn't."

I pat Bruin's head, then pat my chest. He flips into spirit mode and bonds with me, making my lungs flutter a little while he finds a comfy position.

"Bruin is a non-issue. Tell your members to leave us alone, and they don't need to worry about him. They can Elsa their way through their fear and just, *Let it go. Let it go!*"

I'm not sure how familiar Garnet is with *Frozen*, but when I sweep my arms through the air and do the actions, he laughs. Whether it's *at* me or *for* me, I can't tell.

As if he remembers something, Garnet sets his hands on his hips and pegs me with a look. "Speaking of letting things go. Why do I feel like your 'trust me' moment a few hours ago was an ambush to cast an emotional cleanse on me?"

"Who, me? Never. Did it work?"

He rolls his eyes. "Well, for the first time in almost fifty years, my heart and mind feel far less burdened. No Humvee sitting on my chest. No tight jaw from gritting my teeth. I fought just now and didn't get consumed by anger and violence. I had a clear-headed goal to triumph."

Play it cool. Fight the smile... Must. Not. Fist pump.

I shrug and feign innocence. "You know what they say about time healing all wounds. It's hella restorative."

"Hella restorative, eh? You're sticking with that?"

"It's plausible."

"Not really."

I shrug. "Picture me as the little mouse who pulled the thorn out of the angry lion's paw. *Squeak, squeak.*"

Anyx joins us, and Garnet lets it go—for now at least.

"Okay, Thaor identified two of our dead from the Guild database. They're both members of the West Village Wizards and fall under Salem's rule."

Garnet nods. "You two take him in and clean up these bodies. We have an antidote to find."

I cast a glance around and sigh. "It's a proverbial needle in a haystack. We need reinforcements."

I pull out my phone and post in my family WhatsApp chat room. Then I text Zxata and Dora the update. Next, I call up my playlist and connect to the store audio system.

As the music pumps out of the speakers above, I hold out my hand to Garnet. "Care to give a girl a lift to the third-floor Antidotes and Remedy section? With any luck, the book we need didn't get tossed."

He takes my hand and bows. "It would be my pleasure."

Two hours later, the adventure of the hunt has faded, and the search for a third-floor book with a hollow core has become far more back-breaking. Dora and Emmet are taking on the second floor. Calum and Dillan are working on the main floor, and Da finished up in the front of the shop and had to head for his shift in the surveillance van.

Zxata and I have repaired and shelved the books littered onto the third floor's catwalk and have started on the stacks of books Sloan and Garnet have been bringing up.

"So, it was about the *Eochair Prana* but only because the West Village Wizards believed they could find a spell in it that could resurrect a demon?" Zxata finishes fanning through the pages of a text, then follows the reference number on the spine to determine where it belongs.

I grab another and do the same thing. Rinse and repeat. "And when that didn't pan out they went after Myra."

Sloan *poofs* up and sets down another pile. "What I don't understand is why they thought she would know? There are hundreds of new age and occult bookshops and hundreds of authorities on things like demonic resurrection. Why target Myra? Why not move on and ask someone else?"

Zxata slides another book onto the shelf and smiles. "Because my sister isn't simply a bookstore owner—she's a Historian."

I shelve my book and go back to the pile. "Okay, but Sloan's point still stands. It's not surprising that the West Village Wizards pegged Myra as the Yoda guru of exotic books, but why her? There are lots of historians who could've helped them."

Zxata fans the next book and walks down the aisle a ways to find it's place. "No, not simply a historian who knows details of the past. Myra is a Historian with a capital 'H.'"

The capital H thing makes me stop and straighten.

Sloan looks like he might faint.

"I take it this is one of those preternatural world big deal thingies that I don't understand. What's a Historian?" I finish with the book in my hand and slide it in place.

Sloan takes the top book off the pile and checks the spine. As he reads the numbers of the books in my section, he fills me in. "A Fae Historian is a very rare occurrence when a truly pure-blooded child can access and recall all that came before. In some cases, they are bards and can sing and recite the histories long forgotten. In others, they are healers and recall potions and remedies from thousands of years ago, and in still others, they know everything there is to know about subjects like lineage or military events or—"

"Books," I interrupt.

Sloan nods. "Exactly. You see, as a Historian of the written word, she would magically know every book that holds the capability to not only resurrect *a* demon but *the* demon they're interested in. Her knowledge would be invaluable."

Zxata frowns. "But how did they know? It's certainly not

something she would've ever shared with anyone, for exactly this reason."

Sloan opens his book and smiles, then tips it for us to see the hollow core and the glass vial we saw in her memories. "Why don't we wake her up and ask her?"

CHAPTER TWENTY

With the antidote in hand, we call it a night and lock up the bookstore. I want to go with Garnet and Zxata to see if it works, but they say there's no sense. The antidote for necrosis root might take days to bring her back.

"And you're exhausted," Garnet adds. "Between being attacked at the pub and fleeing to Ireland, then being thrown back in time to collect the book, you've done more than enough. Go home and get some rest. Magical stores deplete. You may be young and strong, but you need to take better care of yourself."

Sloan lets out a *harumph* I've heard many times in my life. It's an Irish catch-all phrase that can mean anything. In this instance it could be, "She'll never listen," or, "I've told her that a million times," or, "Yer preachin' to deaf ears, my friend."

I've faced off with enough stubborn men to know when to pick my battles, so for tonight, I accept defeat. "Fine. Home to bed it is."

Sloan's brow arches in disbelief and I revel in the ability to surprise him with my mature, level-headed reasonability.

"We'll *poof* to your place and pick up my truck, then straight home."

Too tired to drive, I hand Sloan the keys and pull out my phone. *Order pizza. We'll pick it up. On the way home now.*

Dealio.

We arrive home twenty minutes later, pizzas in hand, and flop on our asses in the family room with the other tired troops. "Thanks, guys. I appreciate your help. I don't want Myra waking up from one nightmare to be smacked in the face with another one."

"Not a problem, Fi." Emmet stuffs his face. "Her life got hijacked by evil wizards. Could happen to you any day now. The least we can do is pay it forward."

I snort. "You're not wrong."

I finish my second piece and go for a third. "At least we know why it happened now. Hopefully, if we're lucky, that'll be the end of it. Garnet and his men are looking into the wizards now. Maybe they'll leave us alone."

Dillan finishes his slice and pushes back from the coffee table. "Damn, Fi, I wish ye hadn't deleted the pictures on your phone. I want to see the pictures of you in Camelot."

"Hells yeah. Me too," Emmet agrees.

"She didn't delete them," Sloan reminds them. "She never took them."

"Says you." I reach for another slice of Hawaiian. "And don't start on your astrology stuff, crazy man. I was there. I know I took pictures."

"It's astral projection, and yer the crazy one."

I chew my pizza, make zany eyes at my brothers, and make them laugh.

"Is that yer fourth slice? Have ye got a tapeworm?"

I frown at Sloan lounging back on the couch with Kevin and Calum. "Exsqueeze me? If you want things to go smoothly between you and me, Mackenzie, comments like that end now. Tapeworm? Seriously? That's gross."

"Yeah, dude," Dillan says. "Bad call."

Sloan finishes his second beer and sets the bottle with the other fallen soldiers. "She took up a seat at the buffet at Garnet's a couple of hours ago, and now she's eating like she's starving. I'm not judgin'. I'm concerned she's unwell. After what she's been through, and the possession of the book, I simply find it out of character."

The boys slide their frowns from Sloan to me. Dillan passes Sloan a freshie and gets him set up. "Well, yeah, that is odd. You don't usually eat like that, and a lot has happened to you over the past couple of days."

I wave that away. "Honestly, I'm fine. I threw up all the buffet food while I was in with Myra. Trust me. I've got a rumbly in my tumbly."

Sloan's brow creases as his focus intensifies. "Is admittin' ye threw up yer last meal supposed to make us feel better about yer well-being?"

I roll my eyes and reach for my beer. "One amazing, panty-dampening kiss and you're getting annoying. This isn't boding well for you for getting to second base."

My brothers snort, and Sloan's expression drops. "Are we talking about that now? Here? With yer brothers?"

Emmet chuckles, shifts the empty pizza box to the bottom, and brings a whole pie to the top. "Trust me, dude. In this family, we all know what's going on anyway. I'm surprised you're only getting to the locking of lips. The two of you have thrown off fuck-me vibes for months."

If the look on Sloan's face wasn't so mortified, I would've given my brother shit for that one, but yeah, his discomfort is funny as hell.

I set my beer back onto my coaster and swallow. "Okay, two things. One, Sloan doesn't have siblings so he's unaccustomed to the interjections of thoughts and opinions regarding our current status on horizontal hijinks or lack thereof. Take it easy on him. He lives in a stone castle with a bed built like a fortress. They don't creak as things do in our humble Victorian, so he has no idea about that of which we speak."

Dillan groans. "You will. Emmet tends to bring home very vocal girls."

Emmet shrugs and drops into the club chair. "Maybe. Or maybe I'm that good and know how to make a lady—"

"Stop!" I point my finger at Emmet. "Don't finish that sentence. While I like to think of you all as skilled and giving lovers, I don't want any images in my head."

Kevin raises his bottle. "Agreed. Good save, Fi. You said two things. Sloan's not used to sibling chaos, and..."

I grin. "And two, if you guys think you're in the loop on who's doing whom in this house, I'm about to blow your freakin' minds."

The peanut gallery sits forward and eyes one another.

"Who's doing whom?" Calum asks. "And if you say Emmet's back with Moaning Myrtle, I'm going to kill him."

They all turn to Emmet, who shakes his head. "Rude. Her name was Marta, and I haven't seen her in months. Whatever bomb Fi has, it's not me."

"No. It's not. I'm telling you right now that I expect an Oh! Henry from each of you tomorrow."

Dillan's brow pops. "That's quite a demand. You sure you have the goods to back that up, sista?"

"Oh, I have the goods. When Sloan *poofed* me and Liam home this afternoon, I thought Da would be sleeping off the night shift. The house was quiet, so we crept up the stairs to put our stuff away. We caught Auntie Shannon coming out of the bathroom in a towel and Da full monty in the hall. The two fessed up. They're doin' the deed."

"Fuck off." Dillan sends me a stink-eye glare. "You're full of shit."

"Brownies honor." I raise my fingers in the pledge. "Sloan will back me up. He *poofed* away like a scaredy-chicken while Liam pretty much had a stroke."

"That's..." Calum stalls out. "I don't even know how to process that."

Kevin puts an arm around Calum and leans close. "I think it's nice. It sorta makes sense. They've practically been a couple for years."

Emmet tips his beer back and drinks it down. "Am I the only one freaked out by the image of that?"

Cue the shaking heads of everyone in the room.

"Aunt Shannon is an angel. She doesn't have sex," Dillan declares, "and certainly not with Da."

I go back to finishing my beer. "That was Liam's take on things too. Wrong and wrong. Da copped to them being occasional friends with benefits over the years. They progressed into coupledom this summer under the stress of me going missing and losing Brenny."

"Holy shit." Dillan flops back on the couch.

"You remain the reigning Queen of Amazeballs, Fi," Calum admits. "Oh! Henry bars coming your way."

I take my bow, then remember one important point I neglected to mention. "Da said any flack or temper-fueled opinions go through him, not Shannon. He doesn't want blowback on her."

Calum waves that off. "We wouldn't do that. We're okay with it, aren't we?"

Everyone in the room looks around to test the expressions and body language of the others.

"It might slow down his drinking," Dillan offers. "You know, if he has her to focus on instead of Brendan's death."

That gets a few male grunts and hopeful nods.

"I'm not family," Sloan interjects, "but I think it's nice that the two people ye look at as parents fancy each other. I'm not sure mine do. Yer Gran and Granda are my examples of what a real family looks like. Maybe ye should be happy fer them."

Emmet nods. "You're right, Irish, and yer pretty much family. You've saved our bacon a dozen times over, and now that you're snogging our sister, I'm sure you'll be settling in."

"Yeah, make your move, man," Calum encourages. "Fi's had a rough few months. She could use an outlet."

I snort. "Hey, stop trying to pimp me out."

"No, Calum's right," Dillan adds. "Sloan needs to make it happen. Plant that flag before the competition comes back around."

"And when he says flag, he means—"

"He knows what you mean, Emmet." I hold up my hand.

Sloan waves that off. "There's no competition. Yer sister knows her mind, and Liam is part of yer family. He loves her too. We chatted after he was shot and—"

"Wait. What? You and Liam discussed me?" I interrupt.

"You said, loves her *too*. Are you dropping the L-bomb?" Emmet chimes in.

"I didn't mean Liam," Dillan says. "I meant the immortal god offering her carnal pleasures."

My jaw drops, and all the chatter of talking over each other comes to a grinding halt. It's like one of those moments when the needle scratches across the vinyl of a record and everyone tenses.

Sloan frowns. "A god's offering you carnal pleasures?"

I glare at Dillan. "You bring that up *now?*"

Dillan shrugs. "Hey, you just finished telling him there are no secrets in this house. What's the matter? You like to drop the bombs, but we can't join the fun?"

I look at Sloan, and I can't decide if he seems more hurt or pissed. "Ignore Dillan. I have no interest in Nikon. For one, he looks like an eighteen-year-old going through an emo fetish, and for another, he's bored with life and I get the feeling his moral code has worn thin since his time in the Parthenon."

"Nikon?" Emmet says. "Like the camera?"

"Yeah, I used that one on him, and it didn't hit his funny bone. I'd advise against it."

"Hey," Calum jumps in. "If he's from Pagan Greece, he's probably game to join you two. Why choose, right?"

I blink. "Not helping, Calum."

He looks at my face and bursts out laughing. "Ha! The subject has already come up. *Noice.*"

I hold up my finger to lie, but my cheeks are flaming and Sloan already said he could read me like a book. "You suck. This was my moment with the gossip about Da and Shannon, and you sucked all the joy out of it for me."

Dillan laughs too. "Nah. You still win the chocolate bars."

Calum sinks deeper into the couch and raises his beer. "Wow, this is a night for revelations. Fi and Sloan are finally off the blocks, Da and Auntie Shannon are canoodling, and an ancient Greek god is interested in a threesome. Maybe Kevin and I should meet this immoral immortal."

Kevin cracks up, and now he's blushing. "What? I'm not enough for you, archer? Do I need to up my game?"

Calum chuckles. "I have a roomie this week. I don't think Sloan's up to being a voyeur."

As the room devolves into ricocheting comments and suggestions, I wave them a good night, tug on Sloan's wrist, and head toward the bottom of the stairs. With my foot on the bottom step, I glance back. "I'm tired and not seducing you, but do you want to come up?"

He shrugs, his shoulders rigid. "I suppose I will. My room is upstairs."

"Okay. Right. Sorry." I climb the steps and head into my room, not sure if that meant he is or isn't coming in to talk before bed.

When he passes my door and heads to Calum's room, I take that as my answer.

Allll righty then. Good start.

I jolt in the wee hours of dawn and stare wide-eyed at Sloan in a pair of flannel lounge pants and a tight t-shirt lying on top of the bed beside me. I run a hand over my face and push back my hair. "Hey," I say, my voice graveled with sleep.

"Hey. I came to talk after I cooled down, but ye were lost to slumber."

"Time-travel and evil possession can do that to a girl."

"That's what I've heard." He brushes a chunk of hair out of my face. "Close yer eyes. It's not time to wake up yet."

"Will you be here to talk when I do?"

"If that's all right with you."

"It is."

"Good, then. Sweet dreams."

I close my eyes and feel the drugging pull to sink back into sleep. "Sweet dreams."

The next morning, I wake to the buzz of my phone vibrating on my nightstand. With a reluctant groan, I roll over and grab it. "Garnet? Dude, you can't order me to go home and rest, then phone and wake me up. That's counterproductive."

The rumble of his lion's growl has me opening my eyes. "What's wrong?"

"You have trouble coming your way. I need you dressed and at the druid standing stones as soon as you can get here."

I blink at the time on my phone. Oh, damn. It's almost ten o'clock. "Yeah. Okay. Give me twenty minutes."

"Make it ten."

When the line goes dead, I blink at the end screen. "Manners matter, Guild Governor."

Still, he wouldn't be so short with me if it weren't urgent.

"Trouble, Red?" Bruin is star-fished and sleeping belly up, eclipsing most of my bedroom floor. He lifts his head and stretches, his massive paws reaching to the window seat.

"Looks that way." I grab a pair of olive khakis, an ivory knit sweater, and my underthings, then hustle my butt across the hall and into the shower.

"Where's the fire?" Dillan asks as I jog down the stairs eleven minutes later.

Sloan stands from where he's sitting at the kitchen table, and I smile at the spread laid out on its surface. "Aww, you boys made brekkie."

Emmet, Calum, and Dillan all point at Sloan.

I grab my shoes and bring them in to sit and put them on. "And I slept through it. I'm sorry."

"If it mattered, I would've woken you. Sleeping was far more necessary." Sloan's up and putting his shoes on without knowing why.

"What's the dealio, sista?" Dillan asks.

I relay the call from Garnet, and the boys are up now too.

"You don't all need to come."

Calum frowns. "When the leader of the Justice League gives you a heads-up that there's trouble coming at you and calls you to the site where we were held hostage, and you were almost a blood sacrifice, there's cause for alarm."

Dillan nods and grabs his military boots. "No way we're sitting here eating French toast sticks while you're out there facing hostile forces."

"Have ye got yer bear?" Sloan plucks my jacket off the hook and holds it open for me to slide into.

I rub the fluttering presence in my chest. "Present and accounted for."

"All right then, hands in."

I chuckle. This is their new *manly* way to travel with Sloan. Instead of holding hands, everyone gathers round like a huddle and stacks hands. Sloan's hands are the top and bottom bread of the hand sandwich, and away we go.

CHAPTER TWENTY-ONE

I check my Fitbit when we arrive at the druid stones, and it's been sixteen minutes. Yeah, well, I did my best.

"Miss Cumhaill." Garnet waves me over to a group of people gathered near the altar stone.

Miss Cumhaill? Since when has he called me—oh, the terse tone of his call makes more sense now.

Several Guild Governors are glaring at me.

"Mr. Grant." I take his lead on keeping it formal. "I'm here, per your order. What's this about?"

"Where were you last night between the hours of eight o'clock and midnight?"

The subtleties of social cues aren't always my best event, but saying "with you" seems an obvious thing to avoid. "Sloan and I visited a sick friend from eight until about twenty after nine, then we went to the bookstore where I work and spent a few hours organizing it. We got home about a quarter to one. Why do you ask?"

"Can anyone verify that?"

I finger through my still-damp hair and sigh. "Sure. Sloan and my friend's brother were there for the visit, and there were eight or nine of us cleaning up the bookstore."

Garnet nods. "Very well. Give those names to my man, Anyx, and he'll report back to the council as to whether or not your alibi checks out."

"My alibi for what, exactly?"

"Oh, you wily bitch, you know for what." I follow the vitriolic remark to meet the icy gaze of Droghun rounding the altar. "You did this, and you'll hang for it."

"I haven't got a clue what you're blustering about."

"Lies," he shouts while pointing. "The only thing this bitch spouts is lies."

"Hey, fuckwad," Dillan snaps and calls his dual daggers to his fists. "Call her a bitch again, and you'll spout something other than lies. How far do you think I can fountain your blood across this clearing?"

"Inquiring minds want to know," Calum adds, his bow raised and arrow nocked. "Give it a go and we'll see. Emmet, you can measure the distance."

Sloan and Emmet are tight on my back.

The attention of everyone milling around the site is now firmly locked on the standoff. Just for fun, I release Bruin, and he swirls around the crowd in a gusting gale before materializing between Droghun's Black Dogs and me.

Bruin rears up and lets out a violent roar. Whether they want to or not, all the smug assholes take a step back.

"Do you want to continue with your threats now, fuckwad?" Emmet asks. "Or do you need time to go home and change your underwear?"

Droghun straightens and shrugs his reaction off. "Scare tactics only serve to prove how weak you truly are."

"The skid marks in your drawers only prove how tough you're not."

Garnet's brow creases.

Whatevs. This is us. I raise my hands and reclaim center stage. "You asked me to come. I came. You asked me where I was last night. I answered you. Now, what is this heinous and unforgivable act I supposedly committed?"

Three Black Dog assholes back away from a body on the ground at the head of the altar. His throat is sliced wide, and his expression is frozen in a look of horror.

It all becomes clear. *Surprise.*

"Okay, can I have all the Moon Called and anyone else who can scent lies, bring it in? It's lie detector time." I wave my hands, and Garnet, Anyx, and two other men come close.

Garnet gestures at an older beer-gut-TV-and-recliner-type guy fancied up in an expensive suit. "Stanton reads lies through touch. Are you good with that?"

I hold out my hand and nod. "Allll righty then, from the top. I have never seen the dead guy in my life. I told the truth about where I was last night. And Droghun is acting like a big dick to compensate for his tiny dick. He's painting me as the villain in every crime, and I'm sick of it."

Stanton nods. "All true."

Garnet, Anyx, and the other guy nod too. "All true," Garnet confirms. "We're sorry for the accusations, Miss Cumhaill. You're free to leave."

"Wait!" Droghun snaps and breaks out into a smug grin. "You hexed the altar stone. That's how you did it. Maybe you weren't here, and you didn't know Brahm, but you did this."

I roll my eyes and give Stanton my hand again. "*Annnd*, I also didn't hex, spell, or do anything to the altar stone. But, as a druid, and looking at the damage, I'd make an educated guess that your dead guy was about to slaughter an innocent and his ill intent bounced back. Seems like your sacrifice stone is now a justice stone. I won't pretend to be sad about that, but I didn't do it. And hey, you're a filthy necromancer. You enjoy dead bodies, amirite?"

I check with Garnet and Stanton, and they all nod. "She speaks the truth. You are *again* free to go."

I nod, pat my chest, and when Bruin takes his place, my party puts our hands in, and we flash to the back hall.

"You totes did that, didn't you?" Emmet says.

I grin. "Hells yes, I did, but I only came up with the idea. The level of magic to ricochet their intent back on them is way above my paygrade."

"So, who has that kind of mojo?" Dillan asks.

Sloan frowns. "I assume a Greek god with questionable morals and an attraction to yer sister."

I shrug. "I'm not a snitch, but I must say, your intuitive power never ceases to amaze me, Mackenzie."

———

After heating up and eating my French toast sticks with fruit and plenty of syrup, I grab Gran's book about keeping a healthy and happy sacred grove and haul everyone outside to have some family time.

Sloan is still stewing about me going out on a vigilante run with a Greek god I barely know, so I figure the longer I keep my brothers around as a buffer, the more time he has to realize he has nothing to stew about.

When we've all gathered around, I sit in my wicker basket chair and close the book. "How do we keep our fae warm through a Canadian winter?"

I open the book, and spells fill the pages.

"That's freaking cool," Calum says while reading over my shoulder. "Gran's awesome."

We all smile and nod. She is.

I scan a few of the headings and give the boys the highlights. "It says here we can create a natural hot spring, or a geyser, or seal the canopy with a fae membrane impervious to cold. Anyone have any preferences?"

"Are we late?" Aiden joins us with his two kids. "I thought working on the grove might be a nice way to keep them involved."

I giggle. "And Kinu is at one of her 'alone time' classes, and you've run out of things to occupy them."

"Rude," he complains.

Dillan snorts and bumps knuckles with Jackson. "So, where is Kinu?"

"Pottery. It's glaze and fire day."

I hand Emmet the book and take Meggie from my oldest brother, then sit back in the basket swing and snuggle her. "Okay kids, the same rules apply here as they did in Gran's and Granda's grove. We act nice, and we play nice."

"And I can touch the bunnies?" Jackson asks.

"Do you see bunnies, buddy?" Aiden sets him in the wicker chair opposite mine.

He points. "There's one, and there's one, and...that's not a bunny, and that's a birdy person."

Aiden looks at me, and I nod. "Yep. He sees them."

"Naturally?" Dillan looks put-out. "How? He only has his heritage spark. He hasn't begun to develop his abilities."

I'm not sure if Aiden looks more proud or freaked out. "You're sure?"

Emmet backs me up. "He pointed right at Flopsy and Mopsy, and he knew Nilm was different, then pointed at Nyssa." He scoops up one of our Ostara rabbits and has a few woodland words with him. At the end of the conversation, Emmet nods and sets him in Jackson's lap in the wicker swing. "Mr. Bunny says you can pet him on his fur, but he doesn't like people touching his wings. If you do that or if you're not nice, he's going to fly away and not let you touch him anymore."

Jackson nods and looks somber. "Promise. I be good boy."

"I'll watch him," Aiden says.

"No, I'll watch him." Sloan sits in front of the swing. "I can see the animals so there's that. And I can see if they're getting stressed."

Emmet nods. "Okay, Sloan and Fi are watching the monkeys. The rest of us are winterizing this forest. I like the sound of a hot spring. Shall we vote?"

I roll my eyes. "I hope fae aren't easily shocked. I have a feeling our grove is about to become clothing optional."

An hour later, Da gets home from doing paperwork at the station, and the grove loses all interest for the kids. Aiden heads inside with them to help with hot chocolate with marshmallows all around, and I join the winterizing brigade.

"How's it going?"

Pip climbs down from one of her favorite trees and holds her arms up.

Pip and her mate Nilm are *brunaidh*, or brownies, and are similar in size and body to a two-year-old child. Except they have wide-globe eyes and antennae that bob when they walk. "Are you getting warmer, sweet girl?"

She chatters something to Emmet, and he responds. Pip grins and presses my cheeks together while chattering happily.

"She says for you to feel how toasty warm her hands are. Yes, they are very thankful to have heat and are blessed to have such a wonderful host family." He laughs as she says something else and nods. "She wonders if we have any of those salty treats we brought out for movie night."

"Pretzels? No, sorry, sweetie. I don't—"

"Did somebody ask for pretzels?"

The whole group tenses and I step to block any bravado about to be thrown around. "It's fine, boys. This is Nikon."

"Your Greek threesome candidate?" Dillan eyes him up and down. "Not bad."

I facepalm and shift closer to Sloan. "I never said that."

Dillan chuckles. "I wasn't talking about you, Fi. I meant Calum and Kev."

Okay, at least I'm not the only one blushing now.

"You're an ass, D." Calum shakes his head and offers the newcomer his hand. "You'll have to excuse my brother. We Cumhaills tend to omit the stage where we filter our first thought."

Nikon shakes his hand and smiles. "It's what first drew me to your sister. In a room full of pompous asses and powerful people, she said all the things people kept to themselves."

I snort. "Most people find that rude and annoying."

"I'm not most people." He tosses Emmet two bags of pretzels. Then his interest moves from me to Sloan and his smile broadens. "You must be the boyfriend. Fi mentioned you were tall, dark, and handsome."

"No. I didn't."

"Well, you *thought* it."

"As you pilfered through my mind."

"I was bored, and you were the only bright and shiny thing in the room. And, I didn't pilfer. Your thoughts for him are front and center."

"And yet, ye still made yer offer to hook up," Sloan challenges.

He chuckles. "No. It was when I brought up having some fun that her mind flipped solidly to you. I didn't have a chance. Sorry. After thousands of years, my social skills have suffered. I asked, and she promptly declined. Then we moved on to solving a few of life's injustices."

True story. "Is that why you're here? You heard about what happened at the druid stones?"

He surveys the crowd and seems hesitant. "Yeah. The Guild is in a tizzy about Droghun and what happened."

I wave away his concern. "It's cool. My brothers know we were co-conspirators and hexed the altar stone. Apparently, I'm easy to read."

His brow pinches. "Didn't you say your whole family works for the police department?"

Dillan chuckles. "There is the law, and then there is justice. Seriously, an eye for an eye spell won't get you in trouble here. Especially when the dead guy was obvi about to slit someone else's throat."

Nikon assesses the rest of them and nods. "So, it worked as you wanted?"

"Yeah. I doubt anyone will be volunteering to run a sacrificial ritual at the stones anytime soon."

"Mischief managed." He holds up his palm, and I can't leave him hanging. I slap him a high-five even at the risk of earning me a scowl from Sloan.

"Kids," Da shouts from the back porch of the house. "Get yer asses in here and join the hunt. Jackson's run off with the marshmallows again. If ye don't find him, there'll be none left for ye."

Emmet, Callum, and Dillan take off like a shot.

Sloan folds the blanket and places it back into the swing seat. When he straightens, he gestures toward the house. "Shall we? There's hot cocoa gettin' cold."

I meet his gaze to double-check. "Yeah? You're okay with Nikon joining in?"

He offers Nikon his hand. "I can't blame any man for floatin' the idea by ye. Like he said, he asked, and ye promptly declined. End. Of."

I slide in for a hug and kiss his cheek. "Point for you, Mackenzie."

He squeezes me in a side hug and gestures toward the house. "The way I figure it Nikon, after two thousand years, ye might even be ready for an afternoon with her family."

I snort. "True story. A Cumhaill event is not for the faint of heart."

CHAPTER TWENTY-TWO

My family makes me proud, as always. They welcome Nikon in, and the hilarity ensues over hot chocolate and Baileys, the latter growing in steadily heavier pours as the afternoon passes. Aiden takes the kids home after Kinu's pottery class, Dillan and Emmet head upstairs to get a few hours of sleep before they start nights, and Kevin swings by to pick up Calum for their Saturday afternoon plans.

"This was fun," Nikon says a couple of hours later. He stands and eases around where Bruin takes up most of the floor. "Thank you for including me."

I'm more than a little bloaty from chocolaty bliss, and I have a lovely, warm spin going on in my head. Whatevs. "S'all good. You stood up well under the Cumhaill scrutiny. You should be proud."

Nikon laughs but then sobers. "No. Seriously, Red. This was the most fun I've had in centuries."

I hug him and smile. "Anytime you need a dose of loud, nosy, and inappropriate, pop over. We've got you covered."

He nods, and fist bumps Sloan. "Thanks again, Irish."

Sloan dips his chin. "Good to meet ye."

Unlike how Sloan *poofs* out when he portals, Nikon kinda

snaps out. It's like the air snaps its fingers and in the wake of the crack of the noise, he's gone.

"Alone at last." I flop on the couch.

Sloan sits with me, and I lay my feet on the coffee table and lace my fingers with his. "You did good, Surly. Thanks for always being the better man."

He squeezes my fingers and brings my knuckles to his kiss. "It's easy. Yer the most loyal and honest person I've ever met. I trust that ye'll tell me if and when there's something I need to know about other men makin' advances. Ye said Nikon's a good guy, and he obviously is. Yer first impression of people hasn't been wrong yet."

I let my head fall back and stare at the painted tin on the ceiling. "What time is it?"

"Almost five. Should we think about dinner?"

"I'm not hungry. Are you?"

He laughs. "Hardly. We've done nothing but fill our faces all day."

"True story."

The ring of my doorbell has me sitting up. "Are you expecting anyone?"

Sloan laughs. "This is your house. Who would *I* be expecting?"

"Good point. Okay, I'll get it."

Bruin dematerializes from where he's lounging on the floor and flutters in my chest as he settles. I pat my sternum and head for the door. When I open up, Anyx is standing on my porch. "Miss Cumhaill. If you're free, Garnet Grant would like to see you."

"Yeah? What's up?"

"That's for him to explain. I brought a car. If you would."

I eye the black Navigator sitting at the curb and even through the fog of afternoon drinking, my Spidey-senses are tingling. "Okay, let me grab my jacket and my purse."

I stroll through the house to the back hall and get ready to leave. After tying the belt of my jacket, I loop my purse over my head. "One sec. Let me turn off the kettle."

In the kitchen, I pull out my phone and text Garnet. *Anyx is here to pick me up. What's up? Something feels off.*

Here where?

My front door.

Sloan finishes with his shoes and grabs a thick sweater that he pulls on. *Hello*, that's a good look for him. "All set?"

"Uh... Yeah, I guess."

Sloan's attention falls serious. He steps between me and the front door and magic snaps in the air around us. He pegs me with a look. "Speak freely. What is it?"

I unzip my purse and look down as if I'm searching for something. "Deja vu. Garnet was supposedly sending for me the night Liam and I got jumped at the back of Shenanigans. Fool me once. Fool me twice. You know?"

"What do you want to do?"

"Stall. I texted Garnet."

The wooden floor creaks as we head back to the front of the house. The more I focus, the more I know the squirreling in my belly is more than too much hot chocolate. Whatever this is, it's not Garnet.

He always calls or texts me when he needs me.

Sloan steps outside first, and Anyx backs up enough for me to get my keys out and lock up. When that's done, my palm warms against the doorjamb.

Ward of Protection. "All set." I point toward the awaiting truck. "Lead the way."

When Anyx turns to descend the steps, another Anyx pops in beside me with Thaor.

I point at the one heading down the steps.

The new Anyx sees the other Anyx and does a flying tackle off the porch. He takes him down in a bone-jarring thump to the ground, and they begin an all-out brawl on my front lawn.

I must be drunker than I thought because I press my fingers under my tongue and let out a whistle that could shatter eardrums. "Huge points for air on your takeoff, dude."

"What's going on?" Janine picks up her barking mop-head and shouts over from her porch next door.

I point at the two men pounding on each other in the grass. "They're fighting."

Skippy is yipping his fool head off under her arm, and she pats him. "Are you drunk? It's not even dinner time."

I glance at Sloan and frown. "I fail to see what that has to do with them fighting."

Janine scowls. "Are they twins?"

The barking makes it hard to think. I squint and try to tell them apart. "You'd think so, wouldn't you? Let's say yes."

Thaor strides past the fight and is speed-stalking straight for the idling truck. The driver must see him coming because he peels out with the pedal to the floor and lays a giant black skid trail in front of my house.

"That maniac is going to kill someone," Janine shouts.

"At least it won't be me." I flash a thumbs-up, but I don't think she sees the humor.

"Should I call the police?"

Thaor jumps into the mix and gets an elbow to the nose. Blood sprays in the air and I wince in sympathy. "No. I'm sure they'll sort it out. You know how brothers are."

"My brothers would never act like—"

The Anyx bookends flash out, and everything falls silent.

"Where did they go?" Janine points, her mouth hanging open, her face screwed up. "They just—"

"Crap on a cracker."

"I've got this." Sloan *poofs* from my porch to hers and reforms behind her.

She screams. Skippy loses his shit. Then a ball of white fuzz bolts off the porch and heads straight toward the forest beside my house.

"Skippy!" Janine shouts.

"Feckin' hell." Sloan grabs her and knocks her out.

"What the hell?" Dillan snaps.

I ignore Dillan, jump off the porch, and race toward the wild space at the end of our street. Before I get halfway across the lawn, a coyote zips out of the trees and snatches Skippy up.

"Oh, nononono. That's not good."

Dillan catches up to me. "What should we do?"

"Any chance we can save the dog?"

Dillan blinks at me. "All signs point to no."

"Shit. Okay, then I'll help Sloan with Janine. You go back to bed."

"Did I see Skippy get taken by a coyote?" Mrs. Graham asks from across the road.

"Yeah. It happened so fast. Sad, eh?"

"If you say so. In my day, a dog came up higher than your shin." I know where she's coming from, and yeah, coyotes gotta eat, but I feel totes responsible for this one. "Hey, Dillan. Lookin' good, sexy boy."

Yep, Dillan's in his boxers on the front lawn. "Hey, Mrs. Graham. Thanks for noticing."

He's still tossing her a wave when I turn him around and push him toward the porch. "Stop flirting with old ladies."

He snorts. "Hey, I'm all about community service. Besides, cougars are in."

"She's not a cougar. She's a sabertooth tiger."

"Ouch. Harsh."

By the time I get Dillan back in the house and climb Janine's porch, Sloan has her sitting up, and Mark's coming out. "What happened?"

"Skippy got away from Janine and ran off. I'm sorry. A coyote got him, and she fainted."

"A coyote?"

"Mrs. Graham saw it." Yeah, I totally pass the buck on that one but don't even care.

Mark takes Sloan's place and helps Janine to the porch swing. "We were reading in the paper last week about another case where the coyote took a dog right off the front lawn while the owner stood on the porch."

I nod. "It's a thing."

"I…I can't believe it." Janine's still visibly foggy from Sloan clearing her memory of two shifters and a wizard teleporting off my front lawn. "Why would Skippy run off?"

"No idea. It was a cray-cray moment. Maybe you should go in and lie down. It's been a shock."

Mark nods and pulls Janine under his arm, then ushers her into the house.

When Sloan and I get back to my house, I sit on the top step and drop my face into my hands. "What a shit show. I can't believe I killed the neighbor's dog."

Sloan groans. "Ye didn't, and ye know it. That was beyond yer control and a circle of life moment. I agree with the shit show part though. That was classic Cumhaill chaos."

I run my fingers through my hair, shake that off, and stand. "We'll worry about that later. Right now, I want to go to Garnet's and find out who that guy was and check on how Myra's doing."

"Then I'm going with ye." Da comes down the stairs. "I'll not have ye goin' to that man's home like yer a friend of his. If ye don't have the sense to keep him at arm's length, I'll have to do it for ye."

I fight the urge to stomp my boot against the floor but settle for crossing my arms with a bit more steam than usual. "Da, I'm grown and capable of watching my back."

"I'm goin', young lady, and I'll not hear another word about it."

"Why aren't you at work? Don't you have a shift in the stakeout van tonight?"

"Och, the stakeout got canceled on account of a cross-gang shootout. The men we were watchin' got themselves in more hot water than catchin' our notice. That case is closed."

"Oh, sorry. You spent a lot of time working on taking those guys down."

Da shrugs. "Sometimes they take themselves down too. No bother. Besides. We're one step closer to riddin' the city of the men who killed yer brother."

"I won't mourn them, that's for sure."

"Me either." Da grabs a nylon windbreaker off the hall rack and pulls it on. "So, that frees up my night, and I'll be happy to escort ye to Garnet Grant's."

"Awesome. Just please don't get standoffish. I'm trying to build a relationship with him and the Lakeshore Guild that doesn't put us in the crosshairs."

Da arches a russet brow. "I'll try to contain myself. Ye do remember that it was me who taught ye the art of makin' nice with people, don't ye?"

"Yeah, and you also taught us how to get behind an unsuspecting opponent and choke them out with a sleeper hold."

"Another valuable life skill."

I eye him and wag my finger. "Play nice, Da. I mean it. If ye can't behave, I'll not trust ye to take ye back."

Da chuckles. "I think an extremely wise man might've said that a couple o' times or so."

I take my father's hand, then hold out my other hand to Sloan. "Ready when you are, hotness."

Sloan squeezes my fingers. "Aye, blossom. As ye wish."

"What happened?" Garnet asks as his men usher us into his compound home. He's coming out from the back bedrooms, and he looks a little more frazzled than usual. He sees my father with us and nods. "Niall, welcome. Come. Eat. Make yourselves at home, and Fiona can start at the top and tell us her latest tale."

I scan the buffet spread laid out, and it blows my mind. Does he always have this much food set out? Does he feed his whole pride of feline friends?

"I think you got the whole story. Anyx One showed up on my front porch to pick me up and said you needed me. I didn't like the vibe, so I texted. Then Anyx Two came with Thaor to stop whatever was happening."

"How'd you know it wasn't me?" Anyx asks.

"He didn't feel like you. He lacked your swarthy feline swagger." Anyx's mouth quirks up at the side, but my father seems less amused. I ignore his arching brow and continue. "Thanks for the save, by the way. Next time, try not to flash out in front of the muggles next door."

Garnet gives Anyx a scathing glare but his second doesn't respond in any way.

"But ye got yer man, right?" Sloan asks.

Anyx nods. "We're interrogating him, but he's still wearing my face and hasn't said anything so we haven't been able to identify him."

"What sects do ye have in yer community that can take another man's form?"

Garnet points at the food and hands me a plate. How sweet. He's learned I never say no to food twice. "Witches, mages, and wizards could do it. A few fae species could cast a glamor. The Greek could do it. We have a few followers of Freja who could."

I grab a croissant and a stack of roasted turkey. "Nikon was drinking with us all afternoon and has no beef with me. I can sense fae glamors, so I don't think it's anyone from that crowd.

My guess is we're dealing with the wizards who've been harassing Myra, or the witches."

Garnet frowns. "Why did you add witches to the list?"

"Um, because witches be bitches."

Garnet ignores the wisdom of my words and finishes his drink. "If you gentlemen will excuse us for a moment, I think Fi might like to take her snack into the back to eat. There's someone eager to see her."

I finish hogging all the specialty cheeses and squeal. "Myra's awake? You didn't tell me."

"Just now, and I just did."

I take my plate, grab a can of ginger ale from the ice bucket, and follow his lead. "You made my night, Garnet. Seriously."

He chuckles. "I had nothing to do with it."

I follow Garnet to the back and find Myra sitting up in bed. I rush inside, set my plate on the dresser, and jump onto the mattress with her. "You're here! You're back!"

Myra giggles and hugs me. "Thanks to you, I hear."

I ease back and take a closer look at her. "Are you all right? Did the antidote fix you up completely?"

"Completely and totally. I thought I'd have a shower and get back to the world."

"Shower, yes. Back to the world, no." The growl in Garnet's voice leaves no confusion as to his opinion about that. "You're my guest until we get a handle on who's involved in this demon-raising plan."

Myra stares past me. I'm not sure what unspoken conversation they have, but Garnet wins. She rolls her eyes and points at my plate. "What have you got on there? I'm starving."

"I *asked* you if you wanted anything," Garnet protests.

"I didn't then. I do now."

He huffs, but there's no real heat to it. "I'll make you a plate. Chat amongst yourselves, ladies."

I wait until Garnet leaves before I burst out in a fit of giggles. "Ohmygosh he's so cute when he's all growly and protective."

Myra rolls her eyes. "I know. Stupid lion."

"So things are good then? Between the two of you?" I lean back and reclaim my plate and my soda and get us started on the gossip session.

Myra rips off the end of the croissant and snags some turkey. "He told me what you did, clearing our grief. That was sweet of you."

"Sorry. I know that maybe I shouldn't have—not without your permission at least—but I wanted you to feel better, and I could feel the pain weighing you both down. I'm sorry about your son."

She smiles. "Me too. Grant was the light of our lives, and when we lost him, it consumed everything. I couldn't look at Garnet without seeing my little boy, and Garnet couldn't look at me without taking on the guilt of losing him."

"What happened?" I raise my hand. "Sorry. That's none of my business."

She shakes her head. "It's okay. Sometimes hybrid Moon Called don't survive their transition from human to their base animal. Grant's mixed blood brought complications, and we lost him. It happens. That's why Moon Called don't often mate with other sects. It was doomed from the start."

"But you love each other."

She nods. "Sometimes love isn't enough."

I finish a wedge of cheese and shrug. "Sometimes it is."

Myra blushes. "Don't get ahead of yourself. Garnet and I are ancient history. Nothing to see here."

I snort and swallow a chunk of cheese. "Keep telling yourself that."

She grabs another wad of meat and pops it in her mouth. After she's done chewing, she grips my hand. "Seriously, Fi, you're a lifesaver, and I love you for it."

"Do you know who all the players are? Do you think Garnet

and the Guild can round them up and figure out what this demon resurrection stupidity is about?"

"I told him what I know."

"Which you should've done weeks before now." Garnet returns with a plate heaped with food. "Maybe this could've been avoided if you trusted me enough to take care of things."

Myra reaches for the next plate of food and wrinkles her nose. "You don't have to take care of things for me, Gar. I'm an independent female."

"You're a *stubborn* female, and you miss the point. I wouldn't take care of things because I have to. I want to."

"So cute. The big, scary lion man is a pussy cat in love."

Garnet growls at me. "Why do you think you can get away with saying shit like that to me? A week ago, you accused me of being the head of the Toronto crime syndicate."

I snort and grab a couple of grapes from Myra's plate. "No. I told you my *father* said that. I've always seen the true heart of the lion."

He growls again.

Myra giggles. "I told you she's special."

"She's a thorn in my paw."

"No, I'm the little mouse who took the thorn out of your paw, remember? *Squeak, squeak.*"

Garnet chuckles. "So you say. If that were true, why have I never had so many problems and so many bodies within the Guild membership? Ever?"

"You're blaming me?'

"If the massacre fits… Oh, and speaking of massacres, how did you deny the responsibility of cursing the altar stone and get away without getting caught in the lie?"

"Because I didn't lie. I didn't curse the stone."

Garnet frowns. "Please don't lie to me."

"I'm not lying. Hypothetically, it might've been my idea, and I might *know* who did it—but it wasn't me."

"A fine point of distinction but an important one." He relaxes a little.

"It's just desserts as far as I'm concerned."

"It really does offend you, doesn't it?"

"They call themselves druids, but druids are keepers of nature. They slaughter innocents for power. They harness fae creatures and siphon power, desiccate forests, and suck living things dry of their life forces. That's not being a druid—it's the exact opposite. And then, to take a sacred site like the Drombeg Stone Circle and use it for ritual sacrifice? It's disgusting. Seriously. Yes—it offends me."

Garnet nods. "Point taken, Lady Druid. Consider your objections noted."

I look from him to Myra and back. "Sorry. A little of the old Irish ire leaked out on that one."

Myra chuckles. "Don't be sorry, duck. The Lakeshore Guild could use a few more ethically passionate people. It's gotten a bit heavy with complacent dead wood over the decades. Present company excepted."

"Speaking of…" Garnet gestures at the door. "It's time we pay a visit to the West Village Wizards and get to the bottom of things. I assumed you'd like to come along."

"Yes, please. You assumed right." I kiss Myra's cheek and roll off the bed. "Feel better."

She lays back and gathers her plate into her lap. "I do, Fi. Better than I have in years. Be careful. The men who did this to me are a nasty, vile bunch."

I cast a backward glance as I join Garnet. "Don't worry. We've got this."

CHAPTER TWENTY-THREE

Garnet, Anyx, Sloan, Da, and I pile into Garnet's big black truck and head out. Another truckload of men in another big black truck pulls in behind us as we drive away.

"Why are we going the route of old-school travel?"

Garnet turns in the shotgun seat and smiles. "The West Village Wizards have their entire community warded in a magical web of protection. If we try to transport into their territory, we might get thrown back out, or we might get inside the perimeter. From there, we'd have to walk for blocks. It's safer to drive."

"Cool. Good to know."

"I don't suppose ye'd share the neighborhoods and boundaries of the empowered ones in Toronto, would ye?" Da asks.

Garnet shifts his gaze to my father. "Why do you ask?"

He tilts his head, and I'm happy to see he's not looking hostile or offensive. He has his cop "problem solving" face on. "I was thinkin' the West Village has had several public disturbance calls, and there's an uptick in misdemeanor complaints especially around Hallowe'en and the Sabbat holidays. It makes more sense now that I know there is a coven of wizards there."

"What good would knowing the locations of the other sects and guild members do you?"

"From a policin' standpoint, if I knew some of the key players and where they circulated, I might be able to shift the attention of beat cops and investigations that fall under yer jurisdiction back to the human issues and stop the waste of resources. I expect I wasted the past week in the back of a van surveillin' a group the human police had no business tryin' to take down. Am I right? Were Issac North and the men workin' out of Ainslie Street Automotive your problem?"

He nods. "A rugaru nest that delves in gang behavior: guns, drugs, and girls. There was an incident this morning."

Da nods. "My people were the ones sittin' in a van in a parkin' garage across the road for the past week. And my son spent five months undercover investigatin' them, which indirectly got him killed. I'll not let that be for nothin'."

"Understood. Yes, I can certainly give you a bubble map of who's where and what they're into. Nothing specific, of course."

"Still, it might give me an idea of what's happenin' on the preternatural scale of crime in the city."

Huh, who would've thunk it? Da is initiating a cooperative goal with Garnet Grant. Go, Da. "So were the people who killed Brendan not human? Did he get caught up in something on Garnet's side of the fence?"

Da frowns. "I'm still workin' through that, *mo chroi*. Don't worry. I won't stop until everyone who contributed to yer brother's death is off the streets."

I sit back in my seat and stare out my window. I'm not sure how I feel about that. Why did I feel more at peace thinking Brendan simply stepped into a bad situation caused by a bad man? Does it matter if that man was part of the empowered community or if he was working with or for them?

I still have so many emotions twisted around Brendan's death. It'll take more than a few months to sort through them.

Sloan takes my hand and squeezes my fingers.

I squeeze back.

The truck pulls to a stop along the curb, and we prepare to get out. The West Village is a busy shopping district in the city. It encompasses a tight corridor of over four hundred restaurants, shops, and services along Bloor Street West from High Park to Jane Street. It's also one of the city's historic areas, much of it dating back to the nineteenth century.

"We're across the road." Garnet points at the brick building on the opposite side of the street.

"A funeral home. That's comforting." I look at Sloan and my father and shrug. "What? There's no way I was the only one thinking that."

"Not to worry, Lady Druid. This is a polite visit to test the waters and discuss plans and expectations."

I chuckle. "Like, hey wizards. Whatever your plans are to release an evil demon of the Hell Realm, we expect you to stop doing it."

Garnet nods. "Something like that. Perhaps let me do the talking. We're going for subtle inference and a diplomatic meeting of the minds."

"What? I can't be diplomatic?" Sloan and Da both flash looks so hilarious I crack up. "Okay, fine. No Oscar de la Hoya impressions. You won't even know I'm here."

Garnet gestures for Anyx to get the door to the entrance. "Follow my lead."

Da scowls. "We'll do that. Show us how it's done."

The electronic door chime announces our arrival and brings a lanky skinhead in a silver suit out of the offices to greet us. "Grand Governor," he says in a raspy voice I recognize. "My sentries said I could expect a visit from you, but I told them they must be mistaken. You're far too courteous to arrive in my place of business unannounced and uninvited."

Garnet lifts one shoulder in a shrug. "I suppose it's one of the privileges of being Grand Governor, Salem. I can go wherever the fuck I want whenever I want to."

I bark a laugh, then cover my mouth and cover my gaffe with a cough. "Sorry. My bad. Spit went down the wrong pipe. Don't mind me. I'm not even here."

Garnet flashes me a look and holds out his hand. "Let's start with introductions, shall we? Salem, you'll remember Lady Cumhaill from the luncheon last week. This is her father, Niall Cumhaill, and their associate, Sloan Mackenzie. Everyone, this is Salem Markdale, High Priest of the Toronto Wizarding Council and Guild Governor of Wizards."

As soon as Garnet places Salem at the luncheon, I connect the dots. "Oh, you're my heckler. The one shouting snide remarks the whole time I was talking."

Garnet leans forward. "What aspect of diplomacy escapes you? Should we have read the definition aloud before coming inside?"

I hold up my palms. "In my defense, I haven't drawn blood. I didn't even say he acted like a total douche-canoe at the meeting. I'm totes being nice."

"I'd say ye must excuse my daughter, Mr. Markdale," Da joins the convo, "but honestly, I taught her to speak her truth, so perhaps I'm to blame if her lack of delicacy offends. She also has an uncanny knack for sizin' people up, so if she found yer behavior wantin' at the luncheon, odds are, she has good reason."

Aw, thanks, Da.

Garnet seems to agree but still holds himself to a level of formality he saves for Guild-y things. "Perhaps we'll all be more comfortable if we come inside to talk."

Salem raises a hand to stop the inflow of traffic and steps to block us. "Now is not a good time, I'm afraid. We have a private ceremony going on, and my clients deserve to mourn their loss in peace."

My shield weighs in on that and I wriggle a little under the sudden discomfort. *Bruin, it's recon time, buddy. Something's not right. Be careful though. We're in the wizard's den. I have no idea what they might be able to do to you.*

On it. Don't worry about me, Red. I live for danger.

I release my bear to go check things out and tap Sloan's shoulder. "Would you mind scratching my back? It's crazy itchy all of a sudden."

Da and Sloan both clue in immediately. "It is, is it?" He scrubs his nails down my back. "Perhaps ye should take off yer jacket and hang it on the rack there." He points at an open closet, and I follow his suggestion.

"There's no need to get comfortable," Salem protests. "If your back hurts, you should likely go have it checked out."

"Oh, I'm checking it out." I smile. "It'll take a bear moment to investigate and figure out what's going on."

Garnet and Anyx are both fully caught up with that comment, and I feel better when the good guys are all on the same page. Garnet offers me a smile and turns back to our host. "While Miss Cumhaill sorts things out, perhaps we could address a few recent events I've found troubling. Like the allegations that you and some of your people pressured Myra D'anys for information about demon resurrection."

Salem stiffens and slides his hand into his pocket. A moment later, the front entranceway of the funeral home floods with men in suits. "I think it's time to leave, Governor. If someone filed a complaint, I have twenty-four hours to counter the charge."

It's happening now, Red. There are a dozen men in robes in the basement, blood sacrifice made, sigils painted all over the place, and the book on the altar is open to a spell of resurrection.

"Oh, shit."

Everyone turns to me. My mind is spinning, looking for a

clever way to convey this. *I give up.* "They're performing the ritual downstairs. Sacrifice made. Bad mojo brewing."

The fight breaks out in a flurry and Bruin takes form at my side. My bear loves to beat the living snot out of people, and I love it when he's happy.

I call my armor forward, and when Birga manifests in my hand, I choke up on the shaft to compensate for the close quarters. *"Bestial Strength."* I raise my arms to block the crack of a bat to Birga's staff. The vibration of the connection rattles my bones from hands to wrists to elbows.

My armor saves me from the pain of the blow, and I take advantage of the moment to bring my knee up as hard and fast as I can. As my attacker groans and curls forward, I grab the bat and toss it away.

"Always with a man's knackers," Sloan calls while in full swing of his hand-to-hand. "Yer obsessed."

I ignore the jibe, pleased when Garnet's men burst through the door to join us.

Salem is a slippery snake and slithers through the crowd. I give chase and Garnet is hot on my heels. I'm only seconds behind him as I round the corner and run down an empty hall.

I pull up fast, searching for any sign of where he went. "I lost him. How could I lose him?"

Garnet curses. "I have his scent. He should be here."

I lean back to the other hall and shout, "Bruin, I need you to show me where."

A moment later my bear barrels down the hall with a wizard hanging out both sides of his mouth. He looks like a happy dog running with a stick.

Follow me, Red.

He doesn't stop when he gets to the end of the hall. He drops his head and plows through. The wallpapered drywall doesn't stand a chance—it swings wide to grant him access.

This way.

I run full-throttle behind Bruin, and if we weren't trying to stop these dickwads from unleashing minions of evil into my city, this might be fun.

For once, I'm on the offensive.

It's new, and it's way more entertaining.

By the time we arrive to break up the party, Salem has the book in his hand and prattles off some ancient tongue as fast as he can spew the words.

Bruin cuts a swath through the dozen men coming at me, but I'm not sure how we'll ever get through the blockade in time.

Garnet roars behind me, and the vicious snarl scares the bejeezus outta me. I pat my chest and try to get reacquainted with oxygen. "Peed a little there. Not gonna lie."

The shield on my back lights on fire and the fact that the exhumed tattoo of darkness on my thigh weighs in is troubling. Static has my hair rising into the air around my face, and the air over the altar starts crackling with magic.

"*True Trajectory.*" I raise Birga over my head and spear-chuck her into the air. She flies fast and true with the power of my *Bestial Strength* behind her.

Salem stands at the altar, his hands resting on the book before him, his eyes down, his lips moving. He doesn't see the green of the Connemara marble until Birga's spear-tip pierces his chest.

The force of the hit knocks him off his feet and pins him to the wall three feet behind him. The *thud* of him hitting the concrete block is gratifying. The look on his face is one of total shock. He's locked in place with Birga's tip buried in the wall.

Good girl.

Garnet roars, and I see why. The crackling air above the altar swirls and whistles with kinetic energy out of control. I back away from the lightning show, the shrill screech of whatever was starting to come through echoing its displeasure.

I'm on the opposite side of the room from the exit, and things are getting wild. I raise my arms to block my face while pushing forward, but the force of the magical fallout is too much to get through.

"Fiona, get down."

I don't argue with Da. Some commands in life you obey instinctually. When my father shouts at me in that tone of voice, it doesn't even occur to me not to do exactly as he says.

The air isn't quite as chaotic on the floor, but there's still no way for me to get out of here. This place will implode or explode, or something equally bad and I have a front-row seat to Ground Zero.

"Ye need a lift?" Sloan *poofs* in beside me.

"My hero." I throw my arms around him, and a second later, we're upstairs with Da and Garnet.

"Thank the goddess," Da gasps and pulls me away from Sloan to hug me.

"Her and Sloan Mackenzie." I ease back. "Okay, next problem. How do we stop the Hell vortex from swallowing up our city?"

By the blank looks coming back at me, I'm not enthusiastic about the next five minutes of my life. They might be the last five minutes, but whatevs. Semantics.

"Is there someone we can get down here to help?" Da asks Garnet.

"Not that I can think of."

"I have an idea." I pull out my phone and call up my contacts.

"Who ye goin' to call?" Sloan asks.

"Ghostbusters?" I ignore the looks. "Sorry, it's the pressure, and it had to be said." With the urgency of the situation, I get straight to texting.

Hey. You any good with patching the veil between our realm and Hell to keep demons from invading and our city from exploding? Just wondering.

Hypothetically or actually?

Actually.

Nikon appears in the huddle wearing a cosmic bedsheet with

a kitten licking a slice of pizza. The length of colorful cotton is gripped tight at his hip, but other than that, the dude's in the buff. "What the fuck, Fi? Can't you get through a week without blowing up the city?"

I hold up my hands. "Totes not my fault. Is this a toga fail or did we catch you in a moment?"

"The second. And it was a very good moment, so what do you need?"

I point toward the basement. "I hoped you could *deus ex machina* us out of this little problem we're having with the fabric of our realm in the basement."

Nikon blinks. "I'm an *immortal*, not a god. Why can't people get that straight?"

"Well, you have more juice than everyone else in the city. That's why you get the head seat at the table."

He frowns. With the wave of his hand, the sheet is gone, and he's wearing a badass, red leather devil costume. "Fine. For you, Fi, I'll see what I can do."

"You rock, Greek. What's with the tights and horns?"

He flashes me a grin. "If somebody slips through the rift, maybe I'll look like the home team and not get fried."

I raise my thumb. "Yeah, very convincing. Nailed it."

Nikon snaps off, and Garnet shakes his head. "I've known Nikon Tsambikos for over forty years, and he's never spoken more than ten words to me in all that time combined. How is it that he's your beck and call boy in a week?"

"Ha! First, he's not my call boy—I said no. Second, he's nice. He's bored with an unending life, and for some reason, he finds me not boring."

Da side-arm hugs me and kisses my temple. "If there's one thing in life yer not, *mo chroi*, it's boring."

Nikon snaps back, and he has a regular outfit on and the demon spellbook in his hand. "Mischief managed."

"See, I knew you could stop the apocalypse."

He snorts and hands me the book. "No god powers needed."

"Then how?"

He holds up the book. "Can you read, Nikon? Why, yes I can, Fi."

I scan the spell, and none of it is in English or legible. "What does it say?"

"You don't read Enochian?"

I giggle. "I love how you say that with surprise in your voice and a straight face."

"Okay, then, I'll give you a pass. There's a reversal clause at the bottom of the let's open a rift to Hell spell. I followed the instructions, and our seams are sealed. Done deal. Now, can I get back to my evening?"

I bow. "You win the day, dude. As you were."

CHAPTER TWENTY-FOUR

"Sorry, Red. Ye need to wake up."

My eyes pry open one at a time, and I wait for the fog to clear. It's morning...the smell of bacon makes my tummy grumble...there's male rough-housing downstairs. Bruin is sitting at the end of my bed and has his head flopped on the mattress. "Hey, buddy. What's up? You just getting in? What do you need?"

"Yer hurtin', Red. I don't like it. Ye need to see to it."

I sit up and wince as I swing my legs off the side of the bed. My thigh is throbbing, and yeah, I need to have Sloan look at it again. "It hurt last night after the battle with the wizards, but I was too tired to worry about it."

The floor is cold on my bare feet, and I toe my favorite Costco slippers closer and slide my feet in. Standing up, I shuffle over to the mirror and shuck my flannel pajama pants down my—"Holy shitters. That is *not* good."

The flesh that briefly hosted the *Eochair Prana* is gray and looks like it's dying. When I prod it with my fingers, a layer flakes off as if my thigh is shale and not skin. "*Really* not good."

I head over to my door, open it a crack, and stick my head out. "Sloan? Are you around?"

"He's in the basement playing air-hockey with Emmet," Da yells up. "Do ye need him?"

"Uh, yep. Can you send him up, please?"

"Will do. Are ye all right, Fi?"

"I think so. I need Sloan's opinion on something."

I'm staring at the mirror when the footsteps on the stairs tell me I'm getting more than the man I asked for. I roll my eyes, but it's no surprise. There's nothing in this house that isn't everyone's business.

"Knock-knock." Sloan does a knock and walk. "Finally decided to join—oh, Jaysus-fuck, Fi." He crosses the floor in two long strides and drops to his knees. "Why didn't ye tell me it was givin' ye trouble?"

"That's what I'm doing."

The peanut gallery arrives, and a round of gasping inhales and muttered curses light off as my father and brothers catch a glimpse of the macabre peep show.

Dillan scrunches up his face and winces. "Dayam, that's gnarly, Fi. What's happening?"

"I'm trying to figure that out."

Sloan pulls my pajama bottoms down and frees my legs. Then he scoops me off my feet and lays me on my bed. "Calum, fetch me the black kit tucked at the end of my bag. Someone text Dora and ask if she's at her apartment and if I can come to get her."

The urgent aggression in Sloan's movements is putting me on edge. "Dude, your bedside manner isn't comforting. Aren't you supposed to fake it and make me feel better?"

"What is it, son?" Da asks. "Is it that damnable book?"

"Aye, it most certainly is." He reaches back and takes the toiletries kit from Calum and lays it on the bed beside me. "Where's Beauty?"

"She's here." Dillan grabs my spellbook off the cushion on my window seat and hands it over.

Sloan flips through it.

I admire how he knows right where to find what he wants. Most of the time, I'm still exploring the pages, trying to figure out what spells I could use for things.

Emmet hangs up his phone and leans against the footboard of my bed. "Dora says she's at the soup kitchen next door. You can take me with you, and I'll fill in on the serving line while you need her here."

Sloan nods and holds his finger up at me. "Don't move. I mean it. I'll be right back."

Da moves in and sits on the bed. He grabs my hand, and the worry in his gaze makes my eyes sting. "She'll not move an inch. We'll make sure of it. Safe home, son, and be quick about it."

Sloan grabs Emmet's wrist, and the two of them *poof* out.

The rest of us sit in silence and wait. It feels like the room is holding its breath until he gets back. He's only gone maybe two minutes, but it feels like an eternity.

Dora's fashionable in pink camo pants and an angora sweater. A perfectly sensible soup kitchen server outfit. She looks at my leg and pushes out her glossy lips. "Oh, girlie, I'm so sorry."

Dora's sympathy brings on the sting of tears, and I have to blink fast to keep from crying. "Not your fault. Eyes forward. How do we fix it?"

Sloan is doing his healer thing, and Dora climbs onto my covers and starts doing her cleansing routine. "Have you got any whiskey handy or something to numb the pain?"

I bark a laugh. "Whiskey is something we always have in stock in this house."

Two seconds later, Dillan pours me a tumbler, then he takes a swig and passes it around. I tip mine back and swallow fast, letting the burn of the liquid sedation take hold. "Wow, that's powerful stuff for breakfast."

"It's good you haven't eaten anything, girlfriend, because this won't be pleasant. Remember the first time we did this?"

I swallow as a wave of dizzy hits at the memory. "As if it was only last week."

"Funny girl." Sloan offers what I know is supposed to be a reassuring smile. It's not—but it's supposed to be. "The tissue is dying from the surface inward. The tattoo might be gone, but the taint of it is still very much present."

"I was afraid of that. All right, it's not like I didn't know it was a possibility. Hotness, if you can portal yourself into my apartment. Do you remember the cupboard where I keep my cards? There are three more vials of that red cleansing solution in there. Bring them here."

Sloan is gone and back in a flash.

I stare at the vials and groan. "That stuff tastes like festering assholes."

"It should. That's what I used to make it." I stop with my hand at my mouth, and she chuckles. "I'm kidding. Drink it."

I show everyone what a good little patient I can be and do as instructed. My mind fills with a dozen colorful and creative curses, but I have my fingers pressed over my lips to keep from barfing.

"I know that look." Sloan passes his hand over my thigh as intense heat bubbles to the surface of my skin. "I'm sorry, Fi. This is going to hurt like a bastard."

He no sooner says the words than I arch back on my bed and cry out.

Da grabs my hand and squeezes. "Focus on me, *mo chroi*. Look at me and think only happy thoughts."

Dillan and Calum stand behind Da, then Aiden rushes into view.

Okay, now I'm crying. "You didn't need to come over here for this."

"Shut up, stupid. Where else would I be, baby girl?"

While Dora and Sloan do their thing, my family keeps me distracted the best they can. Da never lets go of my hand and

Dillan, Calum, and Aiden entertain me with tall tales of the tortures they suffered at my hands over the years.

Lies. All lies.

I laugh when I can manage, and Da wipes my tears like a champion when I can't. I don't know how long it all takes, but in the end, the pain subsides.

Sloan takes Dora home and exchanges her for Emmet.

He crawls onto the bed, and I roll over and snuggle against his side. The two of us are the closest in age and grew up doing the same things with the same people. He's not only my brother, but he's also one of my best friends.

"How you doin', Fi?"

"I feel like a steaming pile of shit."

He smiles. "That's good because you look like it. No mixed messages there."

"Glad we're clear on that."

My phone rings and I chuckle as the Lion King theme song plays. "Pass me that. It's Garnet."

Da picks up the phone, answers it, and walks out to the hall to take my call.

"Rude. My phone. My room."

"Tough. My daughter. My house," Da calls back.

I snort. "The oul man has a point."

The excitement dies down, and we all sit around looking at one another. "Okay, you're dismissed. I'm fine. The excitement is over. S'all good."

Sloan scowls at me, then gets up and heads out into the hall. The thing about living in an old house is that I can follow Da's and Sloan's movements as they head downstairs to talk. That doesn't fill me with confidence.

I give Emmet one final hug and sit up. "Okay. I'm getting dressed. Aiden, since you're here, will you make me one of your groovy grilled cheese sandwiches?"

"I'd be happy to." He kisses the top of my head and strides off toward the door. "Ready in ten."

"Can't wait." I look at the others and wave toward the door. "Okay, freak-show peepshow's over. I'm getting dressed. Then we'll all pretend everything is fine."

"That's the Cumhaill spirit." Emmet rolls off the bed. "Fake it 'til you make it."

Emmet, Dillan, and Calum reach out to steady me when I stand, then smile and head for the door. "We're downstairs. Holler if you need us."

"I'm good. Honest. See you down there." When I'm alone in my room, I sit on my bed and try not to think about it. "Bruin, would you mind riding inside for a while? I feel stronger when you're with me."

"My thinking, exactly." Bruin dematerializes and breezes into his place in my chest.

With him where he belongs, I grab a clean outfit and head to the bathroom. I'd like to see my leg, but Sloan has it poulticed and wrapped, so there's no peeking.

For today, at least.

By the time I get downstairs, the kitchen smells like grilled cheese heaven, and Aiden has heated tomato soup too. "You're my hero."

Aiden shakes his head. "No, Fi. You're our hero. Now sit and eat."

I take my spot, and the four of us eat. It feels like when we were kids—only without Brendan. "Where did Sloan and Da run off to?"

They all shrug and continue to spoon in the soup.

I squeeze a puddle of ketchup onto my plate and dip my grilled cheese. "Not buying the silence, boys. What's up?"

Dillan frowns. "Sloan and Da are having a passionate difference of opinion."

Calum grabs another stack of Ritz Crackers and crumbles

them into his soup. "Sloan wants to *poof* you back to Ireland to have Wallace work on your leg. Da is opposed. He doesn't want you so far away if there's something wrong."

I see both their points.

"Does he think Wallace will know what to do?"

Aiden is finished putting away the bread and remaining cheese and bacon, and slides over to the sink to start dishes. "I don't know if he thinks his da can fix it specifically or if he feels Wallace is your best shot at fixing it, but he's pretty worked up."

I pop the last bite of my sandwich into my mouth and chew. "He gets that way when he's worried. He's a little tightly wound."

They all laugh.

"You think?" Calum says. "He almost went apoplectic this morning because my socks don't match."

I giggle. "It's fun to set him off though."

Cue another round of chuckling.

"Do we know where my phone is?"

Aiden wipes his hands dry and picks it off the top of the microwave and passes it over.

I pull up Garnet's number and hit send. "Hey, sorry. You called?"

"Lady Druid, are you well? Your father seemed unduly protective of you not being disturbed earlier."

"Yeah, I'm fine. There was a situation, but we're handling it. What did you need?"

"I've called an emergency meeting of the Guild to discuss what almost happened with the wizards last night. I'd like you to meet with the Governors afterward. I think it will go a long way with the other sects to know how integral you and your people were in stopping that clusterfuck."

Garnet's voice must be carrying because four scowly brothers shake their heads.

"Sure. When and where?"

"The location of the Guild conclave is protected information for obvious political and safety reasons, but how about the druid stones at noon?"

"High noon it is. See you there."

I end the call and face the ire of my wonderfully overprotective brothers. "It'll be fine. I feel better already. There's nothing Aiden's groovy grilled cheese can't make right. I'm fine."

"No. You're not," Aiden disagrees, "but we'll respect your right to bullshit your way through for now. We'll also go to that meeting with you."

Dillan's clearing the table, so I hand him my plate. "You don't need to come. I'm sure Sloan will be there, and I'll have Bruin."

Emmet shrugs. "You'll have us too. Lucky you."

"I'm sure it'll be fine. I don't want to derail the day more than I already have."

Calum frowns and squeezes my hand where it rests on the table. "We watched you writhe in pain while fighting the aftermath of taking on an evil manifesto on your own. When we can be there for you, it's what we want to do."

"What we *need* to do," Aiden amends. "Fionn may have drafted you to represent Clan Cumhaill, but we're all part of that. We're a package deal. We have your back."

"Always," Calum agrees.

"Fo shizzle my nizzle," Emmet adds.

I giggle and check my watch. "I'm lucky to have you. Okay, I want to spend an hour in the grove before it's time to leave. If anyone's looking for me, feel free to track me down."

I get four big brother hugs between the table and the hall and feel the love by the time I slide my feet into my shoes and grab my jacket off the hook. It's only been a couple of weeks since the grove took root and my fae immigrated to help us make it great, but they did their jobs.

It *is* great.

I feel the energy of fae prana the moment I step under the

shade of the trees and breathe deep. The ambient power in the air fills my lungs and feeds my cells.

Yep. This is what I need.

"Hey there." Sloan unfolds his long legs to rise out of his chair. "How do ye feel?"

"Better. What are you doing out here?"

"Centering myself. Yer healing took a bit out of me."

"Not avoiding Da? I heard the two of you saw things differently about my next steps."

He holds up his thumb and forefinger, giving me a measure, and smiles. "I might be a little afraid of yer father when he locks horns."

I shrug off my jacket and toss it onto the cushion of my chair. "That proves how smart you are."

I give him a long, tight hug and absorb a little of his strength. When I ease back, he looks equally pleased and confused. "I'm sorry. I've been a dismal girlfriend so far. I should've realized healing me took a lot out of you. I may get swept away when the world's closing in, but I never miss how dedicated to me and my family you always are. Thank you for everything you do."

He eases back and smiles down at me. "Yer not a dismal girlfriend. We haven't even gotten started down that road yet, and that's fine. We know where we are, and it'll come. Fer now, ye have enough balls in the air without tossin' mine into the mix."

I chuckle. "I see what you did there. Good one."

"The point is, I'm fine with that. Ye said upfront a relationship wasn't a priority. Don't feel bad because yer standin' yer ground and focused on yer changin' world."

He slips his fingers under my hair and cups the nape of my neck. The pressure to pull me forward is gentle enough that I could resist if I want to, but I don't.

The kiss is welcome and unrushed, and when everything else in my life is about people coming at me with expectations, this isn't that. It just is.

"Man. Why aren't we doing more of that?"

Sloan chuckles. "Maybe we can work harder to make time. In between you saving your friends and the city and all of history, that is."

"You joke, but I'm serious. That was lovely and exactly what I needed to slow my mind."

"Slow yer mind? Huh, it had the opposite effect on me."

I reach up on my tiptoes and brush my lips across his once more before retreating to my chair and settling in. "Do you mind if we sit with nature for a while and absorb? I feel drained after this morning myself."

Sloan picks up Flopsy from the ground beneath my basket swing and sets the fluffy furball with wings onto the blanket over my lap.

I scrub her velvety ears between my fingers and sit back and close my eyes.

"When I was little, I used to cry in my sleep. When you were here last time, and you and Calum both said I was doing it, it made me wonder what started it again after almost twenty years."

Sloan settles into his swing and folds his legs to cross in front of himself, then sets his wrists on his knees in a meditative lotus pose. "What did you come up with?"

"It's not hard to figure out that I miss Brendan and my life from before. I'm trying to navigate my relationship with Liam now when it used to be so easy to be besties. Now I'm a druid, and he wants things to be like they used to."

"I think he's coming around. We talked a fair bit in Ireland. He's a good guy, and he values yer friendship and yer family more than anything else."

I stretch my neck from side to side and chuckle. "I'm not sure what to think about the two of you becoming buddy-buddy and chatting about me when I'm not there to defend myself."

His smile is easy and relaxed. "One of the most important lessons ye've taught me over the past five months, Fi, is that wherever yer concerned, there's always enough love fer everyone. There's no need fer either of us to worry about being left behind. Yer heart is big enough to include everyone."

"Aww, that's sweet."

"It's true. I'm still glad I'm the one who won out on the kissing part, but hey, I'm not totally evolved."

I chuckle. "Yes, you won out on the boyfriend side of things, but honestly, Liam and I would never have worked in the long run. We love each other and always will, but he likes his world to be comfortable and something he can count on. With me around, he'd never get that."

"I see the allure of comfortable, but I agree. That shield of yers seems to draw the world of chaos right to yer feet."

"Which is why I wanted to come out here and center myself. The Lakeshore Guild is having an emergency meeting right now and called me to appear. We're heading to the druid stones for noon."

Sloan checks his watch and frowns. "All right then, enough chatter. Let's find our inner calm so we can prepare for the next disaster."

"Exactly what I was thinking."

CHAPTER TWENTY-FIVE

It's eleven-forty-two when Clan Cumhaill gathers in the back lane. Everyone's wearing their druid garb, and I have to admit, even as twenty-first-century urban druids, we look like an ass-kicking, awe-inspiring bunch.

Kevin was the one who first thought we needed branding, and he coordinated our look. Black stretch combat pants, black Under Armour shirts, and forest green, lightweight combat vests.

The boys are used to wearing vests, so it's only Sloan and I getting used to them. The fact that Kev included Sloan in the outfitting is yet another reason I love him so much.

We're definitely visibly branded.

I'm not sure we need to look like a SWAT team, but the boys like it, so I play along. Then, of course, Dillan tops his outfit with his beloved cloak of knowledge, which he's wearing with the hood up.

No surprise there.

"Weapons out or in?" Calum asks.

Everyone looks at me, but I look at Da.

"This is an invitation to speak to influential members of the community, *mo chroi*. Intentions are everythin'."

I nod, understanding exactly what he means. "Weapons sheathed. We're there to talk and build bridges. We're confident enough in our skills that we can call on our weapons if we need them."

"Wait!" Kevin waves from where he's parking his car on the dirt lane beside our house. He grabs something out of the back seat and runs to catch us. "I'm glad I didn't miss you. Fi and Emmet, I have something for you."

"Yikes." Aiden raises his palms. "Kev, don't run with knives. We're waiting."

Calum shakes his head. "He probably zoomed through the streets to get here too."

I laugh. "Can you imagine that traffic stop? 'You were going sixty in a forty, young man. What's the hurry?' 'My boyfriend forgot his knives and is leaving for a big meeting.'"

They get a kick out of that.

I catch sight of Janine standing on the balcony of her bedroom next door watching us. "Everyone wave to Janine and try not to look like we're heading off to meet a league of empowered beings to discuss demon resurrection."

They get a kick out of that too.

Kevin joins us with two impressive knife sheaths in hand. He takes a knee in front of me and hands Calum the second one. "Fi, let me finish off your outfit before you go. Cal, you do Emmet's."

Kevin straps the thigh sheath around my good leg and straightens while Calum finishes hooking Emmet up. "Calum said you two don't have close-range weapons, so I researched melee knives. These are supposed to be good."

"That's so sweet, Kev." I reach down to test where my palm falls in relation to the grip of the knife and wriggle the sheath a little toward the outside of my thigh.

"I gotta keep my warriors well-equipped," he says. "Oh, and Em, I'm working on a lot of really cool sharp and pointy weapons for your battle vest for you to defend with."

"You rock, Kev." Emmet holds out his knuckles for a bump.

I check my watch. "Yikes, okay, we gotta go. Thanks, Kev. I love the knife and the thought behind it."

We get to the druid stones with two minutes to spare and not one other car in the parking lot. Calum, Dillan, and Emmet pile out of Dillan's truck, and me, Da, Aiden, and Sloan climb out of my Hellcat. "Huh. So, either we're being punked, it's an ambush, or no one wanted to show up to our party."

Da rounds the hood and chuckles. "Or the meetin' ran long, and they'll transport here as a group in a minute."

"Yeah, it could be that too."

The seven of us climb the small incline to the grassy plateau that highlights the circle of seventeen stones.

Seeing the replica of the sacred Drombeg Druid Stones raises the hair on my arms as it always does. It blew my mind the first time I saw it. The visual affected me down to a cellular level, but I felt and smelled the tainted stink of dark magic even then.

"It's a crime that they use it as a sacrificial site."

Da nods. "It is."

I reach up to the inscription on the left stone at the entrance of the circle and smile. "Hey, I can still read Celtic Britonnic."

"Still?" Calum asks.

"Yeah, Fionn and I cast a spell back at Carlisle Castle so I could understand what people were saying around me."

"Well, fess up, sista," Dillan says. "Let us all in on your little Fionn shortcut. Stop hoggin' it."

I giggle. "I'll try to remember. It was fifteen hundred years ago and all."

Sloan rolls his eyes. "Ye realize that joke has worn thin."

I stick my tongue out and try to remember. "Okay, plant your feet, connect with nature, and repeat after me."

Ancient tongues of pasts long gone,
Fill the air like Babylon.
Charm my ears and bless my words,
To sing their tune like sweet songbirds.

They all do, and a moment later, I know it worked because Emmet runs his fingers down the stone face on the left of the entrance. "While these stones bask in sun, trees will grow, and water will run."

"Yeah, that's the good one," I say. "The one I'm guessing Barghest messed with is the one on the right."

Da shifts over a couple of feet and frowns as he reads the text. "Marked by the past, ordained the exalter, magic released by death on the altar."

I crinkle my nose. "Yeah no, we need to fix that. Anyone have any ancient stone White-Out?"

Sloan chuckles and moves to stand next to Da. He reaches up with his arm and slides his palm down the inscription of the stone. A golden glow ignites between his hand and the surface of the right rock, and as he lowers his hand, the words change. "How's this?"

Da reads the revision. "Marked by the past, ordained by nature, magic released through reverence of creature."

I smile. "Much better. Nature and creature aren't a slam dunk rhyme, but they are meaningful and close enough."

Sloan laughs. "It was a poem on the fly. I'll work on it."

"No need." Nikon joins us from within the circle. "It sets a good tone. I hereby lock it into place. From now on, these stones will be true druid stones and will only empower those who abide by the base tenets of your sect."

"Dude!" Emmet steps in for a fist-bump. "Point for the good guys."

I agree. That's a huge win in my book. "That's amazeballs. Suck it, Barghest."

Nikon blinks, and Calum and Aiden stiffen opposite me. I close my eyes and feel the warmth of heated gazes behind me. "They're all standing right behind us, aren't they?"

"Yep."

Awesomesauce. I turn and face the hostile glares of the majority of close to forty people. I recognize most of them from the riverboat luncheon because they have the same looks of disdain on their faces.

Some seem amused. Whether that's because I stepped in it or because they agree, it's hard to say.

"Sorry. That was uncharitable. While I'm super pleased that no one can use this symbol of druid power and history in ways other than originally intended, I shouldn't have made that personal by speaking out against Droghun and the practices of his necromancers."

"Druids." Droghun steps to the front of the group. "We're the recognized druids of this city."

"*Not,*" someone coughs from behind me.

Oh, you gotta love Emmet.

"Maybe when there was no true druid presence in the city you could get away with saying that, but not now. Druids are the keepers of nature—you sacrifice innocents. We are guardians of the fae—you captured and caged fae to siphon their life force. We are neutral to things like wealth and power and politics—you are driven by all three. You can tell yourselves you're druids all you want, but you're not."

"How long have you been a druid, little girl?"

"Fionn marked me almost five months ago."

"Another thing you claim that can't be proven. Anyone can get a tattoo."

I roll my eyes. "You're right. Anyone can be a poser. That's why you have to look deeper." I look at the peanut gallery and smile. "You see what I did there, right?"

Garnet fights a smile and sobers, then drops his professional mask into place. "We catch your meaning, Lady Druid. So, what do you suggest we do to settle this feud?"

"A test." Nikon holds up his finger. "A traditional one-on-one test of druid skills to show us which one or both of them has the right to call themselves a druid."

I blink at Nikon and think at him, hoping he's listening. *Dude. What the hell?*

Come on, Red. You can take him. He's an ass-kissing boot licker that got promoted because you offed his boss. I have faith in you.

That's nice—and thank you—but a couple of hours ago I was flat on my back being cleansed for dark magic poisoning. I'm barely standing upright.

Shit. I didn't know. Sorry.

Not your fault.

Dillan passes his hand over my face, and I jump. "Yo, Fi. Where'd you go there?"

"Honestly, with her, you can never be sure," Zxata says.

I shake the distraction off. There's no way I can back down now. I'm in it to win it. "I accept. When and where?"

Please say next week, or maybe next month...

"No time like the present," High Priestess Drippy Face of the Witches says.

Nice. I have fans. "Sure. Now works too."

"Fiona." Da scowls. I read his gaze, and I know he's worried about my state of fitness too. Can't be helped.

"S'all good, Da. You can knock down a Cumhaill..."

"...but ye can't keep us down," they all finish for me.

I nod and gesture at the circle of the rings. "Okay, let the test be a true test of druid power and connection. Can someone dampen or eliminate access to all other types of magic?"

"Done," Nikon says. "Filters set. Druid magic only."

I nod. "Thanks."

Droghun frowns. "She can't use her battle bear."

I shrug. "Technically, my connection to Killer Clawbearer is completely druid magic, and my connection with nature strengthens my bond, but if you're *scairt*, I'll agree."

I tap my chest. "Take a seat on the sidelines for this one, buddy."

Bruin bursts from my chest and roars on the wind as he circles the leaders of the other sects. As the wind builds around them and whips their hair and the collars of their jackets and cloaks, eyes widen.

Very dramatic, buddy.

You like that? I thought it added a bit of flair.

Sure did. Thanks for being you.

Garnet clears his throat and raises his hand in a circular swoop of our surroundings. "All right, everyone staying to stand witness, move to the outer edges of the clearing. The battle area is anything within the circle of the stones. Winner will be determined by boundary, a clear winner, or death."

I blink. "Seriously?'

"Are you scairt, little girl?" Droghun taunts.

"No. I didn't realize the marking system of this test includes death."

Everyone moves out. My family members each meet my gaze and smile at me or raise their chins in the universal signal of "hey, you got this."

I take off my vest and hand it to Sloan.

He grips my elbow and the moment he makes contact, a rush of healing strength and druid energy feeds my cells. "Only druid power, right?"

"You're adorable."

"Glad you finally realized it."

When he recedes, only Droghun and I are left circling the center of the clearing. "What are the combat rules?"

"No rules," Droghun snaps. "She professes to be the chosen one. If she's the messiah of the Ancient Order of Druids, I want her to prove it."

Aiden laughs. "If that's all you want, trust us, her spear is longer and stronger than yours. And when I say spear... Did you see what I did there?"

I try not to laugh, but yeah, that was funny, and the look on Droghun's face is even better.

"Enough," Drippy-faced lady snaps. "Engage, or we leave."

Fine. Whatevs.

I call my body armor and watch as Droghun's pupils lock onto the veining of the tattoos. Yeah, it's not pretty, but it's hella effective.

Stretching my druid muscles, I reach out to draw power through my connection. The ambient magic in the air is strong since we released it, and it feeds my power.

Bestial Strength. Feline Finesse.

I feel the inking spells on my flesh ignite as my casting takes hold. How cool is it that I didn't even need to say that out loud and tip Droghun off to my plans?

The first strike comes fast from the side. A sinkhole opens up under my right heel, and I dive out of the way. With the dexterity of a feline and the strength of a great beast, I launch into a backward somersault and land in a three-point superhero pose with one knee and one fist buried in the ground.

The crowd goes wild... Well, at least my brothers do.

And, if any of the other stuffed shirts knew anything about being a cool superhero, they would've liked it too.

Obvi, it's over their heads.

I get my head back in the game when Droghun opens his palm, and a staff appears in his hand.

I do the same and Birga appears in mine.

We connect a few times, striking and blocking, setting up our stances, and getting a feel for one another. His first swing is an obvious over-extension meant to draw me off balance.

I don't take the bait. Instead, I sweep his heel and knock him off balance. In all the hand-to-hand hours I've practiced with Granda, Sloan, Da, and the boys, the key is not to commit too much too soon.

I'm happy feeling out Droghun to see what he can do and he seems to be getting pissed about it.

"You're afraid of me," he growls while charging in for a closer pass. "They all see it."

I chuckle and stop his attempt to throw up a stone wall. When the ground rumbles beneath my badass boots, I release the soil and stone from his call.

He grunts and comes at me while swinging his staff.

He lands a few hits, but I barely feel them and my connection with the stones and the forest beyond pulses in my blood. Da's rule about perfect practice making perfect has never hit so close to home.

My father is a druid phenom with a staff. While Droghun is good, he's no Niall Cumhaill.

I hold my own in the battle and meet his attacks with equal and opposite force. While he's strongly offensive, I simply counter each challenge and end his strikes.

"Fight me, bitch."

I chuckle again while feeling the electricity in the air build. It may be a bright, clear, autumn day, but I sense the potential of power in the ozone. "Sticks and stones, dickwad. Remember, you're not supposed to call me that anymore or my big brothers will come after you."

I wear on him with taunts and strategy, meeting his advances, negating his strikes. Eventually, I position myself so he turns from the forest at the far end of the stones.

Call me petty, but the irony of my first true offensive move is genius and sweet revenge. As I swing Birga in a deadly arc toward his face, my Creeping Vine spell wraps around his ankles.

I squeeze my hold on the living ropes coming from the forest and tighten their grip. Droghun realizes too late that my overt offensive was the distraction. The vines have a hold on him and are dragging him faster and faster toward the trees.

With Birga poised, I jab the earth by his face and ribs and arms as he flails. I intentionally miss, making him look foolish. With a parry of my spear, I spin Birga in the air and butt-end him once in the gut to make my point.

When he tried to drag me into the forest in Ireland last month, he was a coward and hid.

I beat him then, and I'll beat him now.

His staff cracks me one in the shoulder, but it bounces off my hardened flesh. The only damage it does is to flick my hair so I look a little like an eighties Pat Benatar video.

Droghun twists and curses as the vines pull him closer to the boundaries of our battle. He fights them off with some efficiency, but nature's response to him is slow and unsure. Nature magic doesn't trust him.

By the time he reaches the ring of the stones, he flips to his knees and manages to get himself free.

I'm sweaty and a little breathless, but I'm used to fighting my brothers two and three at a time. Fighting one opponent that isn't on the best of terms with druid power is a workout but not a threat.

"Accept it, Droghun." I give him the chance to save face. "Barghest lost its way from what the druid sect is all about."

"You impudent little bitch."

"Seriously? I was trying to be nice." I swing Birga in a wild circle over my head and call all the wind and animals I can. The gale of autumn bite whistles through the clearing as a forest flash mob surprises Droghun.

They grab hold of him and drag him out of the stones.

"Out of bounds, asshole. I win."

I release my hold on the weather and send my thanks to the creatures of the forest: the deer, the bear, the raccoons, and squirrels, and skunk. "I am in your debt, my friends."

Droghun is still struggling to untangle himself when I release my call on Birga and my armor to return to the Guild Governors. I'm halfway back to the crowd when—

"On yer back," Da shouts.

I drop and roll to the side, unsure what Droghun has in store, but I don't care. I won fair and square.

Cheating is a bitch move.

I'm still connected with my natural surroundings when my temper flares and calls the fury of lighting to the ground. I grip a fist in the air and throw it at where Droghun stands, eyes wide.

The strike is swift, and the *crack* hits at the same time he drops to the ground and covers his head.

I don't fry him. I don't need to. The point was to prove who had a better command of nature magic and who had the right to claim themself a druid.

That would be me.

I feel Fionn in me. I feel him in the air around me. When I turn back to my family, I see him standing with them clapping. I think it's the stones that allow him to appear. Something about the magic of the stones, anyway.

When I join them, Fionn bows his head. "A class all yer own, *a leanbh*. Well done."

"Thanks, oul man." I rejoin the group. "Da, Aiden, Calum, Dillan, Emmet, and Sloan, this is Fionn mac Cumhaill. Fionn, this is my family—your family too, I guess."

I swear the six of them look like they might stroke out.

Fionn eyes Sloan up and down and nods. "And is this yer man? The one ye told me ye have yer eye on?"

"Seriously? You're bringing that up now?"

"I'm glad he did." Sloan grins. "What did she say about me, I wonder?"

Fionn looks off to the side and smiles. "A brawny male with shoulders as broad as a door and muscles that rise like the rolling Irish hills. He's a warrior, fiercely loyal to his cause, and wildly protective of those he loves."

My cheeks flame hot, and I smack Fionn's shoulder. "You took that completely out of context, and you know it. I was scaring off a flutist by spinning a yarn."

"Ye never mentioned a flirtin' flutist in yer recount of yer castle adventures." Da obviously enjoys my public mortification.

"Why is everyone so interested in my love life?"

Fionn chuckles. "I don't get to come and go as I please, ye know? An oul man gets to make sure his heir apparent is in good hands and good company."

Da chuckles. "She's in good hands, sir. We'll all make sure of that."

Fionn gives him a nod and waves as he wanders across the clearing. He disappears somewhere near the center of the stones, and I smile. "Laters, oul man."

"Un-freakin'-believable," Sloan says. "That was the touch-stone founder of our entire heritage, and yer shootin' the shite with him like it's nothin'."

I shrug. "He's cool, but he's a person."

He rolls his eyes and sighs. "Yer ridiculous. Ye know that, don't ye?"

I giggle. "You may have mentioned that once or twice."

CHAPTER TWENTY-SIX

"Clan Cumhaill, will you join us a moment?" Garnet asks. He's had his head down and has been chatting with the others since the end of the one-on-one challenge. Now, he waves us all over to join them.

"That was quite a display, Fiona," Zxata says. "You didn't even look challenged."

I shrug. "Droghun is a fierce warrior when he's able to access the full strength of his power and ability. Because this was a druid test and Nikon locked all but druid magic, he was at a disadvantage. The Black Dogs have attacked me on more than one occasion. They're dangerous opponents, but they aren't druids. Therefore, I had the advantage."

"It's gracious of you to speak in his defense, Fiona." Suede winks from the front row. "That shows maturity beyond your age and a sense of confidence that isn't dependent on oppressing others. She has my vote."

"Your vote for what?" I ask.

She smiles. "To take the oath as the representative for the Guild Governor position for Toronto Druids. We all witnessed a druid spirit give you his blessing. You've proven that following the sect's foundational tenets makes you more eligible to claim the title than Barghest. I agree with your motion to have them renamed as Toronto Necromancers."

"My motion?" I look around. "I didn't put forth a motion."

"Sure, you did." Garnet raises his gaze to search the faces of the forty people standing there. "Can I get a playback of the motion Lady Cumhaill raised at the luncheon? Where's Laini?"

A tiny girl with pink hair and a round face steps to the front. She closes her eyes, and when she speaks, it's my voice coming out of her mouth. "Barghest doesn't deserve the right to hold a *druid* seat. You are filthy necromancers, plain and simple. Keep your damned seat, but don't associate it with druids or what we stand for."

Garnet looks over at me. "Ring any bells?"

Da frowns at me, and I shrug. "Not my most diplomatic moment. My mouth got away from me there."

Nikon laughs. "Bullshit. It was the best meeting since the mages plucked the tree nymph's leaves, smoked them in the lounge, then lost control of their magic and sent a herd of conjured dragons down Yonge Street."

Suede and a few others laugh.

I manage to keep a straight face. "I wasn't hinting for a seat on the council."

Garnet lifts one shoulder in a lopsided shrug. "Even so, in the weeks and months since you unexpectedly arrived on our doorstep, you've proven yourself a capable power, a fair and just character, and you care as much or more about Toronto and the citizens within her streets than any of us. I believe you are the right choice to fill the druid seat."

I shake my head. "My Da is the head of our family. It should be—"

"You, *mo chroi*. Fionn chose you for a reason. I, for one, think he knows what he's doin'."

"You have my vote, baby girl," Aiden says.

"And mine," Dillan, Emmet, and Calum add in unison.

I meet Sloan's gaze, and he nods. "I don't get a vote because I'm neither a Cumhaill nor a citizen of Toronto, but if I were, I couldn't think of a better representative of what it means to be a druid. I think ye should take the oath."

My head swims. Take a seat as a Guild Governor on the Lakeshore Guild of Empowered Ones? It would allow me to find out more about things I still need answers for...

Like, who's following up on the wizards now that their leader is dead? Did the stupid idea about resurrecting a demon die with Salem? How will the necromancers feed their magic now that I've taken away their ritual site? Where can I put the *Eochair Prana* as a safe final resting place?

Yeah, there's a lot I want to be privy to, but do I have to join the stuffed shirt brigade to do it?

"It's an honor to be nominated..."

Nikon snorts. "You're not winning an Oscar, Red. Take the oath and be the change you want to see."

I swallow and let that sink in. "Okay, but if I take the oath, it's not only me. We all take it. I'll sit on the council, but Clan Cumhaill is a package deal."

"As you wish," Garnet says. "I'll say it once, so you know what you agree to. Then, if you choose, you can repeat it after me. Agreed?"

I nod. "Sounds good."

"I swear on my honor as a citizen of Toronto and warrior of the empowered world, that I will be dutiful in the laws of our community, never cause needless suffering, and will fight until my dying breath against all persons who intend to do harm within the boundaries of my fair city."

I check with my brothers and Da. "It seems okay to me. Any objections?"

"Is yer shield tingling?" Sloan asks.

"No. S'all good."

Da nods. "I have no objections."

I meet Garnet's gaze and smile. "All right, Grand Governor. Once more from the top. Let's do this."

Endnote

Thank you for reading – *A Family Oath*

While the story is fresh in your mind, click **HERE** and tell other readers what you thought.

A star rating and/or even one sentence can mean so much to readers deciding whether or not to try out a book or new author.

And if you loved it, continue with the Chronicles of an Urban Druid and claim your copy of book four – *A Witch's Revenge*

IRISH TRANSLATIONS

Arragh – a guttural sound for when something bad happened
Banjaxed – broken, ruined, completely obliterated
Bogger – those who live in the boggy countryside
Bollocks – a man's testicles
Bollix – thrown into disorder, bungled, messed up
Boyo – boy, lad
Cock-crow – close enough that you can hear a cock crow
Craic – gossip, fun, entertainment
Culchie – those who live in the agricultural countryside
Donkey's years – a long time
Dosser – a layabout, lazy person
Eejit – slightly less severe than idiot
Fair whack away – far away
Feck – an exclamation less severe than fuck
Flute – a man's penis
Gammie – injured, not working properly
Hape – a heap
Howeyah/Howaya/Howya – a greeting not necessarily requiring an answer.

Irish – traditional Irish language (Commonly referred to as Irish Gaelic unless you're Irish.)

Knackers – a man's testicles

Mo chroi – my heart (pronounced muh chree)

Mocker – a hex

Och – used to express agreement or disagreement to something said

Shite – less offensive than shit

Slan! – health be with you (pronounced slawn)

Gobshite – fool, acting in unwanted behavior

Slainte mhath – cheers, good health (pronounced slawn cha va)

Wee – small

A WITCH'S REVENGE

The story continues with A Witch's Revenge, coming soon Amazon and Kindle Unlimited.

Pre-order now to have it delivered to your Kindle on midnight December 27, 2020.

AUTHOR NOTES - AUBURN TEMPEST
NOVEMBER 22, 2020

Thank you so much for reading *A Family Oath*, the third book in the Chronicles of an Urban Druid series—I hope you loved it.

When Fiona's world becomes complicated, she falls back on the two things she depends on to survive: the unshakeable faith she has in her family and her ability to laugh and see the humor in crazy and stressful moments.

In these times of turmoil, I think Fi has the right idea.

May we all love deeper, laugh harder, and accept the people around us without judgment.

A Family Oath is my 40th published novel (JL Madore and Auburn Tempest combined) and releases on my father's birthday —November 29th. I find the timing cool and kinda monumental because he died in 2000, when I was 29, which was more than a decade before I started writing. He never got a chance to read my stories—and likely wouldn't have even if he were alive—still, I think he'd be pleased about how much I love what I do.

When the world overwhelms, dive into a book and let laughter carry you away for a while. Book four in the series promises to bring you more family moments, magic, and mayhem.

A Witch's Revenge is up next, so claim your copy and continue the adventure—with us, with Fiona and the gang, and in the rich lore of Irish mythology.

Wishing you all lives filled with love, laughter, and magic.

Hugs to all,

Auburn Tempest

Thank you for not only reading this story, but these author notes in the back!

Following Auburn's comment about her father not reading her books (not only because he had passed, but that he probably would not had he lived) I thought about my own dad.

I'm blessed that he is still alive, and we have talked a couple of times about him not reading my stories.

In short, he doesn't enjoy the genres I write.

Vampires? Nope.

Science Fiction? Not a chance.

Urban Fantasy? *What am I smoking.*

But, and here is the important part for me, he follows my career and is proud. That's all I personally need.

My mom, when she was alive, also followed my career but didn't read my stories and I never had a problem with this. For some reason, I'm totally ok with a million strangers reading my stories but don't particularly want my parents to read them.

I was ok with my older brother listening to Emily Beresford reading the stories. That worked great.

Thinking about it for a few seconds, I have concluded it might be that the stories are about 10% personal. I don't mind strangers reading because they probably don't know the 10% from the other 90%.

My parents would probably guess and that's just too much information sharing for me.

And I am past fifty years old.

Humans. *We are such weird creatures.*

Ad Aeternitatem,

Michael Anderle

ABOUT AUBURN TEMPEST

Auburn Tempest is a multi-genre novelist giving life to Urban Fantasy, Paranormal, and Sci-Fi adventures. Under the pen name, JL Madore, she writes in the same genres but in full romance, sexy-steamy novels. Whether Romance or not, she loves to twist Alpha heroes and kick-ass heroines into chaotic, hilarious, fast-paced, magical situations and make them really work for their happy endings.

Auburn Tempest lives in the Greater Toronto Area, Canada with her dear, wonderful hubby of 30 years and a menagerie of family, friends, and animals.

BOOKS BY AUBURN TEMPEST

Auburn Tempest - Urban Fantasy Action/Adventure
Chronicles of an Urban Druid

Book 1 – A Gilded Cage

Book 2 – A Sacred Grove

Book 3 – A Family Oath

Book 4 - A Witches Revenge

Book 5 - A Broken Vow

Book 6 - A Druid Hexed

Misty's Magick and Mayhem Series – Written by Carolina Mac/Contributed to by Auburn Tempest

Book 1 – School for Reluctant Witches

Book 2 – School for Saucy Sorceresses

Book 3 – School for Unwitting Wiccans

Book 4 – Nine St. Gillian Street

Book 5 – The Ghost of Pirate's Alley

Book 6 – Jinxing Jackson Square

Book 7 – Flame

Book 8 – Frost

Book 9 – Nocturne

Book 10 – Luna

Book 11 – Swamp Magic

Exemplar Hall – Co-written with Ruby Night

Prequel – Death of a Magi Knight

Book 1 – Drafted by the Magi

Book 2 – <u>Jesse and the Magi Vault</u>
Book 3 – <u>The Makings of a Magi</u>

CONNECT WITH THE AUTHORS

Connect with Auburn

Amazon, Facebook, Newsletter

Web page – www.jlmadore.com

Email – AuburnTempestWrites@gmail.com

Connect with Michael Anderle and sign up for his email list here:

Website: http://lmbpn.com

Email List: http://lmbpn.com/email/

Social Media:

https://www.facebook.com/LMBPNPublishing

https://twitter.com/MichaelAnderle

https://www.instagram.com/lmbpn_publishing/

https://www.bookbub.com/authors/michael-anderle

OTHER LMBPN PUBLISHING BOOKS

For a complete list of books published by LMBPN please visit the following page:

https://lmbpn.com/books-by-lmbpn-publishing/

Lightning Source UK Ltd.
Milton Keynes UK
UKHW020022021021
391519UK00009B/2189